the heart
between us

Center Point
Large Print

Also by Lindsay Harrel and available from Center Point Large Print:

One More Song to Sing

**This Large Print Book carries the
Seal of Approval of N.A.V.H.**

the heart between us

LINDSAY HARREL

CENTER POINT LARGE PRINT
THORNDIKE, MAINE

This Center Point Large Print edition
is published in the year 2018 by arrangement with
Thomas Nelson.

Scripture quotations are taken from The Message.
Copyright © by Eugene H. Peterson 1993, 1994, 1995,
1996, 2000, 2001, 2002. Used by permission of
Tyndale House Publishers, Inc.

The text of this Large Print edition is unabridged.
In other aspects, this book may vary
from the original edition.
Printed in the United States of America
on permanent paper.
Set in 16-point Times New Roman type.

ISBN: 978-1-68324-782-1

Library of Congress Cataloging-in-Publication Data

Names: Harrel, Lindsay, author.
Title: The heart between us / Lindsay Harrel.
Description: Center Point large print edition. | Thorndike, Maine :
    Center Point Large Print, 2018.
Identifiers: LCCN 2018002693 | ISBN 9781683247821
    (hardcover : alk. paper)
Subjects: LCSH: Self-actualization (Psychology) in women—Fiction. |
    Self-realization in women—Fiction. | Twin sisters—Fiction. |
    Large type books. | GSAFD: Christian fiction.
Classification: LCC PS3608.A7794 H43 2018b | DDC 813/.6—dc23
LC record available at https://lccn.loc.gov/2018002693

For my husband, Mike—you help me to be the bravest version of myself. Without you, I would not have had the courage to pursue my dreams.

"Men go abroad to wonder at the heights of the mountains, at the huge waves of the sea, at the long courses of the rivers, at the vast compass of the ocean, at the circular motions of the stars, and they pass by themselves without wondering."

—*Saint Augustine*

Prologue

Amy says in order to move forward, I have to stop clinging to the past.

But it's not that simple, to just stop doing something you've done for years. So instead, she's asking me to focus on the future. On my dreams.

Because the thing about dreams is, they give you something to live for.

That's why she had me write a bucket list, twenty-five things I want to do before I die. Twenty-five things that will make my future brighter, that will stop giving my memories so much power over my life.

I've been in therapy for seven years, but I still struggle. Not every day—like at the beginning. But sometimes still, the memories sneak up on me when I least expect them. They drag me down and pull me under like a riptide.

And even though I long to fight them, my arms and legs get tired. I grow weak.

In those moments, I'm maybe kind of okay with letting go and drifting away, allowing the sea to carry me wherever it wants to go.

But now when that happens, I have a new tool. I can try to focus on the dreams, the plans, the goals I have. And I can say, "Not today. I won't let you rip them from me."

It's not necessarily about avoidance or forgetting. There are some things you never forget. Instead, it's about learning to swim parallel to the shore, to be one with the waves, with the pain. To replace weakness with strength, fear with hope.

According to Amy, hope can be my rescuer. If I let it.

Chapter 1

For the first time in her life, Megan Jacobs felt almost brave.

Her hands continued to grip the steering wheel a moment longer than necessary before she put her Ford Focus into Park and cut the engine. The parking lot at the banquet hall was packed, and people strolled toward the entrance dressed to the nines in tuxedos and ball gowns, ready to enjoy the fund-raiser.

Megan really hoped Caleb was among them.

On the other hand, she hoped he wasn't.

But that was the whole point of coming. Not that a fund-raiser for the very hospital where she'd received her heart transplant wasn't worthy of attendance. Still, the only thing that had prompted her to accept the invitation in a last-minute RSVP was seeing on Facebook that her old hospital buddy was heading home for the weekend.

It was finally time to apologize.

Megan blew out a breath, flipped open the lighted mirror on the visor, and angled it downward. Her natural dark-brown hair hung in waves around her face. She'd filled out a lot in the last three and a half years since her surgery, looking healthier than she ever had. Would Caleb notice a difference in her?

Her trembling hand touched the scooped neckline of her red satin dress. Her fingers found the scar that ran from the bottom of her neck nearly to her belly button. The doctors had said it would fade with time. But more than three years later, it was as prominent as ever, like a plump white caterpillar that never moved.

She snatched the smooth, lightweight scarf that lay on the messy passenger seat and for a moment imagined what it would feel like to leave it behind. But then she sighed, wound it around her neck, and draped it to hide the scar.

When she leaned over to grab her clutch, her hand brushed the letter she'd received last week—the one she couldn't bring herself to do anything about. Megan covered it with a magazine that lay on the floor. She'd think about it later. Right now she had to focus on finding Caleb Watkins.

She opened the car door and climbed out into the fading Minnesota sunlight, wobbling on her brand-new stilettos. The days were getting longer now that summer had finally arrived. Winter had lasted longer than usual this year, with a flurry of snow falling in early May.

Megan loved all the seasons but felt a special connection with winter. Maybe that was because she understood it best—the snow covering the ground, burying it, waiting for something to happen. To grow.

Sometimes it seemed she'd been waiting her whole life.

Tiny pebbles crunched beneath her heels as she approached the hall. Strands of classical music drifted toward her. A few other people converged at the door, where a large sign indicated she was in the right place.

Megan said hello to the greeters and was swallowed into a glamorous room decorated with at least thirty round tables, each one featuring a black shimmery tablecloth, an ornate gold-and-floral centerpiece, eight place settings, and name cards. People milled everywhere, gathering in small clusters and gripping champagne flutes or wine glasses. Servers bustled in and out of a swinging door to the left with silver trays, stopping to offer hors d'oeuvres to attendees. The faint scent of seared beef made its way from the kitchen every time a server disappeared or reappeared through the door.

She forced herself to put one foot in front of the other, sneaking peeks around the room for someone she knew—specifically, a lanky guy with dark hair who'd always had the ability to coax a smile out of her even on her worst days. Megan wandered toward the edge of the crowded room. Dealing with hypertrophic cardiomyopathy for so much of her life hadn't provided many opportunities for swanky social gatherings like this one, and so far she didn't recognize anyone. Maybe Caleb wasn't coming after all.

By instinct, she placed two fingers over her wrist. For fifteen seconds, she counted, then did the math in her head. Ninety beats per minute. Right within range, even though a little higher than normal. She took the small notebook out of her purse and jotted down her latest stat. Some might call it an unnecessary habit, one formed during that first year after surgery when her doctor had suggested tracking her heart rate, along with what foods she ate and when she took her medication.

At her first-year checkup, he'd recommended getting a heart-rate tracking device like a Fitbit— something that wouldn't require her to be so vigilant.

She hadn't. If she left it up to a device, she might eventually forget altogether about the need to track her heart rate—and she couldn't afford to be so lax.

Megan capped the pen and stuffed it and her notebook back into her purse. She took a deep breath. Time to find her seat. With steps that were surer than she felt, Megan found the seating chart, then headed toward the front row of tables, looking for her name card. She was so focused, she didn't see the person in front of her and ran straight into someone tall and solidly built.

"Oof." She closed her eyes at the pain that shot through her nose and stepped back. "I'm so sorry."

Two arms steadied her. "Meg?"

She'd know that voice anywhere. She opened her eyes and craned her neck upward. Caleb stared down with his emerald eyes.

Oh.

No longer was he her pale, skinny friend with a mullet who needed a new heart. His cheeks weren't sunken in, his hair had been cut, and his skin had a nice bronze to it. He filled out his suit with muscles she'd never seen before. There hadn't been any recent pictures of him on Facebook. The only photos he'd posted were those he'd taken as a professional photographer. She was wholly unprepared for this transformation.

Because frankly, he was gorgeous.

Megan blinked in rapid succession and stood there like an idiot, unable to say a thing. Their easy camaraderie was gone, now that she and Caleb hadn't spoken in over a year.

Not since he'd called and asked her to come work with him in London like they'd always dreamed—and she'd said yes, only to change her mind a week before the trip, leaving him to scramble for another writer at the last minute.

"Meg? You okay?" Caleb studied her face, his brow furrowed in worry.

She lowered her hand. "Yes." Her voice squeaked as she pushed the word from her lips. She cleared her throat. "Yes, I'm fine. Sorry about running into you. I mean, literally running into you. It doesn't mean I'm not happy to see you." Oh man. This was getting more uncomfortable by the minute. And what now? Did she hug him? Fist bump like they used to? Turn and run right out the front doors, not looking back?

A different kind of anxiety than she'd been feeling that night zipped through her. Almost like . . .

But that was nonsense. This was Caleb. The guy who had been her fellow-patient-slash-friend since their awkward teenage years, who'd maneuvered his wheelchair into her hospital room at two in the morning to share his forbidden pizza more times than she could count. The friend who had spent hours and hours in the hospital's children's center looking at old copies of *National Geographic* with her, dreaming of what life would be like once they got their new hearts. He'd received his five years ago, and she'd been thrilled for him.

But oh, it had been so hard to watch him go on almost immediately to do what they'd dreamed of doing, together—without her. Of course, it didn't make sense to begrudge him. It's not like he'd stopped calling her and giving her encouragement during her presurgery and recovery days.

Well, not until a year ago, when he'd asked her to join him, and she'd chickened out.

So tonight she'd come to make amends.

Enough. Megan stepped forward and wrapped her arms around his chest. His arms encircled her, and for a moment, she was home. The loudness in the room faded.

When she pulled away, the noise came careening back. Caleb smiled, but his features seemed tighter. "It's good to see you."

"You too." She wanted to say more, but how could she go from "Hi" to "I'm sorry" in two seconds flat?

Crystal would have known what to say. She'd have walked into the room completely competent, like she owned the place. Unlike Megan, who shifted from one foot to the other and picked at her cuticles.

But then, her twin had always been Megan's opposite in every way, hadn't she?

Megan tugged at the short waves at the nape of her neck. "H-how are you?"

"You know, living the dream." Caleb chuckled, but something about his laugh sounded off. He fiddled with his bow tie.

"That's great." The words had a ring of fake brightness to them. "You're working as a freelance photographer still, right?" As if she didn't stalk the gorgeous photos from around the world he posted on Facebook—amazing landscapes, dangerous animals, foreign people, wonders of the world.

All the places they'd talked about seeing "someday," he was seeing. And she was busy . . . doing what?

"Yeah, I just got back from Cameroon." A smile settled on Caleb's lips. "You wouldn't believe how lush it is there. And the people are so friendly. You'd be jotting everything in your journal."

Her memory was filled with so many nights in the hospital with Caleb, watching the Travel Channel together, Megan recording details as they flashed across the screen, then attempting later to form them into a written account. Caleb would read her "articles" and decide what pictures he'd take to complement them.

And now it had been years since she'd even touched a journal.

"I'm sure I would."

"Still working at the library?"

"Yes. Same ol', same ol'." Megan had been an aide at the small library in her hometown since high school, and despite the bachelor's degree in English she'd earned online, she'd stayed in the minimum-wage position.

Not just that, but at the age of thirty-two, she still lived with her parents with no concrete plans of moving out. She'd intended to, once she was "well enough." Then the days slipped into weeks and months, even years, and Megan had stayed put.

Her life seemed more pathetic by the moment.

Caleb frowned. He opened his mouth to say something else.

But she couldn't take whatever he was going to say. It was bad enough she was disappointed in herself. Adding her once-upon-a-time best friend's disappointment to the load was more than she could bear. "It's really stuffy in here. I need air." Megan turned on her heels and pushed her way through the crowd. She burst onto a balcony, inhaling the fresh air, taking it in gulps.

Her lungs burned.

"Meg, wait."

She leaned against the concrete railing, her back to Caleb as he approached.

He placed his elbows next to her on the railing. His cologne floated on the evening breeze—a woodsy scent that wasn't familiar. Not familiar but not unpleasant. Not at all. "Can we start over?"

Megan tilted her head toward him. An apology rested in his eyes. She nodded and chewed her bottom lip.

"You look beautiful tonight."

Her cheeks warmed and her eyes flitted back to the horizon. "Thanks." She should compliment

19

him in return. "You don't look so bad yourself."

"I know."

She laughed. Her hand flew out, playfully smacking his arm. "So modest." Now this—this was familiar.

"I'd much rather be in my jeans and T-shirt, though." He snuck a look around and yanked off his bow tie, stuffing it into his pocket. Then he undid the top few buttons on his crisp white shirt. "There. Now I can breathe again."

His transplant scar peeked from below, but he didn't seem to care.

Silence fell. *Now or never, Megan.* She turned her whole body, still cocking a hip against the railing. "Caleb, I came tonight to see you."

"Really?"

She nodded. "I'm sorry about London."

He remained quiet for a moment. "What happened?"

Seeing him there, strong, resilient, living his dream . . . It broke the dam of longing inside of her. How she wished she had half the courage he did. "I convinced myself my health wasn't good enough yet. That it was an adventure for 'later.' "

"I thought I'd given you enough time to recover. Two years should have been plenty, and from our texts and phone calls, it seemed like your doctor was really impressed with your progress. I never meant to push you."

"You didn't." She started pacing and the words

just tumbled out. "It's true there is always the fear of relapse in the back of my mind. But it was more than that. You wanted me to come to London on this grand adventure—and write about it for a magazine."

Caleb scratched behind his ear. "I don't get it. Isn't that what we talked about doing for years? Me photographing, you writing? But then the perfect opportunity came along and you didn't want it."

"I did want it. But fear took over. Because what authority do I have to write about something like that? Me, who has never been anywhere or done anything? Who still lives at home, working the same job I've worked since high school? Who has written countless articles over the years and has only had the courage to ever show them to you and my family—never to submit them?"

Caleb was quiet for a moment. "You said you're sorry. Does that mean you regret saying no, or just regret putting me in a tough spot?"

Tears welled in her eyes and spilled onto her cheeks. She swiped at them as they fell. "I regret all of that."

"Then why haven't you done anything to change it? Why not submit one of those articles? Go somewhere and get experience?"

All million-dollar questions. "I can't explain it. I'm just stuck. It's like any time I get the desire to move forward, something's holding me back. I mean, it's not just about the writing. I can't even get up the courage to see my donor's family." The image of the letter waiting in the car flashed through her mind. One more failure to add to her long list. She continued taking a few steps, pivoted, walked a few more steps. Then started all over again.

Caleb gently stopped her and guided her back toward the edge of the balcony. "Have they contacted you?"

"Janice Harding forwarded me a note they wrote a few weeks ago. They said they're ready to meet me."

"When I met my donor's family, it was really healing for me." Caleb hesitated. "Of course, everyone has a different experience. But it could be good for you."

"Maybe." Janice, the Donor Family Services Representative for the transplant program, had included her own note when she sent the family's. She'd said the ball was completely in Megan's court. A ball Megan had never asked for, one that had come flying out of nowhere, leaving Megan wincing as it hurtled toward her. But how could she deny these people anything?

It was something Nana would have told her to pray about, if she'd still been alive. But what was the point? God would do what he wanted whether she prayed or not.

Caleb reached out and squeezed Megan's hand.

The tender touch was so familiar, but the fire it sent up her fingertips was not. "If you're looking for a way to get 'unstuck,' this might be a good place to start."

He didn't understand. Except, actually, he probably did. "But how do I waltz in there, a living reminder to these people of all they lost? I don't know much about my donor except that she was an eighteen-year-old girl with her whole life ahead of her. How would her family feel knowing I've done absolutely nothing with my life since she saved it?"

It was true, wasn't it? She'd been hiding. Hiding in her parents' home, hiding at the library, hiding from life.

Megan turned to face the lights of Rochester. Somewhere out there, a family waited for closure. Closure only she could give. And maybe in taking that step toward closure for them, Megan would finally find the courage she'd been searching for all these years.

Chapter 2

As far as stomachaches went, Crystal Ballinger's was off-the-charts painful.

She groaned and rolled over in bed, clutching her belly. With her other hand, she felt in the dark until she located the TUMS on her side table. Like a pro, she unscrewed the cap one-handed, fished a tablet out, and popped it in her mouth, chewing as the awful powder coated her tongue. Then she lay there for a moment, letting the fog of sleep drift from her mind.

Why wasn't Brian in bed? Had her husband left for church already? He normally told her good-bye.

Today *was* Sunday, wasn't it?

No, wait. He'd left last night for a twenty-four-hour shift at the station.

And today was Monday.

"What time is it?" No one answered her, but the cat on the end of the bed protested as Crystal bolted upright and grabbed her phone.

8:16 a.m.

And several texts from Tony asking where she was. Oh no.

Despite the discomfort in her stomach, Crystal launched to her feet and scrambled toward her closet, wincing from the pain. She flipped on the light and located the outfit she'd hung up for today, then tore off her pajamas, throwing her legs into the suit pants quickly—too quickly. Her foot caught on the seat of the pants, and a ripping sound reached her.

"No, no, no." She tugged the pants off and examined them. A tear in the main pant seam rendered this pair useless. Crystal tossed them aside and reached for her matching backup pair—but they weren't on the hanger. She'd worn them Friday, hadn't she? Yes, then stuffed them into the bag to take to the dry cleaner's, along with every other pair of pants she owned. Only, she hadn't had time to go to the dry cleaner's this weekend since she'd been working on the Hoffman proposal from dawn till midnight both Saturday and Sunday.

This was a nightmare.

She had no other choice. With a yank, she pulled the pair of pants from Friday out of the bag and carefully stepped into them. She threw on her white blouse and matching suit jacket, then slipped a pair of heels onto her feet. As she passed her mirror, Crystal groaned. She'd just have to hope Leonard Hoffman was more concerned about her plans for his restored New York City bank than her wrinkled pants.

Crystal raced to the front door, grabbed her laptop bag and purse, and rushed to her subway stop. With every step, her body begged for coffee.

Coffee. Coffee. Finally she reached her train—crowded and smelling of things she'd rather not define—and clung to a bar as the car took off at full speed, which still wasn't fast enough. Crystal shot a text to Tony telling him she'd be there on time. She prayed—no, hoped—she was right.

Thank goodness she carried an arsenal of makeup in her purse. Crystal did her best to throw on some foundation, blush, and lipstick one-handed. Then she popped in a breath mint and ran her hands through her two-day-old hair, coercing it into a loose bun with a pen she scrounged up from the bottom of her bag.

Her stop finally arrived and she disembarked. Checking her watch, she climbed the steps to the top of the subway stop and was met by the much-too-cheery sun. Ten minutes till the pitch was supposed to begin. Crystal maneuvered in and out of the crowd, past kids on their way to school, moms with strollers, and countless businessmen and women. "Sorry. Sorry."

Finally she reached her building. Spying a huge crowd at the elevators, she opted for the stairs and ran up ten flights in her four-inch heels. The stifling air in the stairwell nearly suffocated her.

Her chest heaved as she threw open the heavy metal stairwell door and ran toward her suite. She nearly doubled over at the wrenching pain in her stomach but wouldn't let that stop her. These pains seemed to come at the most inconvenient times. She was almost there, with two minutes to spare. As she entered the front door of Samson Group Architectural, the front office attendant, Todd, did a double take. "What the—"

"I don't want to hear it." Crystal straightened her back and slowed her pace. If Leonard Hoffman was already here, the last thing she wanted to do was startle him. First impressions were undoable—and hers was bound to be awful as it was, thanks to her sweaty armpits and disheveled appearance.

She finally arrived at the grouping of cubicles in the main workroom. Other junior architects bustled to and fro, some chatting at the water cooler. Other voices rang out as they talked on the phone. The intern, Jamie, spotted her from down the hall and her eyes widened. Crystal reached her cubicle, pulled her printed proposal and laptop from her bag, and threw the empty bag onto her chair. She whirled and headed down the hallway toward the conference room, where Tony's voice boomed. As she entered, Crystal blew out a breath when she saw only Tony and Jamie.

"Jamie, I need coffee. Stat. Please."

The girl bolted out of the room.

Her boss's gaze narrowed when he saw her. "Where have you been?"

"Didn't you see my text?" Crystal set her laptop down and bent to grab the appropriate cords. "I overslept. I was here late last night and must have been really out of it this morning. I'm so sorry." She avoided his stare as she popped the cords into the right outlets on her computer. Now was not the time to come across as incompetent, not when she had a possible promotion on the line.

"You're lucky the client is running a bit behind. He just got into town. Flight was delayed."

She flashed him a weary smile. "See? It all worked out."

Some might have said it was because the good Lord was watching over her. But Crystal knew better than that.

She pulled up the right presentation file. It loaded and projected onto the screen behind her. There. She'd done it. She clutched her side and grimaced.

Tony frowned, his eyes perusing her. "Your stomach again?"

"It's fine." Probably a pesky ulcer. Mom used to get them all the time, said they were stress-related. No wonder with all the worrying she used to do over Megan. And it wouldn't be a surprise if Crystal had one too, with all the work she'd been putting in lately. If Brian knew about it, he'd try to get her to see a doctor, but there was never time. Besides, she'd been keeping the pain mostly under control with the TUMS.

"You look awful. Hoffman is expecting 2017's

Junior Architect of the Year, not a hobo off the streets."

Her cheeks flooded with heat. "Let me run to the restroom and fix myself up a bit." Not waiting for her boss to say anything else, Crystal ran out of the room—and straight into Jamie. Coffee from the mug in Jamie's hands splashed all over Crystal's blouse and jacket. She couldn't help the screech that flew from her mouth.

Jamie shrank back. "Oh no. I didn't mean . . . It was an accident. Let me get a paper towel or something."

"It's fine. I'm going to the bathroom anyway." As if wrinkled pants and a half-made-up face weren't enough . . .

She headed toward the lobby but spied a few women sitting on the sofas, briefcases in hand. Not Mr. Hoffman, but it could be other potential clients or Mr. Hoffman's associates. No way could she be seen like this. Crystal turned on her heel and quick-stepped back to her cubicle. What could she do about her stained shirt?

Jamie rounded the corner. "Mr. Hoffman and his team are here." The girl looked positively ill.

Crystal's eyes drifted to Jamie's reddish-orange sweater. It wouldn't match the style of Crystal's suit, but what other choice did she have? "Jamie, I need your sweater. Hurry." Oh, that had come out much more of a bark than she'd intended. "Please."

The girl flew into action, revealing a turtleneck short-sleeve shirt underneath her sweater. Crystal unbuttoned her own jacket and flung it aside, then pulled Jamie's sweater over her soiled blouse. The sweater was made of the itchiest material Crystal had ever worn—polyester, if she had to hazard a guess—but a quick glimpse down told her it at least covered the offending stain. "That'll have to do. Thanks."

She left her cubicle and Jamie behind, turning back toward the conference room. When she entered, Tony and Landon—another partner— were chatting with a distinguished gentleman in his seventies and the two women Crystal had seen in the lobby. The man wore an Armani suit and smelled of Cuban cigars.

Crystal pasted on a large grin and approached him, her hand outstretched. "Crystal Ballinger. So pleased to finally meet you, Mr. Hoffman."

He took her in, one eyebrow cocked, but nodded. "You as well. I've heard great things about your work."

"Thank you, sir. I hope you won't be disappointed."

This was it. If she nailed this presentation, Tony would have to promote her to senior architect. He'd been grooming her for years anyway, and with Karen's departure last week, the job was hers for the taking.

Crystal launched into her presentation.

Dragging any decent ideas from her overtired brain had been a challenge over the last few weeks, but she'd managed to come up with something good. Brian hadn't liked the long hours she was putting in, but she'd promised him she'd back off a little after this Hoffman proposal was in the books, once her promotion was secure. She'd even promised they could finally plan a trip to visit her family in Minnesota. Because Brian didn't have family of his own, he wanted to get to know hers better. But the thought of facing Megan and her parents turned her stomach.

Still, that's what people did when they loved each other—compromised. And she loved her husband with an intensity that sometimes scared her. Not that she was that great at telling him. But she'd get better. It was on her list of things to improve.

She flew through the presentation. Hopefully Mr. Hoffman would see that, despite her appearance, her work spoke for itself. Mr. Hoffman was hard to read, but so were other clients, and she'd never failed to land an account since beginning her tenure at Samson Group seven years ago. Despite her lack of coffee and the ache that pressed into her belly like a needle, her presentation was flawless. She hit the last slide. "I'd be happy to answer any questions you might have at this time."

A silence bubbled in the room. Mr. Hoffman's

poker face fell into a frown, and self-doubt slipped into Crystal's conscious. Still, her smile remained in place.

"I do have one question." Mr. Hoffman steepled his fingers on top of the conference table. His stare bore a hole into Crystal's confidence.

Be strong. Be steady. Don't let him see you sweat. "Yes, anything."

"I want to know where you're hiding the bright young architect I've heard so much about."

Was he referring to Meredith, another junior architect who also happened to be her main competition for the promotion? "I'm sorry. I don't—"

"This presentation. It was something I'd expect from a college student." Each word punctured another hole in Crystal's facade of confidence.

Her stomach cramped in pain, and she had to blow out a breath through her teeth, hissing slightly. "I'm so sorry it wasn't what you were looking for."

Tony caught her grimace and rescued her. "As one of our most talented junior architects, Crystal has been swimming in a sea of work lately, taking on the work of someone with twice her years of experience. Perhaps we haven't given her the support she needs to do your project justice. Would you consider giving us another week to put together a more appealing proposal?"

"I don't think so." Mr. Hoffman stood, and his

two tight-lipped associates followed suit. "Ms. Ballinger, I'd heard you were one of the most creative minds in the business, light-years ahead of your colleagues." He tossed her proposal onto the desk in disgust. "I heard wrong. Good day." He turned and left the room, and his associates scurried after him.

Crystal sank down into the nearest seat. She glanced up at Tony, who frowned. "I'm sorry."

Tony took off his glasses and fingered the frames. "Me too." He tapped the edge of his glasses against the oak table. "He's right. It wasn't your best work."

Deep down, she knew that. "I worked my rear off to get it right. It's just—"

Crystal stopped herself. She couldn't tell her boss she was out of ideas—that as much as she tried, she couldn't find an ounce of inspiration to save her life. Great architects didn't sputter out after only seven years on the job. Twenty, maybe. But seven?

She'd just have to try harder. Make a new plan. Remind herself that she was in control of her own destiny.

That had always worked in the past. And it had to work now.

Chapter 3

Megan couldn't believe she was about to do this.

She faced down the huge brick home—the place her heart donor used to live. Her hands shook as she shut the car door and walked up the drive. The house was located in the center of the Rochester suburbs and was surrounded by large oak trees full of life. A breeze rustled through the branches, and the leaves waved at her.

Almost like they were welcoming her heart home.

This heart would never be hers. Not really. And though it kept her alive, it hadn't seemed to change who she was, however much she might wish it had.

Above her, the sky shone a brilliant blue, dotted occasionally with wispy clouds. It was the kind of day that should be spent lounging on her back in the green grass, daydreaming about the future. But today belonged to the Abbotts.

As it turned out, showing up at the fund-raiser on Friday had resulted in more than just smoothing things over with Caleb. The several hours they'd spent reminiscing and talking had far exceeded her expectations. His pep talk had given her the courage to finally call Janice

Harding and get the Abbotts' number, then phone the Abbotts on Monday.

Mrs. Abbott had answered Megan's call and gently requested Megan visit them at home. Her husband, a physician, was off on Wednesday—would that work?

She'd expected more time to prepare herself but supposed sooner was better. Less chance of chickening out. Mom had offered to come with her, but Megan knew she was supposed to do this alone.

Megan reached the Abbotts' large front door, where a lion's head knocker stared at her. She opted for the doorbell instead. As soon as she pressed the button, the sound of chimes rang inside, merrily announcing her arrival.

A woman of medium height opened the door wearing pressed blue slacks, a sweater, and a strand of pearls around her throat. She looked to be in her mid-forties, and her hair was pulled back in a low bun. Her lips quivered as she took in Megan. "I'm Charlene. Charlene Abbott." The woman's words tumbled out in a light Southern accent. "You must be Megan."

"Yes." For a moment, she was frozen to the step. Behind Charlene a large staircase rose and split in two directions. A dazzling chandelier hung overhead, casting little beams of light every which way as the sunlight reached through the doorway.

Charlene extended her hand. "It's so nice . . ." She gulped. "I'm sorry. I'm just . . ."

"It's okay. Me too." Megan felt instant compassion for this woman who had lost a daughter. It didn't matter how big her house was or how much money she had. Charlene would never get the one thing she truly wanted. Megan took Charlene's hand in hers and without thinking, pulled the woman into a hug.

Charlene's arms tightened around Megan. She was shorter than Megan and her head rested near Megan's chest. For a moment, the woman leaned her head in, as if—oh. Megan's heart picked up speed.

Charlene shuddered in her arms. She pulled back and wiped her eyes. "I'm so sorry. It's just . . . Thank you. I never thought I'd hear Amanda's heart beat again."

Heat welled behind Megan's eyes and she couldn't keep a sob from bubbling up in her throat. "It's my pleasure."

Shaking her head, Charlene straightened. "Look at us, a couple of bawlin' Bessies. Come in, please, and meet my husband." She led Megan down a high-ceilinged hallway to a living room decorated in a country chic design. Charlene indicated for Megan to sit on the light-brown loveseat. "I'll fetch him from his study."

She left and returned with a tall man who had

a salt-and-pepper mustache and a full head of hair. "I'm Gary Abbott, Ms. Jacobs." He shook Megan's hand, and he and Charlene sat opposite her on the sofa.

"Call me Megan, please."

"Megan. Thank you for coming." Gary reached for his wife's hand and took it in his own, gently stroking it with his thumb as he leaned forward. "We appreciate you coming here. I know this must be difficult for you as well, but we were finally ready to meet the people Amanda helped."

It was common for organ donors to save several lives, depending on the nature of their death. "How many were there?"

"Six. One didn't want to meet, and two are out of state. We've met the other two—and you make three." Charlene's lips pulled into a thin line.

"I'm glad I could come." Hard as it was to be here, that was the truth. Megan owed Caleb for encouraging her to step out in faith and contact the Abbotts. Maybe this would help them all move forward. "I'd love to hear about Amanda, if you're willing to share."

"Of course." Charlene looked at Gary, her lip caught between her teeth. Then her gaze swiveled back to Megan. "Would . . . would you like to see Amanda's room?"

A room was an intimate thing. What would Megan discover about the sort of person her donor had been? She nodded her assent.

Charlene beamed, and she popped up from her place on the sofa. "Follow me."

Megan rose and followed Charlene down the hallway and up the front staircase. She ran her hand along the smooth railing as she climbed, imagining Amanda doing the same thing day after day. "How long have you lived here?"

"We're originally from Georgia. We moved here when Amanda was ten." Charlene turned left at the top of the stairs and abruptly stopped at a row of pictures. Her hand moved to swipe a speck of unseen dust off one of the frames.

As Megan got closer, she could see that each frame held a photo of a blonde-haired girl with a huge smile. Amanda Abbott had been a knockout, the kind of beauty every other girl wished she could be. But something in her eyes radiated kindness—and so she also seemed like the type of girl Megan would have felt an instant connection with. In one picture, a young Amanda rode a horse, pride and confidence evident in her stance astride the animal. In another, the girl grinned as she threw her arms around the neck of her daddy.

Megan's heart leaped in her chest—almost as if it recognized the picture and longed to be nearer to it, nearer to the memory.

Megan tore her eyes from the pictures and saw Charlene watching her. She cleared her throat. "She was beautiful."

"Inside and out." Charlene swiped another tear and motioned farther down the hall. "Her room is this way."

Megan followed the woman into the bedroom at the end of the hall. She circled the room and took in all the knickknacks, including framed photos by Amanda's bed of her and her friends, and one of her and her parents. She turned to Charlene, who had picked up a jewelry box with Amanda's name engraved along the front edge. "Do you have any other children?"

Without looking up, Charlene shook her head. "We lost a few babies in the womb before Amanda came along. She was our miracle."

Grief socked Megan in the gut. All of their children, gone.

The things God allowed to happen . . . They sometimes made no sense.

Megan turned to leave the room, but a bulletin board with a huge photo collage caught her eye. She walked closer. Each photo featured something from a different country: flamenco dancers in Spain, gondolas in Venice, Buckingham Palace in London, and more.

"She always wanted to travel abroad." Charlene stood just behind Megan, and her gentle voice floated on the air, almost reverent here in Amanda's world. "She dreamed of being a doctor, you know. Like her daddy. Planned to go to Harvard." Megan had always wanted to attend an Ivy League school, but instead completed her English degree online over the course of eight years in between bouts of illness. "She'd just found out she was accepted on early admission, when—well, the accident was two days later."

Megan touched the edge of the nearest picture, where a herd of animals flooded the Serengeti plain in Africa. "What happened to her, if you don't mind my asking?"

"I don't mind." Charlene walked to the bed and sat. "It was just before Christmas, as you know. We were on our way to a party and were T-boned in an intersection. All Gary and I suffered physically were a few broken ribs. But the main impact occurred right where Amanda was sitting."

Megan stared at the picture of the flamenco dancers. The reds and greens and oranges blurred together thanks to the tears forming in her eyes. The dresses seemed to spin, as if the performers were really there, dancing for her. Dancing for Amanda. "I'm so sorry."

"A nurse actually told me I was lucky I didn't experience more severe injuries, since Amanda and I were sitting on the same side of the car. *Lucky*." Charlene choked on the word. "Can you believe someone would say that to me?"

"People say dumb things when they don't know what else to do." Megan had certainly heard her fill of platitudes over the years.

She pulled her eyes from the photo collage and turned to Amanda's mom, who'd begun to cry. Megan was only making it worse for this poor woman by being here. "I should go."

"No, I'm sorry." Charlene cleared her throat, stood, and straightened her blouse. "Let's go back downstairs. We want to show you something."

She followed Charlene through the hallway, past the photos of Amanda, and downstairs to where Gary waited. He hadn't moved from his spot on the sofa.

"Sit, dear. I'll be right back." Charlene scooted out of the room toward the kitchen.

Gary stared at the clock on the wall—or maybe at the family photo beneath it. How difficult this must be for him.

They sat in silence until Charlene swung back into the room with a plateful of cookies, a book of some sort, and a cup of ice water, which she placed in front of Megan on the glass-topped coffee table. "Please. Take a treat."

Mom always taught Megan and Crystal to be polite, so she took a cookie. This was the first bite of sugar she'd even contemplated eating since her doctor had given her a strict post-transplant diet regimen. She slipped a bite of the sweet into her mouth and let a chocolate chip sit on her tongue. Wow. She'd forgotten how good chocolate tasted.

Settling back onto the couch, Charlene looked

at her husband with raised eyebrows—a cue of some sort. Gary straightened and nodded. "Megan, we are so thankful you've come today. You don't know how much it means for us to see how Amanda's death was not in vain. That others were saved because of her."

Megan swallowed her bite. "Of course."

He hesitated. "Our daughter had trials in life, ones not of her own making. She did her best to deal with them . . ." He stopped, swallowed hard.

Next to Gary, his wife nibbled the edge of a fingernail and stared at her feet.

Gary finally spoke again. "Ever since we moved here, she was in therapy to overcome those trials. Her therapist encouraged her to journal, you see. We discovered the journal from the last year of her life in her desk after her death."

"Not that we were snooping." Charlene leaned forward suddenly, as if desperate for Megan to know they weren't those types of parents. "I found it when I finally got up the courage to tidy her room."

She pointed to the book on the coffee table. It was spiral-bound with a picture of the Eiffel Tower on the cover. "I know it seems a bit unconventional to let you see something like this. After all, it's deeply personal, at times raw. But we decided that if you chose to come see us and asked to know more about Amanda, we'd show this to you."

Megan picked up the journal and traced the picture. She opened to the front, where Amanda's name was scrawled across the page in typical teenage bubbly letters.

Gary cleared his throat. "In this particular journal, she created a bucket list for herself. Things she wanted to do, places she wanted to see. It was Amy's—her therapist's—idea, a way for Amanda to replace her losses and grief with something else. Joy. Hope. Something to look toward instead of always looking backward."

Megan's gaze careened upward and connected with Gary's. Oh, how she could relate to that last statement.

"That's her bucket list on the first page."

She scanned it and saw a lot of dreams—from things as silly as kissing the Blarney Stone in Ireland to adventurous goals like running with the bulls in Pamplona. Number nineteen made Megan giggle: *Kiss a handsome stranger in the rain.*

"Take a look at the last item on Amanda's bucket list."

Megan flipped the page and saw a few more items. When her eyes hit number twenty-five, her mouth fell open.

25. Give my heart away.

Megan covered her mouth with a hand. The air buzzed with premonition. It did not feel like a coincidence that she was here.

Charlene twisted the huge ring on her finger. "We know it's not how she meant it, but she did that—for you. She gave her heart away. She completed one item on her list."

"And you don't know how grateful I am." A tear slipped from Megan's nose onto the paper, thankfully missing the print. She smoothed it away with her thumb.

For a moment, Charlene studied her. Something in her gaze seemed to read something inside of Megan. She glanced at Gary and worried her lip. "Would you . . . would you like to keep the journal for a bit?"

"Oh, I couldn't do that. It's precious to you." And yet something in her knew that she wanted nothing more than to read Amanda's words, to know more deeply this girl who had given her heart away to a stranger.

Charlene stood, approached Megan, and squatted next to her. She reached out, hesitant for a moment, and placed her hand over Megan's— Amanda's—heart. "It is indeed. But I feel a prompting to let it go for a while, to allow someone else the pleasure of knowing my girl, struggles and all."

"Are you sure?" The words came out a whisper.

Charlene glanced back at Gary, and he nodded. She faced Megan again. "I'm sure."

And Megan had the strangest feeling that this visit wasn't going to be the end of one chapter as she'd hoped. It was going to be the beginning of something else entirely.

Crystal was going to be fired. She just knew it.

Come to my office. Now. That was all Tony's instant message had said. Crystal's head spun as she headed down the hallway. It had been two days since she'd bombed the Hoffman presentation. She thought maybe she'd skated by. But by now, Tony would have had a chance to talk with the other partners and realize Crystal wasn't senior architect material.

Maybe she wasn't even junior architect material anymore.

Her stomach clenched as she opened Tony's door and peeked her head inside.

Her boss sat hunched over his desk, fingers to his temples as he studied a report. He'd discarded his tie.

"Knock, knock." Crystal tried to sound confident, but her voice betrayed her.

Tony looked up. "Come in." He began clicking his computer mouse and the printer whirred behind him. "Grab some coffee if you want."

So he wanted her to get comfortable. Maybe this wasn't a worst-case scenario after all. Crystal headed for Tony's personal Keurig and brewed herself a cup, adding a tiny dash of hazelnut creamer. She took the mug between her fingers and the warmth seeped into them. With a sip, the coffee slipped down her throat. But the sweetness of the drink couldn't soothe the sourness in her soul.

Crystal took a seat across from Tony, who was still occupied with something else. As he snatched papers from the printer and stapled them, her eyes roamed his office, took in the wall full of awards, each one lauding his tireless efforts in building the Manhattan skyline as one of the city's best architects. The couch in back where he spent many nights after working like a dog. The framed picture of his boys, now thirteen and fifteen, who lived full-time with their mother. They'd been married for eighteen years when Carrie divorced him last year—because he worked too much, or so Crystal had heard.

A stab of anxiety rolled through Crystal's veins. But that would never be her and Brian. She wouldn't let it. They'd figure out their differences, settle into a better routine soon.

He'd been sweet on Monday night, comforting her after she'd bombed the Hoffman project. He'd made her favorite dinner, and one thing had led to another . . .

Her cheeks warmed at the remembrance. It was the first time they'd been together in weeks. Or was it months?

Maybe doing so poorly on the Hoffman presentation was a blessing in disguise.

Although she couldn't help but wonder—and

hate herself for it—if Brian secretly hoped her failure would mean she'd move on from her goal of advancing at the firm. He supported her dreams, yes, but she knew he also longed for a wife focused on the same things he was. Career advancement had never been at the top of his priority list.

It hadn't always been at the top of Crystal's either. But the last few years especially had lit a fire in her, and more and more she'd become attached to the idea of gaining a promotion to senior architect, then achieving partner by the age of forty. And now that a spot had finally opened for senior architect, she could practically taste the victory.

Or had been able to, before the Hoffman presentation had gone awry.

Tony finally swiveled in his chair, holding a file. "Knowing you, you're still reeling from the Hoffman rejection."

She forced a chuckle. "I guess you know me pretty well."

"I'm not going to lie. It would have been a decent-size account, and Landon and the others are not happy about losing it. They questioned my decision to trust a junior architect with such a large venture in the first place."

She gulped. There was nothing she could say to defend herself. Even her promise to do better seemed inadequate.

He continued. "However, I reminded them how talented you are and that everyone is allowed one screwup. That was yours. Let's move past it." Tony held out the file toward Crystal. "I just heard about this exciting new opportunity."

She set her mug on his desk and took the file from his outstretched hand. Inside was a call for proposals from the Jeff Lerner Corporation. "Isn't this one of the top investment firms in New York?"

"It is." Tony leaned forward, light and extra energy in his eyes.

Crystal scanned the proposal and got a funny feeling in the pit of her stomach. "They want to tear down the James Lawrence building?"

How many times had she walked past that run-down building in the heart of Manhattan on her way to work, often stopping to stare at it and imagine what it once was—what it could be, with a little help?

"No, no, not tear it down. Refurb it. Expand it. Revive it, if you will. There are several surrounding apartment complexes the company has purchased as well. They want to make it into an entire community unlike anything else in the city."

Every architect had a dream project: add a skyscraper to the Big Apple skyline, or create a glitzy gallery frequented by the elite, or build monuments to great leaders. Something in

Crystal told her that this project was why she had become an architect. She'd seen the James Lawrence building's potential the first time she'd discovered it as a first-year grad student new to the city. It was a hidden treasure, overshadowed by the buildings around it.

But given a little love and attention, it would shine. She just knew it.

"I want this project, sir." She tried not to let the giddiness in her bubble to the surface. But it was the first time in forever that she'd felt excited about a project. No way could she let anyone else work on it.

"Glad to hear it. Because it's going to be an important one."

"In what way?"

"It could be your ticket to a promotion."

Crystal sobered. These were the words she'd longed to hear.

"As you know, being a smaller boutique firm, we take a long view of things and tend to groom our senior architects for partnership. They also take on some management responsibilities, so it's not just about being creative. It's about communication, dedication, hard work—all of which I believe you have in spades."

Tony raised an eyebrow in her direction. "It's no secret I've been singing your praises for years now, but the others aren't convinced. Yes, you've done fabulous work in the past, but lately . . .

49

Well, they want to know you can really handle the senior architect position."

"I can, Tony. You know I can."

"As I said, I have faith in you, but a few others believe Meredith would be a better fit. Given its size, the Lerner project is a good opportunity to test your merit. I'm going to ask both of you to prepare proposals separately, and we'll present them to Mr. Lerner and his team. If he chooses one over the other, the selection will be clear."

Okay, so not exactly what she wanted to hear.

But even though her work had been subpar lately, the fact she had a chance to work on the James Lawrence building in order to secure this promotion had to mean something. If she believed in divine signs, she'd take this as one. That job was as good as hers. "Understood, sir. When is the proposal due?"

"That's the good news. We have some time. About two months, in fact."

"Why so long?"

"The CEO himself wants to sit in on the presentations, and he's out of the country until August."

Good. Not only did that give her time to perfect the proposal, but she should be able to honor her promise to Brian of more quality time. Mostly. There would be some late nights, but he had to understand that. After all, the promotion was directly tied to this project's success.

Achieving her goal would be a testament to who she was as a person—someone who had something to offer the world, who took life and made it what she wanted it to be.

Crystal stood to leave. "I'll get started on it right away."

Everything was finally going according to her plans. All of her hard work was about to pay off. She'd blow Jeff Lerner away with her proposal for the James Lawrence building, get to work on the project of her heart, make senior architect, and someday partner—and finally establish herself as someone worthy of remembrance.

Now all she had to do was convince her husband that any time spent working on this new proposal would be worth it in the end.

Chapter 4

Megan walked through the large oak door of her parents' home and kicked off her brown sandals in the entryway. The hour-long drive from the Abbotts' to Little Lakes had given her lots of time to think—and cry—as day became dusk.

The house was quiet, despite the presence of her parents' cars in the drive. Maybe they were next door, enjoying the first part of the evening on the Johnsons' back porch. Good. She loved her parents, but Mom would want to know everything about her visit. And right now, Megan didn't have the energy to share all she was feeling, partly because she wasn't totally sure herself.

Megan headed to the kitchen, which always brightened her mood with its yellow walls and smooth white granite countertops. The shabby chic curtains floated in the breeze coming through the open window. The evidence of an early dinner still hung in the air, which smelled like lasagna. Since Megan hadn't known when she'd be home, she'd told her parents to eat without her.

Megan rummaged in the fridge and pulled out some veggies and a head of lettuce. She chopped the vegetables, threw them over the lettuce, and poured vinegar and extra-virgin olive oil on top. Then she headed down to the basement where the comfiest couch in the world sat before a fifty-five-inch television. She plopped down, set her salad on the couch next to her, and used the remote to scan channels.

She settled back and watched a few minutes of a *Gilmore Girls* rerun. She crunched bell peppers and carrots, barely tasting anything. With the flick of her wrist, she flipped through channels again. When she found herself pulled in by a documentary on the Travel Channel, the old familiar pang nearly rent her heart in two and she hit the Off button. The room grew dark.

After getting a new heart three and a half years ago, she'd often wondered if she'd ever be "well enough" to travel. But after her conversation with Caleb on Friday, she was seeing things a lot more clearly. It all boiled down to fear . . . and what she was going to do about it.

Maybe her sickness had nothing to do with her physical heart—and everything to do with her emotional one. She placed a hand over Amanda's heart and sat still for a moment. It beat steadily inside of her. Today it had almost felt like it was trying to tell her something. But that was ridiculous.

Still, it had once beat inside a girl who, like Megan, had dreamed of adventure. *"Would you . . . would you like to keep the journal for a bit?"*

Charlene's question reverberated in her mind.

Megan snatched her bowl and took it back to the kitchen where she'd left her purse. She grabbed it, headed for her bedroom, and sat on the foot of her canopy bed. The room still featured the soft lavender comforter she'd had for the last fifteen years. In fact, the entire room was a monument to teenage Megan. The Backstreet Boys still grinned at her from a poster above her desk, and her boom box sat on her white fairytale dresser with a stack of outdated CDs beside it. A Minnesota Vikings hat hung from the side of her dresser, a gift from her football-loving father trying to get at least one of his daughters to cherish the sport as much as he did.

She pulled Amanda's journal from her purse and cracked the cover. Just after the bucket list, there was an entry that began: *Amy says in order to move forward, I have to stop clinging to the past.*

Megan read the passage—and was hooked. She moved to the next entry.

1. See the world from the top of the London Eye.

When I was eight, Daddy took me on my first Ferris wheel ride. It was awe-inspiring, seeing the world from such a different point of view.

And that's what I need now: a perspective change. For seven years, I've battled depression. So for seven years, I've had my fill of therapy sessions, of journaling, of processing. And I've come a long way. I'm seventeen now, healthier than I've ever been. Stronger. I sometimes look back at my old journal entries, and I can see the progress I've made. I can see myself becoming someone entirely different, being rebuilt one page at a time.

But there are still times I can't get out of my own head. I can't see past what's right in front of me. I can't forgive Uncle Joe for what he did to me, the way he splintered our family forever. For the way Mom still thinks it's her fault, because she allowed her troubled younger brother into our lives.

See? The old me would have said it was my fault. Progress.

But still, I fight that stupid depression monster. Sometimes I find myself walking around my bedroom and staring at my pictures, seeing a blonde girl I don't recognize. Who is she? She looks like me, and I can imagine she talks like me, but she doesn't smile like me. She really means it—in those moments. But when I look back and see her in those frozen frames, I can't remember the joy.

Will the joy ever come naturally? Will it ever be my first instinct? Will I ever be able to give myself fully to it without being sucked into a vortex of pain and guilt?

My childhood is almost over—has been over for years, really, and I've walked around in a child's body, knowing things I shouldn't know.

If only the not-quite-adult-not-quite-child me could go back and rescue the ten-year-old me.

But one thing I've realized in my years of therapy: if-onlys don't exist.

And I kind of think that's the perspective I need to embrace if I'm ever going to really live.

Megan couldn't relate to the kind of awful situation Amanda alluded to—no one should have to—but she found herself nodding along with the girl's words. Her own childhood had been sucked away too, in a different way, every spare moment spent in the hospital, watching from afar as Crystal lived the life she wanted.

But Amanda was right. If-onlys didn't exist.

The only thing that did exist? Right here, right now. And Amanda didn't have that anymore. It had been taken from her. She'd only been able to complete one item on her list, and not even in the way she'd meant. Amanda would never have the opportunity to do the other twenty-four things on her list.

And suddenly an idea popped into Megan's mind. An idea too crazy, too scary to really contemplate.

It wasn't realistic.

It overreached her bounds.

Surely it wasn't even feasible.

It would take time. Money.

And courage. Lots of courage.

But Amanda's heart inside Megan picked up pace at the idea, as if urging her along.

"Is that what you'd want, Amanda? To complete your list?"

Ba-dum, ba-dum, ba-dum. The girl's heart pulsed beneath Megan's fingers in agreement.

"Then maybe . . . maybe you can. We can." Megan's breath shuddered in and out at the eerie sensation. "Maybe I can do it for you."

Crystal headed down the dim hallway of her office building after yet another grueling twelve-hour day. Excitement over the Lerner project had pinged through her whole body all day, ever since Tony told her about it. Motion-sensor lights popped on as she passed. She stepped onto the elevator and rode down ten stories, leaning her tired body against the wall as she watched the numbers flip by on the digital screen above the doors.

But the anticipation of her needed conversation with Brian lodged in her side like a large splinter. She felt the discomfort no matter which way she bent. And she wouldn't even be able to talk with him till tomorrow thanks to his overnight shift at the fire station.

A janitor mopping the floors in the lobby nodded hello as she passed. Crystal pushed the heavy front door of the building open and was met with the bustle of a busy street. Taxis honked and moved like snails through downtown Manhattan, and people of all kinds wound their way down the sidewalk—theater-goers, performing artists, girls in slinky dresses headed for the local bars and hottest clubs. The smell of Italian food from the fine restaurant down the street mingled with the scent of hot dogs rising from the vendor's cart in front of Crystal's building.

How she wished Brian would be home when she got there. They could order a pizza and watch their DVR'ed episodes of *Survivor*. And maybe, when the timing was right, she could tell him all about the Lerner project and how much it would mean for her to work on it. She'd explain her heart, he'd explain his, and they'd work through their differences, like all married couples did.

Suddenly a fierce ache for her husband attacked her. She missed him, and she didn't want to wait until tomorrow to see him. Maybe . . . was that dumb? No, why not? Unless the crew was out on a call, everyone should be awake.

It had been a while since she'd visited him at work. Too long. Yes, that's what she'd do. Surprise him. Show him their marriage still had a little mystery left. A thrill of pleasure wound through Crystal as she headed toward the subway and took the train to the right stop. She climbed the stairs and emerged in front of Brian's station. The trucks were parked inside, which meant the guys were there.

She pushed through the front doors and took in the flurry of activity before her. A few guys shot a ball back and forth across a ping-pong table, others cheering them on. Some lounged in overstuffed chairs and read or chatted, sodas in their hand. Two men watched *Top Gun* on the beat-up television set that looked to be from the nineties. Several crew members stood in the kitchen, prepping a late dinner. Crystal's eyes landed on her husband, chatting and laughing as he chopped vegetables.

Brian looked up. "Crys." He put down his knife, wiped his hands on a towel, and made his way around the island. Her husband was such a good-looking guy with his short blonde hair, broad shoulders, and sun-kissed skin, and she didn't often notice the effect he had on her.

But right now her pulse raced and her mouth felt dry.

When he reached her, he threw his arms around her. "You're here." The faint scent of his vanilla-rum cologne enveloped her.

She laughed into his neck. "I just thought I'd stop by—"

"Crystal, long time, no see." She pulled back to find Ben, a skinny redhead with a bulbous nose, sauntering up. He'd started on the crew the same day as Brian. "How ya been?"

She felt the eyes of everyone in the room on her. "Good to see you, Ben. And I'm fine. Busy."

"Must be. You used to come around here at least twice a week." Ben popped her in the arm playfully. "You'd bring me a bear claw, remember that?"

"That's right. From Gino's down the street." She turned to Brian. "And I'd bring you a chocolate Long John."

"Those were the best donuts I've ever tasted." He winked at her.

She suddenly felt like a schoolgirl with her first crush. "I see there are a few people here I haven't met. Want to introduce me?"

"Not really." He put his arm around her waist and tugged her closer. "I kind of want you all to myself." His whispered words were hot against her ear.

"Get a room already." Ben shoved Brian toward the hallway, and the other crew members laughed and whistled.

Brian grabbed Crystal's hand, leading her down the hall. He opened the door to one of the bunkrooms. Inside the tight quarters, there were two twin beds and two dressers. From the window, the setting sun said its good-byes as it drifted beyond the horizon and gave up the sky to the crescent moon.

Her husband closed the door behind them and pulled her against his chest. He worked his hands into her hair, looking into her eyes with a hunger that hadn't been there in a long time. Had it been there Monday night? If so, she'd been too consumed with her own sorrow to notice.

Whatever had come over him, she didn't mind one bit. "Hi."

"Hi." He leaned in and kissed her, moving his lips to her ears and neck.

She was losing herself in his embrace in a way she hadn't allowed herself to be lost in forever. Going, going, gone. And it was blissful.

Brian trailed his fingers down her arms. "I told Ben there was no way you'd forgotten. You probably left early this morning to let me sleep since you knew I had a shift."

Crystal shook the fog from her brain. Forgotten what? Scanning her mind for promises and commitments, she came up empty. Maybe if she just played along . . . "That's true. I didn't want to keep you from your beauty rest." She winked.

He acknowledged her playfulness with a grin. "You didn't know that I'd planned to surprise you with breakfast. But I couldn't expect you to read my mind."

Oh man, what in the world was he talking about? "Right."

His face fell, hands dropping to his sides. "You forgot our anniversary, didn't you?"

Bile rose in her throat. "Oh no."

It'd been five years since they'd said "I do" at a justice-of-the-peace ceremony in the middle of the day on a Thursday. When she'd suggested they elope, Brian had resisted the idea at first. But the thought of rubbing her happy relationship in Megan's face like that, when her sister was on the brink of death and Crystal hadn't been there for her like a good sister would have been—well, it gave her extra motivation to be persuasive.

Last week she'd made a mental note to buy Brian an anniversary gift. But between then and now, that note must have been covered up by all the other sticky notes piling up in her life. "I'm so sorry, Brian." She stepped forward, reached out a hand to comfort him—but there wasn't any comfort to be had for that kind of screwup. Crystal's hands became fists at her sides instead. "I guess my mind has been elsewhere."

He blew out a sigh and sank to the edge of his bed. "Things have to change, Crys. We can't keep going like this."

Crystal leaned against one of the faux wood armoires in the room. "I'll admit our schedules have been crazy lately."

"Not our schedules. Yours."

Were they really going to have this same old argument again? It never got them anywhere. "I know I've been working a lot lately. But we had some great time together on Monday, and look, here I am surprising you at the station. I'm trying."

"I know." He sighed and reached out his hand to her.

She grabbed it and sat next to him. Her husband tucked her underneath his arm. For a moment, she allowed her body to relax, rest.

"I love you, Crys." His baritone rumbled from his chest through hers.

"I love you too."

"And I miss you." He put his nose to her hair, inhaled. "Do I need to come to work and kidnap you like I used to?"

She smiled at the memory. When they'd first met, she'd been in her third year of graduate school at Columbia, working an internship and keeping up with what had seemed like a massive course load. Brian would plan rooftop picnics or walks in the park and steal her away for an hour or two in between work and classes.

At first, she'd been determined not to date anyone, not wanting the distraction. But he'd slowly worn down her defenses, and she'd liked who she was when he was around.

He snatched a strand of her hair and rubbed it between his fingers. "I've always loved the passion you have for your work and how brilliant you are at it."

"Thank you."

"But I can't help but feel that lately it's become less about that passion and more about . . . I don't know, achievement."

The comment stung. It was definitely true she'd become more focused on becoming senior architect lately, but it was natural for a person to want to progress in her career if she was passionate about it.

"Anyway, I know the presentation at work didn't go the way you'd planned, but I'm glad it's over. It's been stealing all of your attention lately. I'm looking forward to having you home in the evenings and on the weekends I'm off."

And there came that splinter again—except this time it had made its way deep, jabbing her organs and puncturing her lungs. She had to tell him about the Lerner proposal. But how could she, when they'd finally found a moment of peace?

"What's wrong?" He pulled back and looked down into her eyes. "You stiffened."

"Nothing." She'd tell him later, when the blow of her forgetting their anniversary had lessened.

He cupped her cheeks with his hands and kissed her gently. "I just want a little balance in our lives, you know? And once I have a little more of your focus, we can finally talk about moving to the suburbs. Planning that trip to visit your parents and sister. Starting a family."

The look on his face was so earnest, she couldn't watch him anymore. Moving to the suburbs wasn't her favorite idea, but she could do it for him. And she couldn't deny she'd been putting off a trip to see her parents and Megan for the last few years. She'd promised they could finally put a date on the calendar once the Hoffman presentation was over.

And children. He wanted children so badly—he'd been in the foster system and never had a family of his own—and she wanted to give him the desire of his heart. But every time she thought about having kids . . .

Now just wasn't the right time. Someday she'd be ready.

"I've got an idea." He squeezed her knee. "I can see if one of the guys can take my shift this weekend. How about you take off Friday and we spend the weekend celebrating our anniversary upstate? Ben just told me about a romantic cabin he and Kelly rented."

He was an amazing husband, one she surely didn't deserve. But there was no way she could ask off right now, not with Meredith breathing down her neck. "That sounds so lovely, really. But I can't get off Friday. And I was hoping to get a jump on something Saturday since you were supposed to be working. Rain check?"

Brian's arms released her, and she suddenly wished she'd stayed silent. "But we agreed—"

"Yes, but Tony just told me today about an amazing project that I have to work on." The words burst from her lips before she could think a moment more about them. Crystal rushed on. "Remember the James Lawrence building I showed you when we first met?" She explained briefly the merits of the project. "It's like this project was meant to fall into my lap."

Brian ran his hands through his hair and didn't say a word.

"Don't tell me what you think or anything." Her attempt at humor came out flat and sarcastic.

Her husband shrugged his shoulders. "Frankly, I don't know what to say. I thought you were going to take a break for a while."

"It's not like I can stop working altogether." Bereft of his touch, Crystal shoved her hands underneath her legs and squished them until her fingertips grew numb.

"But you said you'd set boundaries. That you'd take time for other things in your life. You always claim busyness, but there will never be a perfect time to start a family."

"There will be better times than this." Crystal licked her lips. "My chance at senior architect is riding on this—"

"And there it is."

"What's that supposed to mean?" She pulled her hands from under her legs. They tingled, numb, asleep.

"That's all that seems to matter to you anymore."

"That's not true. I—"

The thought was interrupted by blinking red lights surrounding the ceiling. A call for paramedics to report to Engine Thirty-Five sounded over the intercom. Brian hopped to his feet. "I've gotta go."

"But—"

"Somebody needs me more than you do right now. Though I'm starting to doubt whether you need me at all."

Then without so much as a hug, he was racing down the hallway, leaving Crystal's heart as numb as her fingertips had been moments before.

Chapter 5

She'd put it off long enough. Megan had to tell her parents about her decision.

She sat quietly at the lunch table on Friday afternoon, shoving small bites of pot roast and potatoes into her mouth. Mom and Dad chatted about Dad's week at work. Since he and Megan both only worked half days on Fridays, they often ate lunch together. Mom had set the table with a purple tablecloth and adorned it with daisies.

Megan hated to ruin the cheery mood. But it had to be done.

"I need to tell you guys something." Megan forced the words out and realized too late that she'd interrupted their conversation.

"Of course." Mom put down her fork, dabbed her mouth with a napkin, and folded her hands in her lap. At fifty-eight, she still looked young and spry, despite the streaks of gray in her blonde hair. "You can talk with us about anything."

Dad's eyebrows raised in expectation. "Absolutely. What's going on?" He adjusted his thin-rimmed glasses.

Megan pricked a roasted carrot and twirled it on her plate. "As you know, I had a great checkup today."

"Yes, and we are so thankful." Mom reached over and squeezed her forearm.

This was the first doctor's appointment Megan hadn't allowed her mother to come to. At first, Mom had protested. After all, her entire life for more than twenty years had revolved around Megan's health. Every time Megan had been admitted to the hospital, Mom only left her side to eat, sleep, and shower. She'd even quit her job as a lawyer to take care of Megan a few years after she'd been diagnosed, once her symptoms worsened and she needed more constant care.

But besides the fact Megan was thirty-two years old and could handle checkups on her own, she'd needed to ask the doctor a few questions. Alone. Specifically, was she physically capable of traveling around the world? And was she well enough to, say, run with the bulls in Pamplona?

He'd assured her the answer to both was yes.

"I talked to Dr. Springer about a few things today." The light from a cookie-scented candle flickered on the wall.

"What kinds of things?" Mom's grip on Megan's arm tightened. "Have you been having problems you haven't told us about?"

"No, nothing like that." Megan paused. It was now or never. "You know I went to visit Amanda's family earlier this week."

"Yes." Mom's lips twisted in sympathy. "Those poor people."

How was Megan going to get through this without crying? "Her parents showed me her journal." Megan pulled it from her lap and placed it on the table next to her plate. "Inside, she wrote a list of twenty-five things she wanted to do during her lifetime. A bucket list."

Mom released Megan, and her fingers drummed along the edge of the table. "Did that make you uncomfortable?"

"A little at first. But they thought I might like to get to know Amanda. The person she was. The things she struggled with. The things she learned."

Mom took a deep breath and drew a tenuous smile across her lips. "What was on the list?" She was trying so hard to be brave, but Megan could tell this conversation shook her. She likely could imagine this being Megan's journal of unfulfilled dreams spread open on the table. Many times it almost could have been.

But Megan had lived, because of Amanda. She owed her this and so much more. And not just that—it was the perfect way to get unstuck.

Megan cleared her throat. "Mostly travel stuff: visit Machu Picchu, walk along the Great Wall of China, see the Taj Mahal, run with the bulls in Pamplona, stuff like that."

"It sounds a lot like the places you used to talk about seeing." Dad took a large bite of his roast and chewed.

Warmth nestled inside her. Even her dad saw

70

the similarities between Amanda and Megan. "I started reading the journal and only got a few pages in when I got an idea. More than an idea, really. Almost like a calling."

"A calling? From whom?" Mom pushed her plate away from her. She then put her elbows on the table—something she'd never normally do.

"From Amanda."

Her mother's eyes widened, and she looked from Megan to her father. "What do you mean?"

"I know it wasn't actually Amanda calling me—"

"Calling you to what?" All color had drained from Mom's face. As if she knew.

Megan's appetite gone, she smashed the carrot on her plate with the prongs of her fork. "I'm going to finish the list."

"What?"

Megan was surprised the chandelier overhead didn't burst with the shrillness of Mom's voice.

"Whatever makes you think that is a good idea?"

Dad lifted his hand and frowned. "Now, Tracy—"

"No, Ken. This is absurd." Mom visibly calmed herself. She turned back to Megan. "Honey, you've done so much lately to get healthy again. This kind of trip would test your limits in a way you never have before. I'm not sure you're ready for that."

"Dr. Springer doesn't agree." The defiance in Megan's tone surprised her—and it clearly shocked Mom. Megan tightened the grip on her napkin. "He said there isn't one thing on the list I wouldn't be capable of doing." Of course, he'd also said he wouldn't necessarily recommend some of them, given her health history . . . but Mom didn't need to hear that.

"I can't believe he would tell you that. Didn't you say running with bulls was on the list? How is that safe for anyone, much less a girl who's had a weak heart her entire life?"

Though her mother hadn't meant the words as barbs, they landed and stung all the same. "I have her heart now, Mom." Megan's throat got all cottony—a telltale sign of tears to come. Great. Not now, when she was trying to present her case logically. She took a sip of water. "The last item on her bucket list was to give her heart away."

Mom deflated a bit. She shrank back into her seat. "You are so incredibly sweet. I know you must feel as if you owe the Abbotts something—"

"Not just something, Mom. I owe them every-thing."

Mom's eyebrows bunched as she searched for the right words. "And we will be forever grateful that you are here with us still. There were times—so many times—I thought we'd be saying good-bye."

"Me too." Megan's vision blurred.

Dad had finished eating, but still he didn't say anything.

"I just don't think you should make a decision based on emotions alone." Mom's lawyer tone came out. "You should be logical about this. How are you supposed to pay for it? You're still working on paying down your hospital bills." She saw a debate and was determined to win. Winning against Megan had always been easy. Crystal was the one with an iron will and the nerve to fight back. How would she handle this?

She'd just leave and not look back. Oh, where had that thought come from? Megan threw it far from her mind. "I'm not sure. I haven't worked out all the details yet. Maybe I can get a small loan. And the hospital has been great about working with me on payments so far. Living here rent-free has allowed me to get ahead on my payments and save a little on the side, so maybe I can delay my next several payments a bit."

"That seems unwise. And also, have you thought about the fact you've never traveled anywhere? Traveling can be very stressful. What will you do when you get to the middle of nowhere and know nobody?"

Mom's words chipped away at Megan's confidence. Just because she'd always dreamed of doing something like this didn't mean she was cut out to actually do it. Maybe Mom was right. Megan hadn't thought through all of this. But she could learn, couldn't she? "I—"

"And what about your job? As a part-time employee, you don't have paid time off."

Here was a question she was prepared for. She'd already run the idea past her boss. "Kara said they couldn't guarantee they'd be able to hold my position for me, but they'd get along without me for as long as possible and offer it back if it's still available when I return."

"Is that the most responsible thing to do—leave a steady job when you've got bills to pay?"

She'd spent hours thinking about that very thing. "The library was never meant to be my job forever. You know I've always wanted to be a travel writer, or at least work for a newspaper in some capacity. And you've always said you believe in me."

"Of course we believe in you. It's just—"

"Wait, Mom. Listen." Wow. Is this how it felt to fight for something? A spark of determination moved her onward. "Every time I showed you an essay or a piece I'd written just for fun, you'd encourage me to submit it somewhere, to share it with the world. You'd tell me I had what it took to succeed. I never believed you. But now . . . I want to try. This could be such a great opportunity for me to build my portfolio."

"How?"

"I could start a travel blog. I've read plenty of them, so I know generally where to begin. And even if no one ever reads it, just writing it will provide me with some pieces to show a newspaper or magazine. I'm hoping that could lead to some freelance jobs." Megan blew out a shaky breath. "At the very least, it's a step in the right direction."

"So is this about Amanda, or is this about you?"

"Both, I think." And that was okay, wasn't it?

Mom was quiet for a moment. She stared at the flowers on the table. Her gaze moved back to Megan, softened, yet pleading. "I suppose we can't stop you, can we?" She gathered a few dishes and stood, pushing her chair out as she did. "I just hope you know what you're doing." Then she headed toward the kitchen and disappeared around the corner.

Oh, Mom. Megan looked at her own plate. The mashed contents were transformed from an appetizing feast to a pile of lumpy remains.

"Your mother loves you." Dad's voice whizzed through the stagnant air and smacked Megan in the face. She gazed up at him. He had pushed aside his own plate—clean as a whistle—and steepled his fingers.

"I know that." And she did. Sometimes she just wished—well, that she'd never been sick. That she'd been born with a different heart. That she had more courage. That she was more like

Crystal. She didn't know anyone stronger than her sister.

"As much as she loves you, though"—Dad snapped Megan back to the present—"she often lets fear get in the way of reason."

"What are you saying, Daddy?" Dad rarely gave advice. But when he did, Megan listened.

"I'm saying your mother has many fine qualities. She's loyal and loving and generous. But she's afraid of losing you. She always has been. She wrestles with God about that every day." He got up and gathered his plate and utensils, then turned toward the kitchen. "If you're going to be like your mom, then copy her loyalty or her love or her generosity. Not her fear."

Megan twisted in her seat. "So you agree with me? That I should go?"

"That doesn't really matter one way or another. Something tells me, Megan Jayne, that you know exactly what you should do." Daddy nodded, as if agreeing with himself. "But be sure you pray about it first." He left the room.

Pray about it . . . sure. She'd missed a lot of church growing up, but she'd tried praying for years that God would make her well—or, at the very least, that he'd make her strong. Finally, she'd given up. It had been years since she'd really bothered to ask God for anything. And then—*bam!*—out of the blue he gave her a new chance at life three and a half years ago. Not because she'd prayed about it but because he wanted to.

Her prayers did nothing to sway an almighty God, so if he didn't want her going on this trip, he'd find a way to stop her.

Daddy was right. She *did* know exactly what she should do.

She walked to the candle, leaned over, and blew it out. Smoke rose and curled in the air, but Megan smiled at things to come.

Crystal checked her watch as she hurried from her office building toward home. It was Friday, and she'd purposefully left before 5:00 p.m. It had to have been months since the last time she'd done that. But she'd heard the concern in Brian's voice Wednesday at the fire station and was determined to do better, to show him he was a priority to her. She'd surprise him with dinner when he got home from playing basketball at the gym.

The air was crisp today, and though tinged with smog, it smelled of cinnamon. When she arrived home, Crystal tossed her purse onto the entryway table and headed into their bedroom. She changed from her business casual wear into a pair of skinny jeans, a loose off-the-shoulder sweater, and a pair of sandals. Then she opened the top drawer of her dresser and rustled through her undergarments until she found the nightie she was looking for stuffed in the very back. Crystal tugged off the tags, smoothed out the lingerie, and placed it on top of the bed.

She hummed as she headed toward the kitchen. From the foyer, her phone rang. Who would be calling her at four in the afternoon? It might be Tony, who had looked at her askance when she'd said she was taking off early. He'd wanted to order Chinese and discuss the Lerner proposal. She'd said they could do it Monday over lunch instead.

See? She could balance work and her personal life. It just took careful planning.

When she reached her phone, the name on the caller ID made her do a double take. Mom? She hardly ever called when she knew Crystal was working. "Hello?"

"Crystal." Mom's voice sounded frantic on the other line. "Thank goodness you answered."

"What is it? What's wrong? Is it Megan?" Crystal turned and leaned against the wall. Her heart slammed into her chest and sweat formed on her palms. Had her sister relapsed?

"Yes, I'm calling about Megan, but it's not what you think. She's okay. Physically, I mean."

Relief coursed through Crystal. "You scared me."

"I'm sorry, hon." A pause. "But I need some reinforcements. Your sister is going on a trip and will be gone for weeks, maybe months."

"Oh. That's cool." Crystal headed toward the kitchen.

"No, it's not."

"What's wrong with Megan taking a trip?"

"Not just any trip. She's going by herself to South America, Africa, Asia, Europe, you name it."

"She's wanted to travel for years. I don't see the problem."

"You don't understand. This isn't just a normal sightseeing trip." Mom briefly described the purpose of the trip as Crystal pulled all the ingredients for stuffed bell peppers and a side salad from the fridge.

Crystal got chills when she heard about her sister's mission. "It sounds like something she really wants to do. She's got a good head on her shoulders. And she's read a lot about travel. I'm sure she'll be fine."

"Maybe, but the emotional stress will be so difficult. What if it causes her to have a heart attack? Or reject her organ? She'll be over there by herself and her doctor is here—"

"There are doctors overseas too. Don't you think you're overreacting?" Mom had always hovered over Megan, so it shouldn't be a surprise that the idea of her being gone freaked Mom out.

"I just worry."

Funny, she'd never seemed worried when Crystal went off to graduate school in New

York City as a twenty-two-year-old. Crystal had agonized over the decision to move away from Minnesota when Megan was so ill, but ultimately knew there wasn't much she could do for her sister anyway. Ever since high school, when Mom had started homeschooling Megan, Crystal and her twin had lived fairly separate lives.

Still, when she'd left for Columbia University, she'd expected more of a protest from her parents. But they'd been so consumed with Megan's health at the time, they hardly seemed to notice she was over a thousand miles away.

Some things never changed. And Crystal was over it. Mostly.

Crystal rummaged in her cabinets and emerged with a cutting board. "You mentioned reinforcements. What do you want me to do?" As if anything she could do would make a difference when it came to Megan. Their relationship was beyond repair, and it was all Crystal's fault. Things had been tenuous before Megan's transplant surgery, but that day Crystal had shown her true colors. And facing Megan afterward had been too difficult.

"She won't listen to me. And I know things are a bit rough between you right now, but maybe you could talk some sense into her."

Crystal let loose a derisive snort. "Rough?" Sure, if that's what you called it when twins who were once as close as peanut butter and jelly now lived in a state of limbo, talking or texting only when necessary—and never about anything important.

"Oh, darling, I do so wish you and your sister could work out whatever is between you. It breaks my heart to see how far apart you've grown."

Crystal plunked the ground turkey onto the counter along with an onion, tomatoes, romaine lettuce, vegetables, and various spices. "I know, Mom." What more could she say? Things were the way they were, and all a person could do was deal with it and move on. Acknowledging the pain only brought more pain.

"Could you just try and talk to her, sweetheart? This would give you a clear reason for talking. Who knows where the conversation could go after that?"

Crystal rolled her eyes. Did Mom really think she could make a difference, or was she using it as another excuse to try to fix what was broken between her daughters? "I doubt she'd listen to me. But maybe I can try."

"I'd appreciate it." A pause. "I'm sorry to have bothered you."

"You didn't."

"It's so good to talk to you." Mom's voice was soft now. "We don't hear from you often. Have you had a chance to check your work schedule yet? We'd love to see you this summer. Or

Christmas. Whenever it's convenient for you. Or your father and I were thinking of catching a few Broadway shows. Maybe we can convince Megan to come with us and we can have a fun family reunion in the Big Apple." Another pause. "If that wouldn't put you out. We could stay at a hotel."

"You absolutely would not—"

"Oh, Crystal, I'm so sorry. Megan's boss is calling on the other line. Maybe between the three of us, we can convince Megan she doesn't need to take this trip. We'll chat soon, all right? Love you, sweetie."

"Okay. Bye." Crystal set the phone down on the counter and stared at it for a few long moments. Should she do what Mom asked and call Megan?

No, her sister wouldn't want to hear from her. Not after what Crystal had done three and a half years ago and how she'd acted since.

Of course, things between them hadn't exactly been stellar before that. An emotion—guilt? regret?—welled up, and for once, she let it linger. What would it be like to once again have the kind of sibling relationship that made talking to each other something to look forward to rather than dread?

But just as quickly, she hushed the question. Emotional what-ifs got a person nowhere.

After flicking on the radio, she started chopping the onion while Adele's voice gathered and swirled around her. The onion's juices rent the air and tears began leaking from the corners of her eyes.

"What's wrong?"

She jumped at the sound of Brian's voice, and the cutting knife clattered onto the counter. She turned to the right and took him in—his gym clothes drenched, hair tousled with sweat. "You scared me. I didn't hear you come in."

"Sorry." He stepped forward and slowly, tentatively, reached out to wipe her tears away. "You're home early. Are you all right?"

The gesture was so gentle, so sweet. An ache tore through her, and she stuffed it back inside. He must have forgiven her for forgetting their anniversary. "Of course." Crystal picked up the knife again and resumed cutting. "Onions make me cry."

"You're sure it wasn't something else?"

"I'm fine." Crying never did anyone any good. What was the point? She rose up on her tiptoes and planted a kiss on his lips. "Go shower. Dinner will be ready soon."

"Crys." His voice was a whisper, even though he stood close. "You can talk to me, you know."

She hesitated. "I just talked to my mom."

"How did that go?" Brian snagged a baby carrot from the counter and took a bite.

She explained Megan's trip and her mom's request as she finished chopping the onion.

"Why don't you call?"

"You know why." The onion done, Crystal opened the ground turkey and dumped it into a skillet. She added the onion and some garlic salt, then clicked on the burner.

Brian leaned against the counter to her left. "Your sister loves you. I'm sure if you'd just talk more often, you'd be able to work things out."

"That's what Mom seems to think too." Crystal broke up the meat with her spatula. Raw meat flung out of the pan. Oops. Too much force. She grabbed a paper towel and cleaned up her mess. "But it's more complicated than that."

"You can't avoid your family forever."

"I'm not." Anger rose in her, but no, that didn't do any good either. She stirred the meat, and it started to sizzle as the burner heated up. This isn't how she'd envisioned the evening going. "Can we talk about something else, please? How was your day?"

"It was good." Brian sighed. "Babe, you have to stop avoiding things when they get hard." His hands encircled her waist as he came up behind her.

Crystal continued to stir the meat and onions together, getting all the pink out. "Things with my family are fine. Yeah, we don't talk that much, but it works for us." Because it was too hard to watch her parents fawn over Megan like they always had and think about the disappointment they inevitably felt toward Crystal and the poor excuse for a sister she'd been. "And like I've told you, we'll plan a trip out there to see them all soon."

"But when? You've been saying that for the past year or two."

"When everything settles down."

"From what I can tell, that doesn't seem likely anytime 'soon.' "

Crystal focused on stirring the meat. Nice and steady. "We'll figure it out." Yes, life was crazy right now, but eventually . . . Well, maybe that wasn't true. But she didn't know how to stop the carousel without jumping off completely.

The meat was finally cooked, so she eased out of Brian's arms, then grabbed a glass jar from beneath the cabinets and carefully drained the grease into it.

Brian folded his arms over his chest. "Do you think maybe you go-go-go so hard because . . ." He furrowed his forehead. "I don't know. Because you don't want to stop and feel? You never really dealt with what happened to your sister and what happened to you as a result."

No, I ran.

Memories socked her in the gut. Crystal put the meat back onto the stovetop to stay warm, then grabbed a green bell pepper and began gutting it. "There's nothing to deal with. Everything turned out okay." Megan was fine now.

"You can't tell me that her being sick your whole lives didn't affect you. That it didn't matter to you that she got all the attention. That you never felt guilty over being perfectly health—"

"I don't feel guilty." Crystal jabbed the knife through the bell pepper, taking off its head and exposing the seeds beneath it.

"Crystal, your sister was on the brink of death when she finally received her transplant. I've seen how the constant fear of her dying took a toll on you, even if you never talked about it."

"But she didn't die." Another bell pepper lost its head. With a firm yank, she pulled the pit from inside and flung it and the seeds into the garbage. "It's pointless to dwell on that now."

Brian groaned. "I'm probably not expressing my thoughts very well here." Then he paused and snapped his fingers. "Crys, why don't you go on this trip with your sister?"

Her head shot up and she stared at him. "Are you crazy? First, no way could I get the time off work right now, especially after what happened with the Hoffman project. Second, I haven't spent one hour in my sister's company in over three years, and you want me to go on a trip with her around the world that will last weeks?"

Megan would never want that. A weekend back in Minnesota was one thing. But being with her sister for an extended trip around the world . . . It was a recipe for disaster.

"You haven't taken a vacation in years, so I'm guessing you have plenty of paid time off stored away. And this could be the chance to make things better between you and Megan."

"Things between us are fine." As good as they were going to get. They could never go back to being those innocent eight-year-old best friends who didn't know what the words *hypertrophic cardiomyopathy* meant.

"There's that word again. Everything's always fine. Even if you never talk to your family, work eighty hours a week, and are physically exhausted all the time." Her husband's voice didn't rise, but the intensity of it increased. "I suppose you think things are 'fine' between us too, don't you?"

"Of course." She heard the lie in her words. But all couples had their issues, and she was trying to make things better. "I got off work early today. Planned a nice dinner for you. Even laid out a . . . Forget it." She turned toward him again. The look in his eyes shoved guilt down her throat. This conversation needed to be over. She was having trouble keeping her emotions in check.

"I appreciate those things. I do." Brian came closer to her. "But one time doesn't change all the times in the future that you'll have to choose between your job and our family. It's bad enough now, but how do you see your demanding career fitting in with our life when we have kids?"

"I'll figure it out."

"Don't you see, Crys? You will never be able to figure out any of this if you don't fix things between you and Megan."

"What in the world does one have to do with the other?"

"All I know is that ever since we came home after Megan's surgery, you've been a totally different person. Sure, you were driven before. But that trip, that experience, broke something in you. You've lost your why, and I'm not sure you can get it back until you heal." He paused. "I'm not sure we can get *us* back until you heal."

Did he really think it was that easy? Things had been wrong for far too long for healing to be a real possibility. And they'd gone wrong long before Megan's surgery. That had just been the straw that broke all their backs.

Crystal picked up the last bell pepper and rammed it through with the knife. A sharp pain penetrated her finger and she yelped, dropping the vegetable and the knife. Blood gushed from her index finger.

Brian leaped forward and pulled her finger under the sink. Her blood mingled with the water flowing from the faucet, turning it pink as it swirled down the drain. He brought her finger closer and examined it. "Doesn't seem that deep." He grabbed a paper towel and wrapped it around her finger, stemming the flow of blood for now. "We can grab a bandage and patch this up quickly."

If only everything were as easy to fix.

She turned her face from his intense gaze.

"Crys." His whisper penetrated her soul. "I just want my wife back."

"I don't know where she went." It was the truth. Brian was right. Something had changed in her three and a half years ago. That day in the hospital, she'd finally come face-to-face with who she really was—and the reality of her utter selfishness, her cowardice, had slapped her full force.

So ever since, she'd been living her life the only way she knew how, the only way experience had taught her to: in survival mode.

Brian seemed to think the answer could be found by taking time away from everything. By facing Megan. Making amends, if it was even possible.

She let herself dream for a moment . . . What if?

Her inner workhorse denied the possibility that leaving behind all her responsibilities could do any sort of good. But given her lack of inspiration at work and the state of her marriage, maybe she really did need to do something drastic. Not that she could totally escape work. She'd have to work on the Lerner proposal from afar . . . and that was only *if* Tony let her take the time away from the office. Besides, the Lerner project was still something her soul yearned for—and not just because of the possible promotion that came with it.

But even if she overcame the obstacle of getting time off work, there was a larger potential barrier at play. "I don't think Megan would want me to go with her." Crystal's finger throbbed with the pressure Brian applied.

"All you have to do is ask her."

But what about Brian? She couldn't leave him, not when they clearly had issues they needed to work through. "I'm afraid of what will happen if I go away for a month or two, especially right now."

The look her husband gave her was so sorrowful, she could barely breathe. "And I'm afraid of what will happen if you stay."

Oh. She squeezed her eyes shut. *Don't cry. Don't cry.*

Maybe Brian was right. They couldn't keep going on like they had been. And if it took this trip to figure things out with her job, her marriage, her family—to figure out what had happened to the Crystal she used to be—then that's what she'd do, if she could get the time off.

Still, how would Megan react to her request?

Only one way to find out.

Chapter 6

Talk with Mom and Dad. Check.
Talk with the Abbotts. Check.
Plan trip.

Megan stared at her woefully inadequate to-do list. Crystal had always been the organized one, Megan the dreamer. Who was she kidding? She had no idea how to plan a trip around the world when she'd only been outside of Minnesota a handful of times. She could ask Mom for help, but given her strong opposition to Megan's plans the day before, that probably wasn't the best way to go. And Dad's rare business trips were arranged by his secretary, so he probably wouldn't be much help.

She tore the piece of paper from her notebook and crumpled it in her hand. Megan aimed at the wastebasket next to her bed and tossed the paper inside. Her eyes flitted to her bookcase. Of course. She'd collected her own miniature library of travel books over the years. She'd start there.

Megan climbed from the bed and crouched next to the bookcase's bottom two rows. Her fingers skimmed the rim of the book spines touting all the places she'd dreamed about visiting. And now she was really going to do it. Her pulse quickened. She pulled books for Peru, China,

Greece, Italy, and France from the shelf, stacking them on the floor next to her. Then her eyes froze on the last book: *The Sights of London.*

A memory surfaced.

It had been 11:00 p.m. Mom had already gone home from the hospital, ending her two-night vigil, but said she'd be back in the morning. Megan couldn't sleep, thanks to the constant beeping of monitors and the cold hospital room. Even with a pile of blankets on, she'd been freezing. Caleb had wheeled himself into her room—like he could sense she was awake, even from down the hall.

He pulled to a stop next to her bed, where a small lamp lit the book in her lap. In his own was something wrapped in brown paper. "Thought you might be up."

Megan laughed softly, then coughed. She snuck her hand out from beneath her blanket and grabbed her cup of water, took a sip. The icy liquid rolled down her throat, making her even colder—if that was possible. "Why are you awake?"

He shrugged. "Couldn't sleep." Though Caleb was usually hooked up to monitors, he was doing a lot better than he'd been when he'd checked in two weeks ago. He was supposed to be getting out tomorrow. Who knew when he'd be back? Who knew when any of them would? "Here." He handed the package to her.

"What's this?" She moved her fingers over the paper. The package was heavy and rectangular—could it be a book?

"Open it."

A smile flitted across her lips as she tore through the paper. She'd been right. A travel book about London rested in her hands. "This is . . . amazing." Her throat grew thick at the last word. Crystal always teased her for crying too much, but she couldn't help it. Not when her best friend had given her such an incredible gift. What would she have done without Caleb the last two years? "How did you know?"

Caleb's cheeks were tinged with red, and he shrugged those scrawny shoulders again. "You're always reading Shakespeare and Jane Austen. I thought London might be somewhere you'd want to travel. Once you've got a new heart."

"It is." Had he really known that just by observing her choice of reading material? Another question surfaced. "Why did you give me this?"

"I thought it was obvious. Tomorrow's your birthday."

He'd remembered. Of course he had. "Thank you, Caleb." She leaned over as far as she could and took his hand in hers. His fingers were rough but warm. "You're the best friend a girl could ever have."

The tips of his ears stuck out beneath his shaggy black hair and they were as red as ever. "Yeah, well, I'm gonna want to borrow it, you know."

She grinned. "Of course. We'll make a plan to visit. Together."

"Just like Paris. And Venice. And the Alps."

"And don't forget Australia."

"And what would an adventure be without Africa?"

"Not an adventure at all." She squeezed his hand and pulled hers away, using it to open her new treasure. The pictures of amazing cathedrals and monuments, castles and gardens, filled her senses. It was all so . . .

She bit her lip, and a tear trickled down her cheek.

Caleb shifted uncomfortably in his wheelchair. "I didn't mean to make you cry, Meg. You shouldn't be crying the night before your sixteenth birthday."

"I shouldn't be sitting in a stupid hospital room either." Her voice trembled. "I should be enjoying a sweet sixteen party with my twin sister. Being silly and

94

dancing the night away. Singing Shania Twain karaoke and dumb stuff like that. Enjoying life. Not . . . this." She looked around.

Her cathedral was the stack of monitors and machines to her right, her monument the toilet behind the bathroom door. As for castles and gardens—they didn't exist here.

She swiped away the tear. "I'm sorry. This is such a sweet gift, Caleb."

"We'll get there, Meg. Someday."

"Will we?" The question lingered in the cold air—a question that neither of them could really answer.

But now, Megan could answer it. She pulled the book from the shelf and cradled it. "I'm going, Caleb."

Caleb.

He'd probably have some advice for her, wouldn't he? Things weren't totally back to normal between them—might never be—but after the fund-raiser last weekend, they'd texted and Facebook chatted a few times. Surely he'd be open to helping her out.

She stood, books in tow, and plopped down at her desk, setting the stack of travel guides to her left. Then she fired up her laptop. Once she'd pulled up her browser, she typed a Facebook message to Caleb. She'd text, but she couldn't remember what time zone he was currently in.

In the message, she told him about her trip—how her visit with the Abbotts had inspired it, and how she planned to start a blog, finally get her words out there. She ended by asking him if he had any tips for trip planning, specifically on cutting costs. Because after her mom expressed concern over how she would afford this trip, she'd taken another look at her savings. They weren't as grand as she'd thought.

After sending the message, she tugged a book on Paris from her stack and began to peruse it. Not a few minutes later, she heard the familiar ping of an incoming Facebook message.

Her heart gave a giddy bump when she saw Caleb had replied:

Meg, that's an absolutely amazing idea! I'm so proud of you for taking this leap of faith and going after your dreams, and for making someone else's dreams come true. The Abbotts must feel so honored. I don't have time right this sec to get detailed with any tips, but I'll be sure to think on it today and write more tomorrow, okay? Oh, but one quick thought comes to mind. What about setting up a GoFundMe? What you're doing is the kind of inspiring story people love to support.

Why hadn't Megan thought of that? It was a brilliant idea. Even if she didn't get fully funded, every little bit would help. She'd just have to ask the Abbotts if they'd mind her sharing Amanda's story in that way. But they'd already agreed to the blog, so she couldn't imagine them saying no to this.

She shot off a quick reply to Caleb and then was reaching to close her computer when a notification popped up. Megan was receiving a Skype call. Who . . . Crystal? Why would her sister be calling, and on Skype of all things? Megan's hand hovered over the mouse for a moment. Finally, she clicked Accept.

Her sister's face—like Megan's but with softer brown eyes and a tiny mole above her lip—filled the screen. Crystal's hair hung long and shiny like always. She'd been dyeing it blonde ever since they'd turned thirteen, her way of becoming "an individual." How dumb that it still stung all these years later.

"Hi, Megan." Her sister's words were stiff. If she was feeling anything, it didn't show.

"Crystal. Is everything okay?"

"Yes." There. A flinch of emotion, but as soon as it came, it fled. "I decided to Skype and if you answered, I'd take it as a sign from the universe that we should talk."

What in the world did she mean by *that?* "Talk about what?"

Crystal flipped her hair over her shoulder. Behind her, Megan could see a perfectly put-together living room painted in bold oranges and reds. The leather couch was accented with designer-looking throw pillows, and the mantle over a fireplace boasted a large picture of Crystal and her husband, a brother-in-law Megan hardly knew.

Emotion clogged her throat. Why was talking to her sister—the twin she'd shared a womb with—so difficult?

The fade between them had happened slowly over the years; as Megan stayed stagnant, Crystal had moved on. When they were in high school, it had meant fewer and fewer visits from Crystal to the hospital, a place Megan frequented. But with the hour-long drive to Rochester and her busy schedule of AP classes and extracurriculars—things her parents encouraged so at least one of their daughters could have a "normal" life—Crystal just couldn't get there much.

It wasn't her sister's fault. It wasn't Megan's either. But they stopped having anything in common. And by the time Crystal decided to go off to grad school, the physical distance between them didn't really matter. Any sort of closeness was already practically nonexistent.

"Megan? Are you listening?"

"Sorry. What did you say?" Megan pulled her eyes back to her sister's face.

"Mom told me about your trip."

"Oh." She paused. "What did she say?"

"That I should try to talk you out of it."

So her sister was calling out of obligation. "I'll let her know you did your due diligence." Megan tried to keep the disappointment from her tone, but she'd never been as good as Crystal at disguising her emotions.

Crystal's lips flattened momentarily. "Actually, I called for a different reason."

"You did?" The fan overhead flung cool air on her, but Megan still felt warm.

"Brian thought . . . Well, we were talking last night, and . . . I mean, it might be a horrible idea." Crystal tugged a piece of hair and wrapped it around her finger—a sure sign she was nervous about something.

Megan straightened in her chair. "What's a horrible idea?"

Crystal hesitated. "He thought maybe I should go with you. I told him you'd probably hate that idea, but . . ." She shrugged, as if Megan's answer made no difference to her whatsoever.

How could her sister sit there so calmly after what she'd just suggested? Every nerve in Megan's body hummed. "Wow." It was the only word that encompassed her thoughts, the numerous feelings that surged and collided. Conflicted. Because on the one hand, having her sister along meant having a companion. She wouldn't have to worry about getting lost in the middle of nowhere by herself.

On the other hand, it would mean having *her sister* as a companion. The sister who was organized but always right. Who would probably act in Mom's stead as overprotective matriarch. Who had once been Megan's closest friend but hadn't held that title for a very long time.

Megan ran her fingers down the stack of books on the desk. She was taking too long to reply. Her eyes found Crystal's once again—and was she imagining it, or did her sister look paler than she had a moment ago?

Megan had thought their relationship couldn't possibly get more strained. But it could. At least they talked occasionally. A no from Megan might sever the fragile connection they shared. She couldn't risk it.

"Sure. Of course you can come." She tried to inject strength into her trembling voice.

No relief flooded Crystal's features, but her shoulders relaxed slightly.

"But it'll be a long trip. I'm thinking about four to five weeks. Can you get that much time off work?"

"Yes, Mom mentioned that. I still need to run it by my boss, but I figured there was no point in doing that until I'd spoken with you. When do you think you'll leave? Do you have an itinerary set?"

"Uh, no. I just decided to go a few days ago, so I don't have any definite plans yet. But I'm aiming for this summer—like in the next month. One of the bucket list items is a set event in early July, so I either have to go soon or wait another whole year."

"All right. I have a huge presentation at work on August 6, so do you think it'd be possible for us to be back by the end of July? Or will that mess you up?"

Megan did some mental calculations. "We're supposed to visit five continents, and that doesn't give me much time to plan . . ." It wouldn't surprise her if Crystal claimed work complications and backed out. The sudden jolt of sadness at the thought—rather than relief—*did* surprise her. "But that could probably work fine if I get to making plans right away."

"If you're sure." Crystal's eyes wandered, as if it was painful to look at Megan for too long. "I can talk with my boss on Monday and let you know what he says as soon as I know."

"Okay."

"And I have a travel agent who can help make arrangements, if you want."

"Oh." Megan had imagined herself putting in the work. She'd started to look forward to perusing her guidebooks again, soaking in the photos and descriptions. "Wouldn't it be better if we planned it together?"

"That would take a lot of time." Crystal straightened, and her voice took on a business-like tone. Of course, now they were discussing facts—something her sister was completely comfortable with. "Don't you think it's best to let a professional handle the arrangements?"

As always, Crystal's logic won out. "I suppose you're right."

"If my boss agrees to my leave, then I can send my agent a list of destinations and she could have an itinerary set within a day or so."

Now, wait a minute. This was Megan's trip. For once in their lives, Crystal was the one tagging along. "I appreciate that, but I can contact your travel agent if you give me her information. I'll have her copy us both on the travel arrangements."

Silence filled the distance between them. Megan longed to say something, share her heart, be chummy in the way they'd been once upon a time. But too much pain filled the void. Would this trip change that? Hope lit inside Megan. Maybe . . .

"I guess we'll be in touch?" Crystal closed her mouth, then opened it, as if she too wanted to say something else.

Come on, Crystal. For once, tell me what you're thinking. Megan waited. And . . . nothing. She sighed and nodded.

"Okay. Bye, then. Have a good weekend."

"You too. Bye."

The line disconnected, and Megan's computer screen went dark.

What had she just agreed to?

Chapter 7

There was something about the passage of time that had the power to fizzle a person's resolve. Especially when that resolve was regarding something as major as requesting time off work in the middle of a career-changing project.

Crystal lifted her hand to knock on Tony's office door, then lowered it. Her heart tap-danced in her throat. What was she doing?

But she closed her eyes and envisioned Brian pleading with her on Friday. Remembered the wistful tone of her mother's voice asking if she could visit, as if she were asking some grand favor that could never be repaid. Saw Megan's quizzical expression on Saturday, clearly taken aback that her twin sister would want to spend time with her.

Even if Tony said no, she had to at least try.

After a swift knock, she heard her boss's baritone from the other side of the door. "Come in."

Crystal opened the door and peeked in. "Do you have a minute?"

Tony looked up from his desk and waved her in as he drew his attention back to his computer screen. "You're a bit early. Aren't we doing lunch in fifteen?"

She sank into the chair opposite him and fiddled with the button on her gray blazer. "We are, but I had something to talk with you about. Something important."

That got his attention. He quirked an eyebrow. "Something that couldn't wait till lunch?"

"Meredith will be at lunch, and this is something I need to discuss in private."

"All right." Tony swiveled his chair so he faced Crystal full-on.

She folded her hands, placed them in her lap, and exhaled. The *tick-tick-tick* of the clock on the wall behind him sounded deafening in the silence. "I want you to know how excited I am about the Lerner project. It's no secret to you that I've lacked inspiration lately." Ugh, that sounded so unprofessional, and admitting it scraped at her tender pride.

"I admit I'd hoped that giving you a chance at this project would light a fire under you. I admire Meredith's work, but I'm a champion of you and your work, Crystal." Tony removed his glasses and cleaned them with a tiny square cloth. He cleared his throat. "We aren't supposed to play favorites, but you are one of the most brilliant architects I've had the pleasure of mentoring, and seeing you faltering as of late has been painful for me."

Oh, Tony. "You're such a softie." Crystal released a nervous laugh. He was going to take this so poorly . . . "Anyway, the reason I'm here is because . . . an opportunity has come up. You know my sister, Megan?"

Tony replaced his glasses. "The one with the heart condition, correct?"

"Yes. Well, not anymore. You remember, she had a transplant three and a half years ago. So, she's planning this trip around the world." Crystal explained the trip and its purpose. "And it occurred to me that maybe I'd like to go. My sister could use the support, especially since her health hasn't really been tested in this way before." So maybe that wasn't the whole reason for going, but Tony didn't need to know everything.

"I see." Tony frowned. "How long are we talking?"

"At least a month. I'm not sure yet." Crystal's knee bounced. It hit the underside of Tony's desk, and she bit her lip to keep from crying out in pain.

Tony didn't seem to notice. "I'll be honest, Crystal. If you get the senior architect position, it will be difficult for you to find time to do something like this. I can't recall the last time I had more than a week off at a time, and I'm always on my phone even then. Of course, I'm a partner, but I know that's something you're aspiring to."

"That's true." Oh, she was going to be sick.

"The thing is, I believe my sister is planning to leave for this trip in a few weeks."

"As in, the very same time frame you're supposed to be working on the Lerner proposal?" Tony's jaw tightened.

Crystal's stomach began to ache and bile rose to her throat. In moments like this, she almost wished she had someone to pray to.

Get ahold of yourself, Crystal. She simply needed to say what she'd rehearsed, use her powers of persuasion to convince Tony this would not only be something that would benefit her as a person, but as an architect too. "Yes. I'm guessing I'd be gone starting mid-June and almost all of July. But I would be sure to work on the proposal while I'm gone. I can log my hours and check in regularly via e-mail, text, et cetera."

Her boss opened his mouth, but she pushed forward. "Think about it, Tony. I'll be surrounded by some of the most amazing architecture in the world. How could I fail to get inspired to create even better architecture of my own? This trip will not simply be some vacation, with me gallivanting around and forgetting about my work. No, it'll be a chance to step out of the office and refresh my creative side."

"And your other projects?"

"I only have a few, and they're at stages that I'm comfortable handing off to our team and overseeing from afar. As I said, I'll make sure

I'm available via e-mail and phone as much as possible."

Tony's bushy eyebrows pressed together as he furrowed his brow. He picked up a pen and tapped it against the surface of his desk. "This won't look good to the other partners. They might decide to give the senior architect job to Meredith while you're gone. There are three of us, and if I'm overruled . . ."

"I understand." She didn't know which hurt more—her stomach or the thought of losing out on the promotion. "But they were willing to wait and let Lerner decide which proposal he prefers. Maybe they still will be."

"They'll question your commitment to this job."

"Do you?" His answer mattered more than she could say. Tony was like another father to her. If he really thought this was a bad idea . . .

"I know you better than that. It does surprise me, but I understand the importance of family." Tony's gaze swung briefly to the picture of his children. "I perhaps learned that lesson too late."

He paused. "So I understand why you want to go. And I see that it could benefit you professionally too. But I ultimately cannot control how this will affect your advancement prospects here. If you're still determined to go after hearing that, then I support you. You'll still have to do your part, though. I expect consistent updates on your progress with the Lerner proposal, and for you to be available when someone here needs you."

"Of course." A surge of something—an unfamiliar feeling—replaced the pain in her abdomen. Could it be hope?

"Okay, then. Let's schedule a meeting later this week and work out the details."

Crystal stood. "Thank you so much, Tony. You won't be sorry."

"I just hope *you* won't be sorry."

The thought sobered her momentary elation. She nodded and left his office, pulling her phone from her pocket as she headed down the hallway. Crystal pulled up Megan's number and sent a quick text:

My boss approved my time off. When do we leave?

Chapter 8

Adventure wasn't all it was cracked up to be.

Megan sat in a plastic airport chair, gripping her cell phone tightly in one hand, her purse in the other. O'Hare's international terminal was crowded and loud. TVs chattered, people blabbered into their phones, and coffee grinders whirred inside the Starbucks behind her. Across the way, a huge window showcased a sunny day.

The first flight had gone well enough. It was short—Rochester to Chicago—but this flight to Peru would take nearly fourteen hours. That wouldn't be so bad, since Crystal was on this flight too.

Or she was supposed to be.

Megan checked the time on her phone again. Ten minutes till boarding and no message from Crystal despite the ten texts Megan had sent her. She'd checked the monitors ten minutes ago, and Crystal's flight showed as delayed with no approximate time of arrival. Would she make it here in time?

"Boarding for Flight 1990 to Cusco will begin in five minutes."

A general shuffling in the seats around her made Megan hop up and grab her things. She texted her sister once more, stuffed her phone back in her purse, wiped the sweat from her hands onto the legs of her jeans, and breathed deep. It would all be okay. Crystal knew the plans, and she'd help make sure this trip was a success.

The gate attendant announced boarding and called out zone numbers. When Megan's zone was called, she rolled her suitcase down the ramp toward the plane. Finally, she found her seat, stowed her carry-on, and sat down.

"Excuse me."

Megan looked up to find a short girl with spiked hair and a nose ring, who pointed to the window seat. "Oh. Sorry." She stood and the girl nudged her way past, sinking into her seat and shoving her backpack underneath the seat in front of her.

"I'm Megan." She stuck out her hand, but the girl just raised a pierced eyebrow and stuck buds in her ears.

Guess not everyone wanted to chat. The lady on the flight from Rochester was extremely talkative. Megan could have kissed her—she'd taken her mind off the fact that Megan was entrusting herself to a big hunk of metal in the sky.

The captain chimed in with a greeting over the intercom, letting everyone know this would be a full flight and they should get comfortable with their neighbors. The girl next to Megan curled up against the window with a jacket as a pillow and closed her eyes.

Where was Crystal? Megan grabbed a book from her purse and settled in. A man caught her eye. He lumbered down the aisle, and something about him made Megan squirm. He looked about her age, maybe a little older, with black hair that had been greased back—or maybe he just hadn't washed it in a few days. His beard was patchy and his lips looked dry, as if sunburned and rubbed raw.

The poor soul who had to sit next to him . . .

And then he plopped into Crystal's seat. The smell of cigarette smoke assailed her.

"Excuse me. I think you might have the wrong seat."

He studied her, one of his eyes lazy. His lip curled into a slight sneer. "Nope. Twenty-three C. That's what's on my ticket."

She forced a smile, ignoring how the smoke seemed to permeate every pore in her body. Her head pounded. "This is my sister's seat, so I'm thinking one of us has it wrong."

The guy held up his ticket. Sure enough, it said twenty-three C. "I was on standby and just got placed here. Sorry, sweetheart. Looks like you're stuck with me. Name's Frank."

"Oh. I'm Megan. I wonder what happened to my sister's flight." She said the last part under her breath as she reached down to rummage in her purse for her phone, which she finally found.

A voice mail that hadn't been there before

popped up. It was from Crystal. "Megan, hi. There was a medical emergency on my first flight, so we had to make an unplanned landing in Cleveland. We sat on the tarmac forever. I tried to text you, but my phone was dead and there was no way to charge it until I got inside the airport. So frustrating. Looks like I won't make it to our flight. I'll catch the first flight I can, but I might not get there until the morning after you arrive."

No problem. Megan could do this. She didn't need Crystal with her. She was thirty-two years old, after all.

Oh, who was she kidding? She'd never done anything like this before. Her mind flashed back to earlier today, when she'd stood near security and said good-bye to her parents. Her mom, tears in her eyes, had hugged Megan tight as if she'd never see her again. Like always, she'd smelled of vanilla and buried her face in Megan's hair as she kissed the top of her head. *There's no shame in coming home if you need to.*

She'd tucked that assurance away, just in case. But for now, she'd stay put—even if it meant riding fourteen hours next to Frank. Megan cracked open the first chapter of her book.

Several times Frank tried to talk to her. He asked her all sorts of personal questions. Once she even found him gazing at her shirt. Megan saw her neckline had dipped, revealing the top of her scar. She made quick work of shifting her shirt upward. If only the girl in twenty-three A would wake up and talk to her. Megan fidgeted in her seat, then tried to close her eyes. But every time she did, she got the eerie sense that Frank was watching her. Eventually she drifted off to sleep and dreamed of oceans and mountains and the Great Wall of China.

And Caleb. Now, why was he on her mind? Probably simply because they'd stayed up on Facebook chatting last night when she should have been sleeping.

"Ladies and gentlemen, we're beginning our final descent into Cusco." The lead flight attendant's voice flickered through the plane. Megan opened her eyes and felt a crick in her neck. "Please ensure your seat backs and tray tables are in the upright and locked position."

"You're very pretty when you sleep."

Megan started at the voice beside her. She turned and took in Frank's curled grin. A shudder raced up her spine.

"I know you were expecting your sister, but since she's not here to meet you, I thought maybe you'd want to grab a drink. It's only five." The smell of beer stained his breath.

The sooner she could get off this plane and safely to her hotel, the better. "Thanks for the offer, but I plan to head straight for the hotel when we land." Megan searched for her book. It wasn't on her lap. She peered onto the floor.

"Looking for this?" Frank held it up.

What in the world?

"Thanks." The pleasantry just flew out of her mouth. If Crystal had been in her place, she probably would have ripped the guy a new one for interfering in her private space. But Megan wasn't that bold.

"I had to get a glimpse for myself at what captivated you so much." Frank pulled out her bookmark: the itinerary Crystal's travel agent had sent her. "And what a coincidence. We're staying at the same hotel."

"Wow." She snatched the book from his hand and pretended to read. She felt the man's eyes on her and flipped the pages every minute or so, hoping his attention would shift elsewhere. Then a thought came. What if he'd rustled through the rest of her stuff? Megan snatched up the bag at her feet and checked. Everything seemed accounted for. Maybe she was just being paranoid.

Eventually they landed and the girl next to Megan woke up. She uncurled from her position—how had she stayed so still for fourteen hours?—and seemed to notice Frank for the first time. She flashed Megan a look of sympathy. Oh sure, now she was sympathetic. Megan stayed glued to her chair until the time came for their row to deplane.

Frank stepped aside and gestured forward. "After you, Megan."

115

Oh, why had she told him her name? Moving her legs as fast as she could, she flew off the plane, up the ramp, and down the halls of the airport toward customs. She got her passport stamped and headed to baggage claim.

Frank hovered as they waited for the bags to slide onto the carousel, and she couldn't shake the feeling he was still watching her.

Once she got her bag, Megan headed to the taxi line. Overhead, the sky was full of clouds that looked as if they might burst at any moment. People hustled everywhere, and the smell of spices clung to the air. Humidity clung to Megan's skin, causing her to sweat even as she stood still.

Finally, a taxi pulled up and she climbed inside.

"Where are you going?" The taxi driver spoke, his eyes reflected in the rearview mirror.

"The Belmond Hotel Monasterio, please."

She settled into her seat and was startled when the other car door opened and Frank got in next to her.

"Since we're going to the same hotel, I thought you wouldn't mind sharing a taxi."

Yes, she did mind. "Actually—"

Before she could do anything, the taxi driver eased out of the parking spot. Frank's foul breath seemed to hover all around her. "Is this your first time in Cusco?" He leaned back and threw his arm along the back of the seat, his hand lightly caressing her shoulders.

Oh Lord, help. She was going to be taken and enslaved, just like the girl in that Liam Neeson movie. Or worse.

She should call 911 or—wait, how would she call for help in a foreign country? But as she was mulling this over, they pulled up to the hotel. Frank winked at her, threw some money at the cabbie, and slipped out the door, disappearing into the crowd with his small suitcase in tow.

Megan opened her door and peeked out. She didn't see him anywhere. As the cabbie unloaded her suitcases, her gaze darted every which way, but no Frank. Maybe she really had overreacted. She paid the rest of the taxi fare and headed inside the hotel.

The high ceilings and crisp air made it easier to breathe. Megan wheeled her suitcases up to the counter and smiled at the young female attendant, who assigned her a room and wished her a happy stay.

She'd done it. Made it to her hotel with only one near disaster under her belt. But she'd overcome. All on her own.

She stepped onto the empty elevator and pushed the button for floor five. At the last moment, someone slipped on with her. The smell of smoke made her head pop up. Frank.

"What are you doing here?" Her voice squeaked. She was frozen to the ground.

He towered over her. She didn't remember him

being that tall on the plane. "I told you." Frank drew closer and whispered in her ear, "We're staying in the same hotel,"

"Look, I don't want any trouble." She'd watched plenty of crime TV shows in her life and should have been paying more attention to her surroundings.

"There won't be any trouble."

"Good."

The elevator door dinged, and she took off down the hallway, Frank hot on her heels. What did she do now? No way was she going to open the door to her room or even show him which room she was in. She stopped at a random room and fumbled in her purse. "Looks like I must have dropped my key card somewhere along the way. I'll have to go back. It was great to see you again."

She turned to leave, and he caught her arm. She tried to tug away, but he kept hold and squeezed. Tight.

"I don't think so, sweetheart." He leaned in to kiss her and she screamed.

A woman stuck her head outside a room across the hallway. "Hey . . ."

Frank looked the lady's way, and Megan darted down the hall. She found her room, slipped the key in the door, and got inside, slamming the door shut. Megan flipped the inside lock and flew toward the phone. She dialed the front desk, her hands shaking, breath heaving.

"Front desk. How may I help you?" The thick Peruvian accent filled the line.

"There's a man in the hallway on floor five . . . He tried to . . . Please have security come and remove him."

"Ma'am, are you okay? Did he hurt you?"

"No. I mean, yes, I'm okay. No, he didn't hurt me." Tears leaked from Megan's eyes. What would she have done if that person hadn't distracted Frank? How could she have let him follow her all the way here? She'd been stupid. She should have known better.

Crystal would have known better.

Maybe Megan should turn around and head home before something else like this happened. She slammed the phone down in its cradle, hot tears welling in her eyes. Then she crawled into the nearest bed, fully clothed, and ducked under the covers.

Chapter 9

When they were growing up, Mom liked to say that anything worth doing was hard.

If that was true, then this whole trip—including an unexpected landing in Cleveland, scrambling to find a way to Cusco, finally getting on a flight only to be seated between a poor mom with a screaming baby and a large man who sweated profusely, and attempting to brainstorm ideas for the Lerner project but coming up empty—was most definitely worth it.

Crystal hoped with everything she had that it *was* true.

She tried to control the yawn overtaking her as she wheeled her suitcase down the hotel hall toward the room where Megan had checked in last night. Crystal had arrived in Cusco around seven this morning and hurried to the hotel. The early smells of continental breakfast and coffee had nearly made her delirious in the lobby, and she longed to curl up and take a long nap.

But before she could eat or rest, she had to see Megan.

Just put one foot in front of the other. She passed a bedroom where a housekeeper's cart propped open the door. Inside, the *vroom* of a vacuum whirred. Crystal checked the room number. Still a few rooms to go.

What would Megan say? Would she get all misty-eyed like she always did—a sight that made Crystal inexplicably uncomfortable? Would she be upset that Crystal had missed their flight? Would she pull Crystal into a tight hug and hold on for dear life, afraid to let go?

Crystal gripped the hotel key card in her hand and it bit into her palm. This time she'd be different. She'd watch over Megan and help her accomplish her task. It didn't mean everything would be totally fine between them again. But maybe it'd be at least a little better.

Room 506. Crystal stopped and slid the card through the slot. When the button flashed green, Crystal took a deep breath and pushed open the door. But it only opened a few inches, clanging against the safety lock. She closed the door and knocked. After a minute of waiting, Crystal tried opening the door again. The lights were on inside, so Megan must be awake. Maybe she was in the shower. Crystal leaned her ear closer but couldn't tell if the water was running or not.

"Meg?" She knocked again. Nothing. Tried to open the door again. *Clang, clang.*

Crystal leaned her head against the door-frame and the wood cooled her. Oh, she was so tired . . . Wait, was that whimpering? Crystal straightened and focused. Protectiveness surged and rationality left her as she banged on the door till her fist hurt. "Meg, are you okay? Let me in."

Next door, a disgruntled man with a thick pair of glasses and a white hotel robe around his husky frame flung open his door. "What in the devil do you think you're doing? It's too early for all this racket."

"My sister may be hurt. I'm trying to get inside." Should she run back downstairs to get hotel security? But there might not be time for that if Megan was having a medical emergency. She rummaged through her purse as quickly as she could. Where was her phone? "Can I use your phone to call for help?"

The man's unibrow dipped on his puckered forehead. "I—"

At that moment, Megan's door closed from the inside. Someone slid the heavy safety lock off the door. Crystal reached for the door handle just as the solid door cracked open to reveal a wide-eyed Megan. "Crystal?" Her voice shook with fear, and she stared at Crystal as if not quite believing it was her.

"Megan." Crystal stepped forward and grabbed her sister, pulling her into her arms. For a moment, the years fell away and they were seven again. Megan had fallen on the playground because Emma Vasquez—the schoolyard bully— had pushed her. Crystal had threatened to de-pants Emma in front of the whole class if she messed with her sister again. Then she'd hugged Megan and helped her limp to the nurse's office where they'd shared a Popsicle.

But the woman in Crystal's arms was no longer a child. And Crystal had lost the right to see herself as any sort of protector. She pulled away. "Are you all right? I was worried when you didn't answer."

Megan's short hair was smashed on one side and her makeup was clearly a day old, her clothes rumpled. Her sister swiped at her eyes. "I'm sorry. I heard you at the door . . . and I thought he was back."

"He who?" Crystal's glance flew to the next-door neighbor, who huffed and slammed his door. Crystal dragged her suitcase through the doorway into their room, shutting the door behind her. "Did that guy next door say something to scare you?"

"No, not him." Megan headed back toward one of the double beds, sat with her back against the headboard, and pulled her hands up to her knees. Her body was visibly relaxing. Had she had a panic attack of some sort?

"Then who?"

"A guy from the plane."

As Megan told her about Frank, Crystal's chest tightened. If only her flight hadn't been delayed. How often was she going to fail to be there when Megan needed her?

Two things were clear. One, it was better to travel in numbers. And two, her sister needed her after all. "It's a good thing I'm here."

Megan stiffened and kept staring at the comforter.

Crystal cringed. "That's not what I meant." Great, now she'd implied Megan couldn't do this alone. This trip was off to such a lovely start. An apology clogged her throat, but it wouldn't come out. Better to say nothing than risk making things worse. Crystal marched to the window and threw open the curtains. A courtyard garden lay below. A tall tree stood planted in the very center, flowers blooming around it in precise rows. Though a breeze shook the branches, leaves didn't fall to the ground. Every thirty feet, an arch of stone rose and fell around each guest room doorway, creating pillared entryways that made each door feel like the entrance to a grand and important suite.

"Maybe I made a mistake."

Crystal turned at Megan's quiet declaration. She longed to pull her into another hug. But her hands remained at her sides. "Look, it's not your fault. There are just some jerks out there who want to take advantage of innocent women like you." Oy, if that didn't sound patronizing.

"I mean maybe I made a mistake in coming here. Was I foolish to think I could really do this?" Overwhelming defeat shone in Megan's eyes.

Crystal could relate to the feeling.

She turned toward the window again and bit her lip. How could she reassure her sister when her own insides shook with doubt? But it wasn't all about her. Megan needed her to be strong.

Her eyes roamed the courtyard again and rose higher. Mountains surrounded the hotel, and the Peruvian sun shone bright today. The grandeur swept over her, and she allowed it to settle into her bones.

"No." The word on her lips surprised her. She swung her gaze back to Megan, whose eyebrows had lifted. "You weren't foolish. And we're not going to let delayed flights or creepy guys stop us from doing what we came here to do."

Nothing was going to keep them from the adventure ahead—or chase them back to the lives they'd been living.

Chapter 10

June 23
Blog Post Title: A Journey Begins:
  Machu Picchu
Post Content:
  My name is Megan, and I'm attempting to do something crazy. And since I'm a writer, I thought the best way to share about my experience is to blog about it. Of course, I'm guessing no one will ever read this. But even if it's just for me, I want to preserve the memory of this journey.
  Today I marked off my first item from Amanda's list. Still, I can't help but feel I failed her . . .

Megan sat in a leather bus seat, smashed between the window and Crystal's legs. She gazed out to see treetops and mountain faces greeting her as they climbed up the hill to the Incan city of Machu Picchu. Crystal's eyes were closed and her head bobbed as she slept. A little boy on the other side of the aisle had devoured some strong-smelling Peruvian food in the first five minutes of the ride and the scent still lingered. All around them, people twittered, their jarring laughter ripping through her consciousness as Megan tried to still her nerves and relax.

She was about to complete the first item on Amanda's list. Thanks to Crystal's pep talk yesterday morning—if she could actually call it that—Megan had let herself get excited again. Her sister had been right. There was no place to go but forward. After all, Megan had already told the Abbotts she was doing this and had started to receive donations via GoFundMe. She couldn't back out now.

But maybe a little extra motivation was in order. She unzipped the backpack on her lap and pulled out Amanda's journal, which she'd read through a few times already. The words oozed strength—and Megan would take all she could get.

4. Visit the Incan ruins at Machu Picchu.

There's something comforting about old things, things that have been standing for years. Things you can count on even when nothing else makes sense.

I want to see things like that with my own eyes. Feel them with my own hands, listen to them with my own ears. And Machu Picchu seems like a good place to start. They're called ruins, but I think there's more to them than that.

Just because something is in "ruins" doesn't meant it's ruined. It's just . . . different from before. It's weathered storms, but it's still standing.

Yes, the past can be damaging, and we don't always want to focus on it, like Amy has told me over and over again. But it can lend strength to us too. I look back at who I was before and who I am now. And even though I see a lot of faults in myself, I do see some strength I might not have had if "sexual abuse" had never become part of my vocabulary.

I may not be the same girl that I was, but I. Am. Not. Ruined.

The bus ground to a halt. Megan stuffed the journal back into the backpack. All around them, people popped to their feet, grabbing their bags and assembling in the bus aisle. Crystal's eyes remained closed.

Megan tapped her sister on the shoulder. "Time to go."

"Huh?" Crystal seemed to shake herself from a stupor. "Oh." She stretched, rubbing the back of her neck.

Not for the first time, Megan wondered why Crystal had come. Did she simply want to take advantage of the opportunity to travel? That could be it, but then why come with Megan when things between them were so . . . awkward? Perhaps she was just being the duty-bound sister since Mom still wasn't totally comfortable with Megan taking this trip alone. Or maybe there was a deeper reason.

Megan couldn't figure it out—and she was too scared to ask.

As Megan and Crystal neared the front of the bus, she could almost taste the high-top mountain air. She descended the bus steps, said thank you to the driver, and gulped in her freedom. "Isn't it amazing?"

Crystal grunted as she stepped onto the caked dirt at their feet. Her designer hiking boots looked brand new, especially next to Megan's old ones, which she wore all the time in the woods at home. Crystal probably didn't have much occasion to hike in New York City. Not that Megan would know since she'd never been invited out to visit.

They headed toward the entrance gate, where fellow tourists were going through a turnstile one by one.

"Do you have the tickets?" Gone was the sister whose face had flashed panic and concern at Megan's frazzled state yesterday. Now Crystal was all professional, just as she'd been when they'd taken the afternoon yesterday to sightsee around Cusco.

Still, a current of tension buzzed in the air, so thin that most people wouldn't notice it. But for Megan and Crystal, it was strung between them like a tightrope, one they had to walk if they were going to get through this journey together in one piece.

"Yes." Megan maneuvered her free arm into her bag and came up with two prepaid tickets.

Trees towered all around them, and the green was luscious enough to rival the beauty in Minnesota. Finally they reached the front of the line, handed their tickets to the gate attendant, and pushed through. They walked around the bend, a long wooden handrail following the dirt pathway as it curved. She could glimpse a few stone ruins below, and there, in front of them, rose a high mountain peak—Huayna Picchu, if her research was correct. Low clouds hugged the top, probably the source of all the moisture that cloistered the air. She caught a glimpse below of the entire Incan city, a series of stone ruins built into the mountainside.

"Can you imagine living here? What a view you'd have every morning." Megan hurried on, maneuvering around tourists who were lingering and taking selfies.

"Hold up, Meg." Crystal lithely avoided everyone in her path. Her hair glinted in the sunlight. "Slow down."

"Sorry." Megan pulled out her map and studied it. "Let's go that direction. We'll start with number one on the map and work our way down."

"Fine by me." Her sister hiked her backpack higher on her shoulders.

They headed to the ruin labeled Nusta's Bedroom. Who was Nusta? What stories, what secrets did his or her house hold captive? Maybe

Megan could tease them out. She and Crystal bypassed an older couple who used walking sticks to keep themselves steady on the rocky stone path.

A memory lodged in Megan's mind. She and Mom had been at the mall shopping for Christmas gifts. A pair of older women had power-walked past them. Megan had felt a challenge arise then. She should have been able to walk just as quickly as they were. But after thirty seconds of picking up the pace, she felt ready to faint with the effort.

Mom had made her sit in a wheelchair for the rest of their outing. The embarrassing *plop, plop, plop* of the rubber wheels was so loud she feared the entire mall could hear her coming.

But now her heart barely picked up speed as she whizzed past the older couple. Crystal protested, murmuring something about how she had to answer to Mom, but Megan didn't care. She kept moving forward until they reached Nusta's Bedroom. From there, they visited the Temple of the Sun, the Tomb, the Palace, the Prisoners' Area, and every square inch of the ruins they could. Finally, they headed toward Huayna Picchu about twenty minutes before their assigned hiking time.

As the sun rose higher in the sky, it grew a little more difficult for Megan to breathe. She stopped frequently and took her pulse, but nothing seemed unusual about her numbers. Her lungs contracted and expanded, at times feeling like a band was wrapped tight around them. She sucked in a breath and stuttered.

Crystal's attention whipped from her map to Megan and her eyes narrowed like a hawk. "What's wrong? Are you okay?"

"Just a little trouble breathing. The air is thinner up here." Megan's head grew light, and she zeroed in on a nearby bench. She managed to make it there without fainting and sank down onto the seat. "I think I'll rest for a minute."

Crystal sat down next to her. "Do you need me to get help?"

"I think it's just altitude sickness. They warned us about that on the way up. We're almost at eight thousand feet."

Her sister peered at her from beneath her blonde bangs. "Let's just rest here for a minute then."

"Good idea." Megan focused on her breathing, and after about ten minutes, the dizziness faded. "I think I'm okay now. Let's head up."

Crystal reared her head back. "If you think I'm letting you go up there"—she pointed to the peak of Huayna Picchu—"you're crazy. No way."

"I'm better, Crystal." She was, right?

"It's a long hike to the top and it's got steel cables, so I'm betting it's a difficult climb. Plus, it's really high up there. That would not be good if you're experiencing altitude sickness already."

"It's only another thousand feet."

"No." The answer came swift and firm, and determination flashed in her sister's eyes.

"We already paid to go up. We're here. Let's just try it. I really want pictures from the top for the blog I'm going to start."

Crystal held out her hand. "I'll go up, then. Give me your camera."

"You hate hiking."

"Yeah, well. The only way you're getting pictures is if I go by myself. We can't risk your health." The grit in Crystal's voice surprised Megan. As the years had gone by, her sister had grown more and more aloof—and seemingly less and less concerned about Megan's health. Maybe she'd just accepted it for what it was.

Reluctantly, Megan relinquished the camera and tickets. "I'll wait here, I guess."

"You'll be okay without me?" Crystal's wary gaze told Megan she doubted it was true.

"Absolutely." If she fainted or had heart trouble, there wasn't much anyone could do unless a doctor happened to be vacationing here. And for the first time today, the vulnerability of where she was and what she was doing struck her.

Crystal stood and dusted off her pants. She placed the camera in her pack and walked off toward the peak. Megan settled in for the wait. Maybe she'd go back and explore the ruins some more.

"Mind if I sit for a spell?" An older woman indicated the empty bench seat beside Megan.

"Go right ahead."

"Thank you, my dear." The lady, who was bundled in a gray jacket and wore an explorer's cap atop her white head, huffed as she lowered herself. "My son told me to meet him here. He went off to hike that peak early this morning." Her wrinkled finger pointed to Huayna Picchu.

"My sister just left to hike it, so I'm stuck here waiting as well." Megan threw the woman a sympathetic smile. "At least it's a gorgeous day out." Surrounded by such natural beauty, she could almost squelch the hint of regret threatening to worm its way into her heart. Maybe she should have insisted on going with Crystal. But her sister probably had a better perspective on things. Megan didn't want to be stubborn for no reason and get herself in serious trouble because of it.

The older woman leaned in. "If I was as young and spry as you look, I wouldn't let anything stop me from seeing the views from up there. I saw them twenty years ago and wish I didn't have this annoying joint problem so I could see them again." She tapped her hip. "After all, what's the point of visiting Machu Picchu if you don't see the view from the top?"

"I . . ." Megan didn't have an answer. Technically, she'd visited Machu Picchu, so

134

she could cross it off the list. But had she really complied with the spirit of the dream? Amanda had longed for adventure. She probably wouldn't have let a little altitude sickness stop her from going the distance.

Why was Megan still sitting here? She could head up now and probably catch up with the group.

But wait. That's right. Only four hundred people were allowed on the peak each day, and tickets had to be purchased in advance for a preassigned hiking time. The hike had already started. And Crystal had Megan's ticket.

She'd missed her opportunity.

Long after the woman met back up with her son and left the bench, Megan sat there and pondered the rest of the list. And when Crystal came back down—her cheeks ruddy, her spirit seemingly refreshed—and showed her a slew of amazing photos, regret kicked her full force in the ribs.

Yes, she'd done what Amanda asked. But she hadn't taken full advantage of the journey. She'd used her health as an excuse.

And she wouldn't let it happen again.

Chapter 11

Today Crystal had two goals.

Get to the Egyptian pyramids.

And talk to Brian.

After a quick hotel check-in and a catnap, she and her sister were in a cab arranged by the concierge. With a strict schedule to keep, their time in Cairo would be short. Her body ached from sleeping in a crunched position on the plane. Somehow Megan had tons of energy. A fire had seemed to light in her after visiting the ruins at Machu Picchu.

Right now, she sat next to Crystal in the back of the old cab, fingers tapping the window as she stared out at the city in the desert. "I'm actually surprised at how much green there is."

"Mmm hmm." Crystal tried dialing Brian's number for the fifth time, but the phone wouldn't connect.

"Probably because of the Nile."

Crystal gritted her teeth as the car hit a pothole and the stitch in her side momentarily caught flame. "Probably." She lowered the phone from her ear.

She hadn't talked to Brian in three days, since she'd landed in Cusco—and it had been a quick call to let him know she'd arrived safely. She missed him more than she thought she would, but what if he wasn't missing her?

"This should be a fun day." Megan was trying so hard to be cheery, but Crystal knew her sister had to be just as tired and worn out as she was. A full day of travel would do that to anyone, and on top of that, Megan had been frustrated with Crystal's protectiveness in Peru. Crystal had read the blog post Megan had written the next day. Her sister felt like she'd failed by not risking her health to go up that mountain. But she refused to feel guilty for keeping Megan safe.

That thought calmed her a bit. If Crystal hadn't been there, Megan might have charged up that mountain and collapsed—or worse.

The cab swerved, and Crystal snatched the grab handle above her window. She caught the cabbie's eyes in the rearview mirror. The man pulled to the side of the road. It was supposed to be a thirty-minute drive to the pyramids, but it had only been ten.

"Where are we?" Megan craned her neck upward to gaze out the window.

The cabbie turned to them. "Papyrus store. You like very much." He grinned at his broken English and gestured for them to get out of the car.

Megan leaned in close to Crystal. "I've read about this. Some cabbies try to double or triple their fare by dropping tourists at undesired locations."

Perfect.

Crystal cleared her throat. "We don't want to go here. Take us to the pyramids, please."

"You will like. Go." The cabbie faced forward again and pulled the keys from the ignition.

Crystal did not like being bullied. "Fine. We'll get out here. But then we are calling another cab to take us there and we will not pay you."

Megan's mouth fell open, and her eyes darted between Crystal and the cabbie. The cabbie frowned and stuck the keys back in the ignition. Without another word, he eased back onto the street and took off, hopefully toward the pyramids. Crystal nodded to Megan, a small smile tucked across her lips.

She dialed Brian's number again, but still no signal. With a groan, she tossed the phone back into her purse. They rode in silence the rest of the way to the pyramids.

As they approached the magnificent structures, Crystal's purse vibrated. She dug her phone out again, but it was just an e-mail. This one wasn't work-related, though she'd received several of those in the last few days. But an e-mail meant she had reception. The car stopped at a signal, and she dialed Brian's number again.

Suddenly, Megan's door flew open and a man about their age scooted into the seat right next to

138

her, pushing Megan up against Crystal. What in the world?

The man had streaks of dirt on his brown cheeks and he reeked of sweat. Megan leaned away from him and her ponytail hit Crystal in the nose.

The man chortled. "Welcome to the pyramids. You want to ride a camel?"

The pandering had begun. Crystal rolled her eyes. "No. We don't. Get out of our cab right now." The cabbie's eyes met hers in the rearview mirror once again, and he continued driving with the man in the backseat. Clearly they weren't getting any help from him.

Crystal glared at the man. His front left tooth was missing and his grin was obnoxious. "Get. Out."

"You have to ride camels to get to the pyramids." The man folded his arms. "Might as well be mine. They are the strongest camels in all of Egypt."

"No thanks." She tapped the cabbie on the shoulder. "Take us to the front gate right now, or you're not getting your fare."

The camel vendor's smile wrenched into a frown. "You wound me. I'm only trying to help."

"We don't want your help."

At that moment they stopped and the man got out, slamming the door behind him. The cabbie kept driving, and the front gate came into view.

Megan turned to Crystal, eyes wide. "You handled that so well. I was ready to pay him to go away."

"After you've been in Manhattan for a few years, you learn how to stand your ground. People there will walk all over you otherwise."

"I guess I never thought of that." Megan fidgeted in her seat. "Do you enjoy living there? I feel like I'd miss the trees and the water."

"There's Central Park. I go there when I can." Not that that happened very often these days. "It's definitely more fast-paced than Minnesota, and it took some getting used to. My first week there I got so lost on the subway that I ended up in Queens when I meant to go to Brooklyn. I tried asking a few people for help, but they just ignored me."

"Rude."

Crystal shrugged. "That's just how it is. Not everyone is like that. But people tend to stick to themselves and not be overly friendly."

Megan studied Crystal for a moment. What was she thinking? That Crystal had become like other New Yorkers? Maybe she had. After you'd grown up in a small town where everyone knew your business—and constantly asked you how your sick sister was doing—there was something rather appealing about living in a city where you didn't have to answer to every person you passed on the street.

The car reached the gate, and the women climbed out. Crystal reached into her wallet and pulled out a one-hundred Egyptian pound note. She wished she'd thought to break the note at the hotel, and she hoped that the cabbie had change since they'd agreed on thirty before the cab ride began.

The man ripped the note from her hands and hopped back into his cab, taking off before Crystal could utter a protest. She clenched her fists and turned to find Megan, trying to regain the sense of calm that she'd felt earlier.

Crystal's eyes swept the landscape. On one side, there stood three Egyptian pyramids and the Great Sphinx with an endless brown desert behind them, transporting them into an ancient world. But that's where the lure and mystery stopped—because across the way, a busy residential area demonstrated how modernity had taken over. There was even a Pizza Hut within view. How disappointing.

But the architect in her wouldn't allow her frustration to ruin the day. She was about to see one of the Seven Wonders of the Ancient World. Perhaps she could borrow some of Megan's upbeat attitude. "Where should we start?"

Megan grabbed the straps of her pack and pointed to a line of tourists. "Over there."

"Let's go." They managed to get through the gates, though it wasn't easy with all the vendors hocking their wares and men trying to convince them to ride a camel.

After they'd paid for admittance to the Great Pyramid, Crystal's pace increased. Her eyes began to catch all the intricate details that others might miss, observing how more than two million blocks worked together to create an awe-inspiring feat of engineering that had been genius at the time.

"Isn't it incredible?" The whispered words slipped from her thoughts to her lips.

"What?"

Megan's voice made Crystal jump. Oh yeah. She wasn't alone. "Nothing."

"Come on. Tell me." Her sister tilted her head and studied the nearest pyramid. "I imagine that to someone with your background, this is a work of art, kind of like *Ulysses* and *Anna Karenina* are to me."

"It's true. Like most architecture students, I studied the pyramids. Many believe they were intended as tombs built for the pharaohs, who were veritable gods among their people. So pyramids don't just symbolize power. They were like a link between people's earthly lives and heaven."

"That's interesting." Megan hesitated. "But what does being here, seeing them, make you feel?"

"It's hard to explain."

"Just try."

Not as easy as it sounded. "I—"

Crystal's phone rang.

Saved by the ringtone. Maybe her husband was finally calling her. "Sorry. Hang on." She pulled out her phone and her chest deflated a bit. Not Brian. Tony.

"It's work. I've got to take this."

Megan nodded. "I'll wait."

"No, go in and start looking around if you want. This could take awhile." Tony was probably calling to discuss the ideas for the Lerner proposal Crystal had sent over that morning. She'd spent a large chunk of time brainstorming on the flight from Peru.

Megan frowned slightly, then nodded and headed toward the opening to the pyramid. Crystal adjusted her sunglasses and answered. "Tony, hi."

"Crystal." Ugh. So much depth in one little word. Her boss's tone revealed a mixture of disappointment and weariness. "I received your e-mail. These ideas aren't original enough."

She sputtered for an answer. "They're just prelim—"

"I realize they're not complete." Tony's voice rustled and cut out a bit. "But Meredith has already come up with five viable options."

Of course she had. Meredith probably smelled Crystal's blood in the water and was circling, preparing to rip her competition to shreds. "The presentation is still weeks away. I'll come up with one idea that will surpass Meredith's five."

"I have faith you will, if you can focus. There must be a lot of distractions."

"Don't you worry. I'll do better, Tony. I promise."

Static came over the line and she missed his next words.

"I didn't catch—" She *oof*ed as a young Egyptian boy with a baggy shirt bumped into her. Where were his parents? She rubbed her side, trying to refocus on her conversation with Tony.

But the phone line was silent. "Hello? Tony?" She stared at her phone and saw "No Signal" blinking back at her.

Great. Here she was, halfway around the world, while someone else horned in on her dreams. She'd just have to figure out a way to best Meredith.

She was almost to the entrance to the pyramid when she realized she still hadn't talked to Brian.

June 25
Blog Post Title: A Bump in the Road:
    Visiting the Pyramids
Post Content:
    Today we had to rely on the kindness of strangers to get by . . .

Inside the pyramid, the world fell away, and Megan could imagine herself as an Egyptian princess in an ancient world.

She examined the stone carvings in the wall in front of her, which showed a row of men and a few children in headdresses and shendyts. Hieroglyphics covered the walls. If she could decipher them, what mysteries would she find hidden there?

For all those years, when she'd read about the various places she wanted to visit, she'd absorbed every detail discussed in her books. But nothing ever told her that the walls and floors had an earthy scent or that the air was cool and slightly wet against her skin or that a person could feel so small inside a monumental feat of architecture like this one.

Thank goodness Crystal hadn't let Megan give up and go home that first morning in Cusco.

Occasionally another tourist would walk by exploring the passageways, but Megan didn't want to go too far. Hopefully Crystal would wrap up her work call quickly.

"You want me to take a picture?"

She jumped at the voice and whirled around. She was alone in the passageway with a large man in a guard's uniform. Megan breathed easier. It wasn't another vendor trying to scare the living daylights out of her. "Oh, that's sweet of you. I thought I saw a sign that said no pictures, though."

The man waved his hand in dismissal and placed it on his rotund stomach. "I can break the rules for a pretty lady."

He seemed innocent enough, so the compliment warmed her. "That'd be great." She heard footsteps, and Crystal came trudging toward them. "Can you get my sister in it too?" Megan dug the camera out of her bag.

The man nodded and took the camera from her. Crystal watched him and her eyes narrowed. "What's going on?"

Megan hooked her arm with Crystal's and dragged her in front of the most picturesque wall. "This nice man is going to take our picture."

"But—"

"Come on. Smile, Crystal." Megan posed, and the camera's flash blinded her momentarily. She grinned at the man and reached for the camera. But he held it just out of her reach and extended his own empty hand. "I'll take the camera back now, thank you."

The man shook his head, the smile gone from his lips. His extended hand remained firm.

Megan opened her mouth to say something, and Crystal groaned. "Oh, for heaven's sake. He wants money for taking our picture."

Suddenly the man's actions made sense. Megan rubbed the bridge of her nose. "He didn't say that before offering." She threw the words toward him, but the accusation didn't move the guard. His eyes were flint.

"It's fine. We'll just pay him and move on." Crystal dug in her purse. "It's not here." Crystal looked up, her eyes full of panic. Crystal never panicked. Something was very wrong.

"What isn't where?"

"My wallet. It's gone."

"When did you last see it?"

Crystal knelt down and dumped the contents of her bag onto the dirt floor. Megan bent to help her comb through the contents. Phone, keys, lip gloss, mascara, tissues, water . . . but no wallet.

Her sister threw everything back in the bag and worried her lip. "That little boy outside. He bumped into me and must have been a pickpocket. It's the only thing that makes sense."

"Maybe we can still catch him." Megan's hand went to her wrist, and it was a full ten seconds before she realized she'd started checking her pulse. It was elevated. She needed to calm down.

"I'm sure he's long gone by now. I'll just have to call and cancel my credit cards when we get back to the hotel and have decent service." Crystal stood again and Megan joined her. "At least I wasn't carrying my passport and had converted only a little bit of money to cash."

"Yeah." Whew, at least the damage wasn't too bad. But then another thought struck Megan, and she clutched the straps of her bag tighter. "Oh no. I don't have my wallet either."

Crystal's eyes locked on to hers. "What do you mean?"

She cringed. "You had yours and we were in such a rush, I didn't think much about it." What kind of traveling moron was she?

"Oh, Megan." Crystal paced. The guard stood by and watched their whole exchange, not saying a word or offering to help. Her sister stopped pacing in front of him and grabbed the camera before he could stop her. "You're out of luck. We don't have any money."

Then Crystal turned on her heel and headed for the outside. Megan scampered along behind her. They burst through the opening to see the crowd had dwindled with much of the daylight. Crystal scanned the remaining people in the vicinity, but most of them were vendors. Her sister slumped onto a bench and put her head in her hands.

Megan lowered herself next to Crystal. "What should we do?"

"I'm thinking."

Megan averted her eyes. This was all her fault. If only she'd thought ahead and been responsible. Her eyes stung. *Do not cry. Do not cry.* "I . . ." Her voice croaked. She waited and tried again. "We can see if any of the guards will help us."

A strangled laugh left Crystal's throat.

"Because that last guard we encountered was such a peach."

Megan had read a report warning tourists, especially Americans, not to be at the pyramids at night. Something about violence and extorting money. They needed to find a way out of here before it got dark. She looked around. Maybe they could find another American family willing to help. But no one really stood out as an option.

"Do you have anything of value to sell?" Crystal's voice broke through Megan's thoughts.

All she had was Nana's ring. She looked at it and twisted it on her finger. "I—"

"Oh. No way." Crystal's features tightened as she saw what Megan was considering. "We'll figure something else out." Did the look of pain flashing across Crystal's face mean she remembered that day in the hospital before her surgery, when Megan had offered the ring to her in case she . . .

Megan swallowed hard. Would she ever know what Crystal was really thinking again?

Focus on the problem at hand, Megan. Think. "What about calling our hotel and seeing if they can send someone? They have our credit card on file, so they'd know we're good for reimbursing them."

Crystal's eyes lit with hope. "That's actually not a bad idea."

Megan's shoulders lifted.

Her sister pulled her phone from her bag and tried dialing. When it wouldn't connect, she banged the phone against her palm. "No service."

After Megan tried her own phone and couldn't make a connection either, she stood. "Let's go see if anyone else has a phone we can borrow."

With a wary glance, Crystal finally rose and followed her. But every person they approached held out a palm, wanting to be paid before they'd allow the sisters to use their phone.

Megan's steps grew heavier. "I've never felt so disillusioned with the human race as I do right now."

Their precarious position was her fault. She had to be strong, find a solution. Giving up wasn't an option.

As Megan was looking around, she noticed one of the vendors looking at them, his head tilted. He seemed to be in his late teens, and Megan saw him turn to say something to the robust woman next to him. They were selling an assortment of drinks, including soft drinks, water, and bottled teas. The ice underneath the drinks had nearly melted away. The woman gestured to them.

"Look, Crystal."

"They just want to sell us a drink."

They might as well try. "Let's go hear what they have to say." She walked toward the vendor cart and didn't wait to see if Crystal followed.

The woman's head was covered, and she gave a

slight nod when Megan arrived at their cart. "My son said you need help." Though accented, her English was flawless, and something about her seemed sincere.

"Yes. Do you have a phone we could use?"

The woman's head moved side to side, quick and tight. "I'm afraid not. Can I help some other way?"

Crystal tugged at Megan's elbow, as if to discourage her from answering. But it couldn't hurt to tell the woman a little bit of information and see if she could offer a solution. "Our wallet was stolen and we have no money. We need to call our hotel for a ride."

The boy clucked his tongue and said something to his mother in Arabic. She answered. Then she turned back to Megan and offered a small smile. "We are almost done here if you can wait. We are happy to give you a ride to your hotel."

Another tug from Crystal. But Megan ignored her. "That would be amazing. We can pay you when we get back there."

The woman shook her head. "No need."

"We'll just wait over there for you." Megan shrugged off Crystal's arm and headed back toward the bench.

Crystal wrenched her around. "Stop, Megan."

"What's wrong? I just found us a way home."

"With complete strangers. How is that safe?"

"Do you have a better idea?"

Crystal swiveled on her foot and faced the horizon. She was silent for a moment, and all Megan could hear was the crunch of the camels' feet moving in the dirt nearby, the squeal of taxi tires, and the constant chatter of the vendors.

Her tone had not been kind. "I'm sorry."

Her sister sighed. "No, I am. I'm worried and not thinking straight. You probably know this about me, but I hate not being in control."

"Oh really? I had no idea." Megan chuckled, though the laugh was strained. "And it's okay. It's a stressful situation, made worse by my forgetfulness."

"Yeah, well." Crystal's eyes seemed suddenly red—almost like she was on the verge of tears—and she cleared her throat. Another unusual flash of emotion from her sister.

They stood there together, watching the sun set behind the pyramids. When the woman and her son approached and led Crystal and Megan to a beat-up brown truck, the girls climbed in. And when they arrived safely at their hotel after a lovely thirty-minute chat with the woman, Aziza, Megan couldn't help feeling maybe a little bit triumphant and brave.

Turns out, she wasn't as helpless as she'd thought.

Chapter 12

If Crystal was going to have a job to come home to, she had to find inspiration for the Lerner project—and fast.

For the hundredth time, she pulled the bangs off her sweaty forehead. Her hand came away wet. Next to her, Megan fanned herself with a pamphlet that espoused all kinds of facts about the Taj Mahal. Crystal's stomach shook with its familiar ache. The spicy laal maas she'd eaten for lunch had not been kind to her. If she did have some sort of an ulcer, it was probably best to avoid troublesome foods in the future.

Their private tour had just ended in the garden out front. From the gorgeous white marble mausoleum encrusted with semiprecious stones to the detailed carvings on the walls, she and Megan had seen all the Taj had to offer. And now, standing in the courtyard near the garden in the fading sunlight, Crystal wanted to scream and uproot every tree.

Because despite her being in awe over this prime example of Mughal architecture, it delivered no inspiration for her own work.

And she needed inspiration, especially after receiving an e-mail from Jamie, the intern, this morning, telling her that Tony and Meredith seemed "really close" and were "always talking behind closed doors."

Of course they were. It made sense. But what if Tony changed his mind, decided Meredith was more deserving of senior architect? Without his support, Crystal didn't stand a chance.

Megan kicked at a pebble on the walkway, scattering Crystal's thoughts. "This place is so overwhelming." Her sister gazed up at the turreted structure.

Maybe she should examine the structure from another angle. Crystal began walking farther away and to the left.

Megan scurried after her. "Where are you going?"

"Trying to see this thing from over there." She pointed to the far end of the giant linear pool on the north-south axis of the structure. The pool was lined with sidewalks on either side and reflected the mausoleum. Surely seeing it from a different perspective would give Crystal some ideas. "I can't squeeze reflecting pools into my design, but maybe incorporating water somehow . . ."

They continued up the walkway, past women in beautiful pink-and-red saris and men in traditional Indian garb, as well as tourists with wide-brimmed hats and big cameras slung around their necks. A few children played a game of tag near the water's edge, threatening to push each other in. As the sun dropped lower in the sky, the air became a little more bearable, though the humidity still clung to Crystal's pores.

"Did you hear the tour guide say the building changes color at different times of the day?" Megan shoved the pamphlet under Crystal's nose as they walked, pointing out a few pictures. "See? It's pink in the mornings and milky white in the evening. I can kind of see it turning now. Oh, and if the moon is out tonight, it will be golden. Obviously I know nothing about architecture, but maybe that's something you could put in your design."

"Not sure that would work, but it's an interesting thought."

Crystal studied her sister. After being together for nearly a week, things were starting to relax between them. Their conversation was still fairly surface level, but Crystal had no idea how to take it deeper after so many years apart.

What had Brian said last night on the phone, once they'd finally had a chance to talk? *Things won't change overnight. Just start small. Share a piece of yourself and see how she responds.*

Once upon a time, that had been easy. Now, after years of stuffing her feelings away and pretending they didn't exist, it felt about as simple as . . . well, figuring out the perfect idea for a career-changing presentation.

But that's why she was here, wasn't it? To try.

Crystal stopped and turned toward the pool, which caught the reflection of the monument behind it. The now milky-white structure sprang up from the ground and thrust forward into the pool, extending beyond its natural reach. It seemed larger than life.

Here goes nothing. Crystal cleared her throat. "You know when I first decided to become an architect?"

"When?" If a word could sound hungry, Megan's did. Perhaps she was just as desperate to find a way to connect.

"Junior year of high school. We took a trip to Washington, DC, remember?" The moment the words were out of her mouth, she knew they were wrong. Because Megan wasn't part of the "we." By then, she'd been in and out of the hospital so much, Mom and Dad had decided she should be homeschooled.

"I remember." Megan's voice was soft, and she stared at the pool, the Taj Mahal towering in the background.

A memory surfaced, one that Crystal had buried deep. Herself, so excited about all the beautiful architecture and monuments she'd seen in DC. She couldn't wait to come home and show the pictures to Megan, who loved the idea of traveling someday. They'd finally have something in common again, something to talk about, something to share—or so Crystal had thought.

But though Megan had tried to act happy for her, Crystal had sensed something shift between them. Her attempts to draw them closer had only made Megan feel worse about her own situation.

In that moment, Crystal had never been more aware of how wide the divide between their lives had become—and how it was something they might never be able to overcome.

"You know what? Never mind. Let's go." She whirled and headed for the exit.

"Wait." Megan caught her arm and tugged, pleading in her tone. "I know it's warm out, but let's just sit here and enjoy this. See if the Taj really turns golden."

Crystal blew out a breath. "All right."

Megan found an empty grassy area under a tree and plopped down, stretching out her legs in front of her and wrapping her arms around her knees. Crystal tossed her backpack onto the ground and then sat beside it. She pulled a few water bottles from the front pocket and threw one to Megan. They both took long draughts. Then Megan removed a notebook from her bag and held her fingers to her pulse, her lips moving silently.

"I've seen you do that a few times." Crystal quirked an eyebrow. "Are you recording your heart rate?"

"Yes." With a quick flourish, Megan jotted something in her notebook, then closed it and put it away. "It was something my doctor suggested I do for the first year after my surgery. I might stop when I get home. But better safe than sorry while I'm away, you know?"

Crystal ran her nail along the edge of her water bottle cap. "Sure." But she didn't know. She couldn't imagine being in Megan's shoes when she was sick.

Being in her own had been hard enough.

Above them, the sky turned from light blue to black, and a few stars popped out overhead. When greeted by the moonlight, the Taj turned a golden hue, like a sparkling beacon to the world. The crowd thinned as people headed to dinner. Spices like saffron and curry floated under their noses, their smell so strong it seemed as if they could be snatched and eaten off the air.

"Crystal?"

"Yes?"

"Thanks for coming with me." Megan worked the label off her own water bottle, peeling it from the glue that held it in place. "It means a lot that you took time away from work and from Brian."

That first day in Cusco she'd told Megan the basics of the Lerner project and the promise of promotion that came with it, but she hadn't exactly said anything about how her marriage was falling apart. A clog welled in Crystal's throat, so she took another swig of the water. "You're welcome."

A slight breeze started up, rustling the label in Megan's hand. "I'm still surprised your boss let you come."

"I told him being around all this amazing

architecture would surely spark some inspiration for my project."

"And has it?"

"Not quite."

The water bottle in Megan's hand creaked as she took another sip. "It seems to me like inspiration wouldn't be something you can force. It'll come to you in the right moment."

"I used to think like that." Crystal pulled her hair off her neck and secured it with a hair tie from around her wrist. "But being in the real world of architecture will wipe that notion right out of your head. Projects have deadlines, and deadlines wait for nothing and no one."

"That makes me sad."

"What?"

"It almost sounds like your job has taken something you love and turned it into a robotic task." Megan rested her chin on her knees.

"That's not true." But then what had happened to her passion the last few years, her ability to conjure up creativity? "It's just sometimes more black-and-white than I thought it'd be when I was a starry-eyed architecture student who didn't know better."

"But why settle for black-and-white"—Megan pointed to the Taj Mahal, which glinted in the moonlight—"or even pink or milky white, when you can have golden?"

Chapter 13

And just as the Taj turned from white to golden, I thought, "What a lovely way to see the world."

Megan tapped the hotel room desk, staring at the blinking cursor, but couldn't think of anything else to add to her latest blog post. She'd written it on their flight from India to Beijing, but something about it hadn't felt complete. Maybe it was the conversation she'd had with Crystal about dreams and passion and living life in color. There was something probing and deep in their discussion that had clearly affected her sister.

How exactly, Megan had no clue. She only knew Crystal's brow had furrowed and she'd become eerily quiet. Not one to wear her heart on her sleeve—at all. Though for a moment there, when talking about Washington, DC, it had seemed like she might be willing to share a little of herself. Maybe Megan just needed to be patient.

She hit Publish and watched her post go live. It was almost time to shower and get ready for bed. Even though it wasn't that late, travel had a way of wearing her out. Since Crystal was in the bathroom right now, Megan had a few minutes to kill.

It was getting darker in the room—the last of the natural light fading outside—so she flipped on the green lamp that looked like it belonged in a newsroom. She'd received an e-mail from their travel agent yesterday asking about officially booking the second half of their trip, but she hadn't had a chance to check her GoFundMe account till now. And quite honestly, she was afraid to look. What if she couldn't afford to complete the whole bucket list?

She logged in—and stared at the screen.

Fully funded.

How was that possible? She scanned the list of donations, and there were several small amounts from people she knew, a few from those she didn't. And then one huge donation, which took care of the balance. Tears sprang to her eyes as she caught the name on the donation: Gary and Charlene Abbott.

And the note that went with it:

We've been so blessed to think of you doing this for our girl. Looking forward to sharing in the adventure from afar! Hope you don't mind, but we shared your blog with everyone we know. Wishing you great success as you honor Amanda's memory.

An ache tore through Megan's heart. The sweet gesture was almost more than she could bear. And it certainly added another layer of motivation to completing the entire bucket list, considering the Abbotts' emotional, and now financial, investment.

Her phone beeped on the desk next to her. A text from Caleb. Though they hadn't actually spoken since before she'd left, she'd texted him a few pictures of Machu Picchu, the pyramids, and the Taj. She hadn't heard from him since sending the last photo.

Now she read his response:

> You've got a good eye for color, Meg. But I hope you took photos with more than just your phone! ☺

She laughed, and her fingers flew across the screen.

> I did, but we don't all have fancy photography equipment, Watkins. I'll leave the professional stuff to you.

> Ha-ha. Oh, hey, I just heard from an editor friend at a small online travel zine. She saw me share your last blog post on Facebook and wanted your contact info. I guess it's not on your website? ☺ I hope you don't mind,

162

but I gave her your e-mail. She said she'd be contacting you soon.

Megan's breath caught.

Wow, what did she want?

Not sure. But her zine is growing rapidly and she's always on the lookout for new writers.

Whaaaaaaaaat?!!!!

She never thought anyone would really read her blog. Sure, she'd had a few comments from people in Little Lakes, her family, and a few of Amanda's friends—which now made sense, knowing the Abbotts had shared her posts with others. But to have an actual editor see her work and request her information . . .

You're so dramatic, Meg. LOL. If I had to guess, I'd say she's seen what I've known all along—you're incredibly talented and need to be published.

Oh, Caleb. He'd always encouraged her when it came to writing, and she'd carried his words with her even at her lowest moments. They made her feel brave, a lot braver than she really was. But that wasn't the point. With him, she'd always been able to imagine who she wanted to be, and he gave her the inspiration to think she could actually become that person.

Megan brushed a finger under her eyes. Oh brother. There she went again.

I'll let you know if I hear from her.

She flipped from her texts to her e-mail, scanning the eighty-three unread e-mails until she saw one from a Sheila Daily.

Ms. Jacobs, I'm the editor for *Travel Discovery Nerds*, an online magazine targeting readers of all ages who love to travel to destinations all over the world.

Caleb Watkins does some freelance work for me occasionally and I got your contact information from him. I'm very interested in your story and would love to chat about the possibility of having you contribute to our magazine. Give me a call if you're interested. I'm in New York City, so call anytime. After all, we never sleep here. ☺

Sheila Daily

Whoa.

Her finger hovered over Sheila's number on the screen. One tap and her phone would connect her to someone who might actually want to publish her stuff. All the possibilities whirled in her mind. They began as fluffy clouds that were light and airy and ripe with refreshing rain. But then they multiplied, bulged, and grew dark, overwhelming her senses.

And just like that, all the fears she'd ever had—all the excuses, the reasons she'd never submitted before—came rushing back.

At that moment Crystal came out of the bathroom wearing a robe with a towel wrapped around her head. A blast of humid air floated out with her. "Bathroom's all yours."

"Thanks." Megan moved to the window, pushing back the curtains and watching the lights of Beijing dance and twinkle in the darkness. What should she do?

"Everything okay?"

"Yes. No. I don't know." She turned to face her sister.

"Well, which is it?" Crystal perched on the edge of her bed as she unwound her hair from the towel.

Megan told her about Sheila's e-mail.

"I don't understand." Her twin finger-combed her hair. "That sounds like a great opportunity. Why don't you sound happy about it?"

"Because . . . what if I'm not good enough?"

"Sounds to me like she thinks you are." Crystal effortlessly wove her hair into a French braid. "And didn't you come on this trip to try to build a portfolio?"

165

"Partially. I also came for Amanda."

Crystal waved off Megan's words. "Yes, of course. But also for you. This isn't just Amanda's journey. It's yours too."

Her sister was right. Megan couldn't—wouldn't—talk herself out of an opportunity, not when it was the very thing she'd been waiting for. "Thanks."

She dialed.

"Sheila Daily speaking."

Megan cleared her throat. "Hi, Ms. Daily. This is Megan Jacobs. I just got your e-mail."

"I'm so glad you called." Papers rustled in the background. "I'm sure you're busy, and it must be very late wherever you are."

"Not too late, but yes. We're in Beijing. Going to visit the Great Wall tomorrow."

"I've always wanted to travel to Asia, but I haven't made it there quite yet." The distant barking of a dog filled the earpiece. Maybe Sheila worked from home. "Listen, I'm always on the lookout for interesting stories and great writers, and when I read your blog, I knew I'd found both."

"Thank you." Megan tugged at the long sleeves of her shirt. "You mentioned me possibly contributing to your magazine?"

"Yes. I'd like to start by having you write a feature piece about your health journey and your decision to take this trip. We'd publish it as soon as possible, and encourage people to follow your blog. Our site isn't like a traditional magazine. We are constantly updating our content. So if the piece gets the response I'm thinking it will, then we could have you contribute regularly along the way, perhaps once a week until you're home. You could still post to your blog, but write something a bit different for our site."

How often had she dreamed of writing for a newspaper or magazine? And here was an opportunity practically leaping into her lap without her sending a single query. "I don't know what to say."

"Of course I'd love to hear a yes." Sheila gave a staccato laugh. "Here's a little more incentive for you. I treat my freelancers very well, and if this relationship works out, I'd be open to more contributions from you. So if freelance travel writing is something you're interested in, we're a good place to start. *TDN* is growing every day, so I will definitely have more needs in the future."

"That sounds amazing." Megan couldn't help the grin that spread across her face. "I would love to contribute as much as you'll allow me to."

"Great." Sheila gave her the details on the piece Megan would write first. Then they exchanged further contact information and hung up.

"Well?"

Megan let loose a squeal. "I did it. I landed my first writing job."

Chapter 14

Why had she let Megan convince her this was a good idea?

Crystal squeezed her eyes shut and gripped the small handrail in front of her as the chairlift shuddered. Only a long, dipping cable kept her and Megan's car afloat over the Great Wall of China's Mutianyu section. Crystal's stomach was already protesting the foreign breakfast she'd eaten. "How did I let you talk me into this?"

"You should really open your eyes. It's gorgeous up here."

"No, thanks. I'm good."

"I didn't think you were afraid of heights."

"This isn't just heights. It's pure madness." Trusting in a foreign country's airborne transportation system had been an egregious error in judgment.

"Come on, Crystal. Just take a peek. You'll regret it if you don't."

Crystal groaned but popped one eye open. Below her, tiny people moved along the wall like bugs in an ant farm. The path rose and fell and went for miles. Mountains and greenery surrounded the wall on all sides. A slight haze covered the sky, but pockets of light shone through. "Maybe this isn't so b—"

The wind rocked their car and Crystal held in a squeal. Thankfully, the end of the line was coming into view. She closed her eyes as another wave of nausea passed.

"Are you okay?" Megan's voice sounded distant.

Crystal nodded and held a fist against her stomach. "Just a little nauseous."

"You don't think . . ."

"What?" She opened her eyes and fixed her gaze on Megan.

"I don't know. Could you be pregnant?"

"No, thank goodness." The words popped out before she could consider what they communicated.

"Oh. Sorry. I just assumed you and Brian wanted kids."

"We do, just not yet."

Brian would be thrilled if she'd agree to go off her birth control pills. But for some reason Crystal couldn't muster enthusiasm for the idea. She'd told him—had been telling herself—she simply wanted to achieve certain career goals before bringing kids into the world, but deep down she knew there were other reasons. Ones she didn't want to explore.

She rushed on. "I think I might have a small ulcer or something like that. It's probably nothing." This morning as she'd looked in the mirror, she'd noticed how her eyes lacked any luster and puffy bags rimmed the underside of her lids. Headaches had come more frequently this last week, and she'd already gone through three bottles of TUMS since boarding that first plane to Peru.

"What? You should go to the doctor."

"When am I going to do that, Megan? We're constantly on the move." If she'd been home, she would have made an appointment with her doctor at this point, no matter how busy she was. But neither she nor Megan could afford a delay.

"We can surely find time for you to get checked out."

"I'm managing it fine. Sometimes I just eat something that irritates my stomach a bit." She'd simply have to suck it up. Besides, how she was feeling was nothing compared to what Megan had been through. Crystal had no room to complain.

They rumbled into the cable car station. Megan chewed her lip and turned away from Crystal. "If you say so."

The cable car swept toward an attendant, who opened their door and helped Megan out, then Crystal. It took a moment for Crystal to get her bearings and steady her legs.

Megan led the way toward the exit. They ascended a few steps and found themselves in an arched doorway. Walking toward the sunlight, they emerged from the cable car station. A brick wall on either side of the path kept them hemmed in. Tourists of all nationalities roamed the walkway, some using the handrails along the edges of the wall to climb the steep path toward the highest point of this section. "Come on."

As Crystal trudged up the path, her nausea subsided. Directly in front of them, a Chinese mom held the hand of a young boy about five years old. He tried to drag his mother toward a viewing machine mounted at the top of a step across the pathway. The woman shook her head and said something Crystal couldn't hear.

What *would* it be like to be a mother? On the one hand, she'd have someone who adored her for no other reason than she was Mom. But children . . . They were so dependent. They required a lot of love and attention. And while Brian would be an amazing parent, Crystal couldn't say the same about herself.

After all, she hadn't exactly been there for the other people in her life.

"Crystal?"

"Hmm?" Crystal looked up to see Megan standing there with a map, a questioning look on her face.

"Are you coming?"

"Oh. Yeah."

Megan led them to the nearest watch-tower—there were twenty-something in this section—and they explored it fully. As they headed upstairs, Crystal caught sight of the mother and her son standing at a window and overlooking the gorgeous scenery below. The mom held the boy up so he could see, letting him stand on the lip of the window, nothing but her arm securing him.

"What are you looking at?"

Crystal jumped to find Megan at her elbow. "The way that woman is holding her son. Mom never would have let us get so close."

"You're right. Remember that hike we took during a camping trip when we were like six or seven? Dad took us out on that rock ledge overlooking the whole forest."

"Oh yeah. And Mom totally freaked out."

Dad had told their mom to calm down, that he was there with the girls and was making sure they were protected. But how had he really known he could keep them safe? As a child, Crystal had completely trusted him, known without question that nothing bad could happen so long as he was there.

Still, the reality was that he couldn't fully protect them. One wrong move and someone could have slipped, fallen right over the edge . . .

Of course they'd been fine. That day. That time.

But one or two years later, Megan had been diagnosed with something that had been completely out of both their parents' control. She'd almost died, and there was nothing they'd been able to do to shield her from it.

"You look pale." Megan bit her lip. "Do we need to go back?"

"I'm fine. Really."

But she wasn't. Every time she allowed a new emotion through the cracks in her armor, it jabbed, rubbing her insides raw. Brian would say this was progress, and maybe it was. But it was painful, and Crystal almost missed the numbness.

She straightened and turned from the mother and son. "Let's get back to it."

That evening Megan took her laptop to the lobby to write her latest blog post and work on her article for the online publication, leaving Crystal behind to try to work on her proposal. Crystal's body ached for sleep, but evenings and flights were her only times to work—and she'd received an e-mail an hour ago from Tony requesting another draft of her proposal.

After she pressed a few buttons on her phone, Norah Jones's voice spilled into the room, ebbing and flowing like the light rain that beat against the window. Crystal settled into the chair next to the window to brainstorm and lifted her hand to her notepad. She closed her eyes, considering all the things she'd seen so far on this trip, thinking about the James Lawrence building. What had she always dreamed of doing with it? How could she pull her recent experiences into this one?

Her old art teacher's voice echoed in her mind: *"What is art about if you don't put yourself into every bit of it?"*

That wasn't as easy as it used to be.

Focus, Crystal. Focus. She pictured the Egyptian pyramids. The Taj Mahal. The Great Wall. All amazing feats of architecture . . .

Her phone rang. Brian. She answered. "Hey, babe."

"Glad I finally got ahold of you. It's been a while."

The time difference had made it difficult to find time to talk. And even when they did, she had a hard time expressing her thoughts. After all the emotions she'd been keeping at bay lately, she felt like a hot mess. What husband wanted to hear about that?

He cleared his throat. "So. How are you?"

"Doing okay." She slid the phone between her shoulder and her cheek and started doodling on the notepad. "How are things in New York?"

"Pretty much the same." Brian paused. "Except you're not here, of course. I miss you."

"That's good to hear." Crystal drew a plane. She pictured herself grabbing hold of the wings and flying along, back to her husband. Back to the comfort zone of work, of progress she could see. "I miss you too."

When things felt awkward or strained between her and Megan—those times it didn't seem like this trip would really change anything—she focused on Brian, on what he'd said before she left: *"I'm not sure we can get us back until you heal."* He'd been certain that healing included patching things up with Megan.

But she felt like she was failing him. Because she still hadn't found a way to open up to Megan, to move past the surface and dive deeper.

How could she, when there was a lingering elephant between them, one that felt like it'd settled there and would never budge, no matter how much she wanted to push?

She was helpless once again. Incapable of fixing this mess.

Her eyes began to burn and an impending headache put pressure on her temples. She slashed through the doodles on her page and closed the notepad.

"What did you do today?" Brian's voice pulled her from her thoughts.

Facts. Those she could handle. She rubbed her forehead. "Today we saw the Great Wall. It was quite an experience." She told him about riding the cable lift.

"I'm surprised you agreed to that. Remember that ski trip when we were dating? You promised you'd never go on another ski lift or anything of the sort ever again."

"Yeah, but Megan really wanted to go, so we did."

"That was nice of you. How are things going between you two?"

"We're getting along, if that's what you mean. No knock-down drag-outs. Just the basic sisterly squabbles." Although, not really even that. Maybe they were both too afraid of what even a small fight might lead to.

"I know it can't be easy." Brian hesitated. "Is she treating you okay?"

"Megan?" Crystal snorted. "She doesn't hold grudges, even when she should." Ah, there came the red-hot eyes again . . . and a single tear, burning a trail down her cheek. Crystal backhanded it away.

"You know, it's okay to have a knock-down drag-out. Sometimes that's what's needed to clear the air. Have you . . . you know, brought up the past?"

"What do you think?" Her voice came out ragged, angry. Brian meant well, but he didn't know what he was asking. "Sorry, I don't mean to sound frustrated. There's just a lot going on. Tony's breathing down my neck with work stuff, we're traveling a lot, which is exhausting, and the emotions I'm dealing with are more than overwhelming. Sometimes I don't think I can do this anymore."

And suddenly she couldn't stuff away the memories any longer. They were coming, curling up from within, bringing images of the day that things had gone from bad to impossible between her and Megan.

There lay her twin, who should be identical in every way but couldn't look less like her if she tried, kept prisoner in a hospital bed thanks to IV lines and monitors, looking nearly dead already. Her eyes had sunken into her pale face, yet somehow still flashed that hope Megan always kept shining. Her hair was dull, so thin and wispy against the pillow. She'd asked to see Crystal alone, so Crystal had left Mom, Dad, and Brian in the waiting room. Every step forward had been torture.

"Crystal." Megan reached out her hand. It looked like one an old woman might have—wrinkled, worn, bruised with splotches of blood just beneath the surface.

Crystal took that hand in hers. A chill burst from it, from Megan. "You're going to be okay." Crystal squeezed, willing some of her own strength into her sister. This wasn't the first time Megan had had to fight for her life. Wasn't the first time Crystal had had to watch. They'd both do it again. Only this time Megan would emerge whole, with a new heart that could change everything—maybe even this distance between them.

She had to. There wasn't an alternative.

Not one that Crystal was willing to accept.

"I know." Megan's voice croaked, thick with emotion and weak from the medications she'd been fed through her tubes. "But if I'm not, you should have Nana's ring. I know you always wanted it."

"Stop it." With a firm shake of her head, Crystal stood, but Megan held on to her hand tighter than she should have been able to. She'd always been stronger than anyone had guessed. "Nothing's going to happen to you."

"It might. And if it does, I just want—"

But Crystal hadn't stuck around to hear what Megan wanted. "You're going to be fine. I promise."

She leaned over, kissed her sister on the forehead, and returned to the waiting room. She waited to hear Megan had made it through surgery and then fled back to New York like the coward she really was.

Silent sobs racked Crystal's whole body as the tears finally streamed out.

"Crys?"

Brian. He was still on the phone. "I've got to go." She barely whispered the words before hanging up and slipping the phone onto silent.

178

Chapter 15

July 1
Blog Post Title: Getting Schooled:
    Visiting the Great Barrier Reef
Post Content:
    We ran into some trouble in paradise
today . . .

Three hundred dollars *should* have paid for a lovely outing on a reliable charter boat.

"What was that clunking noise?" Megan shielded her eyes from the sun as she swiveled her head to the captain, a short man in his fifties sporting a deep tan and bleached hair. Next to her, Crystal sat on the boat's front seat in a half-zipped black wetsuit and pink bikini top. The spray from the moving boat teased their faces as they sped along the Australian coast.

"Nothing to worry about." The captain's Australian accent showcased his nonchalance as he waved his hand in the air. "This old girl has never failed me once."

"Remind me why we didn't book an excursion with a reputable company?" Crystal cocked an eyebrow in Megan's direction.

Her sister had been fairly quiet the last few days

as they'd flown to and explored the Australian city of Cairns—ever since their last night in Beijing, when Megan had returned to their room after writing and found Crystal in tears. She'd rushed to her side, asked what was wrong, but her sister couldn't seem to find the words to tell her.

Couldn't, or didn't want to.

Instead, she'd rushed to the bathroom and shut the door. When Megan had gently brought it up the next morning, Crystal had changed the subject.

Maybe Megan had been a fool to hope things would ever change between them.

Now she shook off what felt like rejection and ran her fingers through her damp hair. "Because if we'd booked an excursion, we wouldn't have control over where the boat goes. And Amanda's list said to 'snorkel a remote part of the Great Barrier Reef,' so we needed that control."

She'd spent time last week researching remote locations with amazing snorkeling and had discovered a small island that fit the bill. Because it was peak tourist season, they'd had to scour the docks to find a boat available for charter. It was a good thing they'd found Captain Donaldson when they did, because their flight to Greece was tomorrow morning.

"How much farther until we reach the island?" Megan looked out over the turquoise water rippling against the boat.

The captain steered with one hand and took a swig from his water bottle with the other. "Another twenty-four kilometers or so."

"Great." The sky was completely cloudless, and there weren't any other boats in sight. Megan couldn't wait to get a peek at what lay beneath—

Clunk, clunk, clunk.

Crystal's head shot up. "That did not sound good."

The captain cursed and banged something metal and hollow just as the boat sputtered to a stop. Megan turned her body again to face the captain. He fiddled with some controls, and the faint smell of gasoline rent the air.

Megan bit the edge of her fingernail. "What's going on?"

The captain ignored her and checked a few more things on the boat. "I won't know for sure until we get back to dock, but I think something's wrong with the engine."

"What does that mean?"

"It means we won't be going to your island." The man picked up his boat phone and dialed. "Mate, we're stuck . . . Yeah, stopped completely." He gave their coordinates and hung up, then scratched his head. The crow's feet around his eyes stood out with his grimace. "Looks like my partner can't come pick us up for about an hour. He'll haul us back to shore and we'll get you a full refund. Sorry for the trouble."

"But we have to get to that island. Can he take us there?"

The man shook his head. "We have to go a lot slower when hauling another boat so we'd never make it back before it gets dark."

But the list—they had to get to that island. "What are we going to do?"

Crystal pulled a strand of hair over her shoulder and wrapped it around her finger. "Isn't our flight early tomorrow?"

"Yes." It was only a balmy seventy degrees, but Megan was beginning to sweat.

"Do you think we'd be able to switch to a later flight so we can snorkel in the morning?"

Megan thought through their travel plans, trying to remember all the details. "The festival of San Fermín starts in five days. The travel agent has everything organized perfectly so we make it to Greece and Italy before we hit Spain." The distant drone of an airplane reverberated overhead. "Plus, when we switch flights, it costs money. And our budget is tight as it is, even with the GoFundMe money."

"I hate to say it, but we might have to leave this item undone."

"We can't." Not when Amanda's family was counting on her, had put up thousands of dollars to financially back her journey. And not when she now had blog readers following along, wishing her success. And especially not when she had another article due to Sheila Daily, who said her first one had hit a chord with readers and she couldn't wait to publish more.

Failure was not an option.

But right now it seemed inevitable.

"Okay." Crystal fiddled with the zipper on her wetsuit. Her eyes narrowed in concentration. "From what you've told me about Amanda, she doesn't seem like the kind of girl who'd give up easily."

"She wasn't." Though Megan had continued to keep Amanda's journal to herself, she'd relayed bits and pieces of her life to Crystal along the way. "But I really don't think there's anything even she could do in this situation."

Her sister chewed her lip for a moment, then stood. She peeked over the edge of the boat and turned to the captain. "Is it safe to snorkel here? Would we see anything?"

"Sure. Though we're out a ways, it's not as deep as you'd think."

Crystal turned satisfied eyes on Megan. "Well?" She shoved her hands through the sleeves of her wetsuit. "Zip me up."

Megan's hands did as Crystal asked, but her spirit wasn't in it. "I had my heart set on going to the island. Weren't the pictures there gorgeous?"

Scooping up a pair of fins from the boat deck, Crystal tossed them at Megan. "Who's to say that this very spot isn't even more gorgeous?" She pulled a pair of flippers onto her own feet. "This is our only chance to snorkel the Great Barrier Reef, and it's remote, just like you wanted. I know it's not the destination we had in mind, but it's where we've landed."

Wow. Did Crystal even realize the deeper truth in her words?

Megan had never thought she'd be here, in Australia, fulfilling the bucket list of a girl whose life had been cut short. That she'd be the one to go on living despite her years of illness.

And yet, here she was. Why she'd been given this chance after years of denial, she didn't know.

But she was done wasting it. Fear and uncertainty had no place in her life, not today.

"You're right." Megan put on her snorkeling gear. She held her finger against her throat, counted. Amanda's heart beat strong, pumping blood in a steady flow.

Megan was ready.

Together, they climbed to the boat's diving deck and sat down. The boat rocked in the gentle waves as the water lapped against their legs. What mysteries awaited them underwater?

They left the boat ledge. Megan kicked her feet, and the flippers helped her move with ease through the water. Her sister pointed down. Sticking the snorkel in her mouth, Megan lowered her face into the water. What she beheld made the heart within her chest skip a beat.

Colorful coral unraveled before her like bouquets of flowers in all shapes and sizes. Yellows and blues, purples and reds, each one bright like paint splattered artfully upon the canvas of an imaginative creator.

Anemones opened and closed, taking cues from the water.

Two sea turtles took their time getting wherever they were going, gliding along without a care in the world. One inclined its head toward Megan.

Crystal swam closer to the reef, and Megan followed. They moved together, pointing out puffer fish, angelfish, orange-and-white Nemos, and a whole host of species she'd never be able to name but would always remember.

A school of pink fish flitted in the currents, performing a graceful dance.

Crystal was right. It wasn't the destination Megan had had in mind.

It was even better.

Chapter 16

8. Skinny-dip.

When we first moved to Minnesota, Mom thought we should make church a priority. So we did, for a little while. Gotta admit, as a ten-year-old fresh from the clutches of sexual abuse, I had a hard time singing songs about Jesus loving me and being strong and courageous when I knew a secret a lot of the kids around me didn't: monsters are real.

One Sunday we heard the story of Adam and Eve, how they were "naked and unashamed." Of course, all the kids giggled when the teacher said the word naked. But I didn't. I started trembling like a freak.

Ever since what happened, I've never been able to be naked in front of anyone, not even half-naked. In gym class, I'm one of those girls who changes in the bathroom stall. Then there was the party Cathi dragged me to last year, where all the cool kids skinny-dipped at the lake behind Manny Frederick's house. I hightailed it outta there so fast . . .

Because skinny-dipping is the ultimate vulnerability. You strip off everything you're wearing till it's just your skin touching water. Your naked body becomes one with the waves. I imagine it's frightening and freeing all at once.

So this bucket list item is, to me, one of the hardest to put on paper. Because I want so badly to reclaim my body.

To prove to myself that Uncle Joe didn't win.

To be naked . . . and unashamed.

Chapter 17

July 3
Blog Post Title: Vulnerability at Its
    Finest: Greece
Post Content:
    Today I did something I've never done
before. And to be honest, I'm a little
embarrassed to write about it . . .

Every muscle ached, but a deep satisfaction welled inside Megan.

She watched the waves break in the ocean beyond the shore of the Greek beach where she stood in the moonlight. Once so powerful, the water trailed along the beach, eventually lapping at her feet and then receding. It was surprisingly warm as it sloshed against her toes. Tiny grains of brilliant white sand coated her wet feet.

Everything else in the world may be in flux, but this, here, was constant. The tide would always come in, and then it would go out. The pull of the moon was too strong for it to do anything else.

"This is more beautiful than I'd ever have imagined it." Megan whispered the words and the breeze tossed them outward.

"Yes, it is." Behind her, where the water didn't reach, Crystal plopped into the sand. As far as their eyes could see, they were alone on this secluded beach Megan had found in an Athens guidebook. "But you say that about everything, you know."

A gentle laugh left Megan's lips. She walked toward Crystal and sat beside her. "I guess I do." She'd definitely said it about the Parthenon earlier today as they'd explored Athens. And the National Garden. And the whitewashed buildings with blue roofs, built into the hills like a modern-day kingdom. And yeah, maybe the Temple of Zeus too. She couldn't help it. The history, the gorgeous setting, the fact that she was here, experiencing all of this—it *was* more beautiful than she'd ever imagined.

And the last few days since Australia, she'd felt closer to Crystal, even if it was one-sided. Yet things did feel easier between them. If it hadn't been for her sister, she'd never have been brave enough to literally take the plunge and experience one of the most magical days of her life in Australia.

Crystal reclined in the sand, propping herself up on her elbows. Her gaze seemed to land to the far left, where the city lights could be seen twinkling in the distance. "This beach sure is romantic, isn't it?"

The comment was so unlike Crystal, Megan nearly laughed. But from the handful of times Megan had seen Crystal and Brian together, they'd seemed deeply in love. She must miss him a lot. "It is."

With a sweep of her hand, Crystal pushed sand aside, then moved it back into place. "Speaking of romantic, what's up with you and Caleb? You guys text each other quite a bit."

Megan wondered if her cheeks were as red as they felt, or if Crystal would be able to make out their color in the moonlight. "We've been talking more lately. He's a travel photographer and has a lot of experience. It's been nice to reconnect with him."

Anytime she thought about him, the biggest grin would pop on her face and she couldn't help but feel lighter inside. But she simply missed her friend. That was all. She wouldn't make a bigger deal of it than that.

"I'll bet it has."

"Stop it." Megan flicked sand toward Crystal at her sister's singsong tone.

"Is he traveling right now?"

She nodded, thinking of their latest e-mail exchange. "He's in Denmark."

"Why don't you see if he can meet up with us along the way?"

"I doubt he'd have time."

But if he did . . . What would it be like to see him again? It had only been a little over a month since she'd seen him at the fund-raiser, when he caught her off guard with his handsome looks and the way his smile had made her feel deliciously warm inside.

Was it really possible? Did she have a crush on Caleb Watkins?

Megan closed her eyes and breathed in the scent of the sea, a salty balm laced with the freshness of lemon. The roar of the ocean beckoned her. What had once been an unfamiliar stranger now called to her like a trusted friend. She opened her eyes and stood. "Let's wade in."

"Changing the subject?"

Ignoring her, Megan walked toward the ocean with purpose. As soon as her feet hit the wet sand, she tingled with anticipation. She would wade in only for a moment.

"You're going to get your jeans wet."

"Who cares?" The water rose to Megan's calves and hit the bottom of her rolled jeans. As the wave left her, the material clung to her skin. She walked farther, this time soaking midway up her thighs. Something urged her to go deeper, but this was far enough. Megan turned and headed back to her sister, who stood on the beach with her hands on her hips. As she walked, the jeans rubbed against her inner thighs, chafing the tender skin.

"What in the world are you doing?" Crystal's look of utter bewilderment made Megan burst into laughter. What *was* she doing? She didn't have a clue. She only knew that some part of her wanted to fling off everything that hindered her—her past, the expectations of everyone she knew, the constant worry that her health would relapse.

The fear of what would happen if she asked Caleb to meet up with her.

And then, like a spark, an idea lit inside of her.

"What's that look for?" Crystal's hands moved from her sides to cross the front of her body.

"An item on the list." One that had given her a bout of anxiety when she'd first read it but couldn't imagine doing anywhere else. "We can check it off right now." Megan's hands shook as she unbuttoned her jeans.

"What item? I thought we already did everything for Athens." Crystal looked at her like she was crazy as Megan peeled off the wet jeans, exposing her damp legs to the breeze.

"We did." With a quick glance around to confirm they were alone, Megan pulled off her sweater and flung it to the ground. "But this one didn't have an exact location."

"Put your pants back on."

Her sister's hiss hopped around her. She looked so flustered. Megan couldn't help the giggle that rose in her throat.

"I can't. The list calls for skinny-dipping."

"What? You're crazy." Crystal's head shot back and forth. "You could get arrested or something."

"There's no one here." With every layer of

192

clothing that left her body, a new sort of lightness came over her. A bird squawked in the distance as Megan lifted her shirt over her head, revealing her scar. For a moment she stared down at it. And even though no one but her and Crystal could see it, letting it out in the open felt like a victory of some sort. "Come on."

"You want me to go with you? Uh-uh. You can be crazy on your own."

"Have you never skinny-dipped before?" Now it was Megan's turn to fold her arms across her chest.

An eye roll from Crystal met Megan's comment. "Sure, when I was young and dumb."

A sudden burst of nostalgia made Megan almost cold. "We never got a chance to be young and dumb together." She'd been too sick. "How about it? Please?"

For a few moments she thought her sister was going to say no. But then, without a word, Crystal began to undress until she and Megan were a matching pair. Megan held out her hand and Crystal pressed her palm in, wrapping her fingers around her twin's. They headed toward the ocean, each step growing more urgent. Megan threw a glance at her sister, whose lips were set in a determined line.

And suddenly they were no longer thirty-two but eight years old, running and laughing their way into the Atlantic Ocean during the last family trip before Megan's diagnosis. Instead of skinny-dipping, they wore matching striped one-piece swimsuits. Back then, everything they wore matched. They'd held hands all the way into the ocean, the cold water slapping their legs and identical small bodies, making them shriek with delight. And even when the waves came, they held fast to each other, never letting go.

This time there were no shrieks of delight, and the water was warm. It encased Megan, hugging her naked torso. Since they were alone, they didn't go beyond where they could stand. They were quiet as they bobbed with the coming waves. So quiet.

Crystal dropped Megan's hand.

What had happened to them? How had they gone from two copies of each other to total opposites who never spoke about anything real? When had the chasm between them become so vast? Was it Megan's fault for being so focused on herself while she was sick? Or Crystal's for walking away?

And was there any hope of real repair, or would they live in this constant limbo forever?

"I was just thinking about our trip to Florida for our eighth birthday." Megan plunged her hands through the water, creating her own waves. "Remember how we went to Disney World and then to the beach? It was the perfect vacation."

Though it was dark, Megan could see a glint

of something in Crystal's expression—longing, maybe? Her sister shifted her gaze to the moon, that glowing source of raw power. But just as quickly, she turned her body toward shore. "We'd better get back. I need to check my e-mail."

The little girl inside Megan cried as her sister left her behind once again.

Chapter 18

The Roman Colosseum was constructed using travertine stone blocks taken from quarries near Tivoli. They were carted to Rome via a wide pathway designed specifically for that purpose."

Crystal rubbed her nose as she listened to their British tour guide, Liam, a young hipster with thick-rimmed glasses and a goatee.

They'd already toured the Colosseum's underground passageways, and now they stood in the shadow of the towering wall above them, all one hundred fifty-seven feet of it. Clouds mostly obscured the sun, casting mystery over the day. Though Megan stood next to her and about twenty fellow English-speakers surrounded her, she felt almost alone in this vast structure that was built to house fifty thousand spectators.

Of course, feeling alone was her own fault. Why did she keep pushing away the people in her life she loved the most? Mom and Dad. Brian. Megan.

Liam slid his glasses farther up his nose. "There are four levels of seating and eighty entrances, though four of those entrances were restricted to the emperor, his household, and other members of high Roman society."

They stood at the bottom of the Colosseum,

where countless gladiators had waited at one time to fight. Crystal's gaze skimmed the walls, crumbling in places but still strong. This structure had endured the test of time for nearly two thousand years. Its strength pulsed beneath her feet, and she could almost feel the vibration of history.

She nudged Megan with an elbow. "Can you believe this place?" Crystal kept her voice low so as not to interrupt the tour guide.

Megan's eyes stayed focused forward. She nodded, acknowledging her but not. No smile, nothing. She'd been quiet all day yesterday as they traveled to Italy—probably upset that Crystal hadn't jumped into the Aegean Sea with both feet. Yes, it hadn't been bad, had almost been fun. But then Megan had to go and bring up their eighth birthday. It was the last piece of normal that Crystal could ever remember having in their family. And she hadn't been able to allow herself to dredge up the memories.

What was wrong with her? She'd come here to repair things, but at every turn she seemed to be making a royal mess of them instead. She needed to be stronger. But every time she tried to meditate on the "strength within"—something her yoga instructor back home always harped on—she couldn't seem to find it.

"As many of you probably know, the amphitheater was used for several events and exhibitions, primarily gladiatorial games where opponents would fight to the death." The tour guide led them down a long path that ran the length of the ground level. "Some of these games included animals such as lions that gladiators would have to kill if they wanted to survive."

Crystal shuddered.

Megan raised her hand. Liam's murky brown eyes lit with interest. "Miss?"

"Didn't the games also include martyrs?"

He stroked his goatee. "That has not been proven, though Pope Benedict XIV endorsed that view in 1749, when he declared the Colosseum sanctified by the blood of Christian martyrs. However, there is evidence of such martyrs at an arena in what is now Lyon, France."

Murmurs from the crowd rose. Liam spouted off several more facts, then checked his watch. "That concludes our tour of the Colosseum. My next tour does not begin for another ten minutes, so if you have any more questions, I'd be happy to answer them."

The crowd dispersed a few people at a time, some asking the guide to take pictures for them, others retracing their steps to study parts of the structure in more depth.

Megan tapped her on the shoulder. "I need to hit the restroom. Do you want to come or should I just meet you back here?"

"I'll wait here." She had no desire to leave yet.

Megan nodded and walked toward the front entrance.

Crystal rotated slowly, taking in the entirety of the structure, far larger and grander than anything she'd ever designed. And while she liked to think she left her own personal signature all over her designs, would any of her buildings be around in two thousand years?

Would the James Lawrence building become something great? Would it change lives for years to come? Maybe, but she wouldn't have anything to do with it if she didn't come up with a killer design—and soon. Tony had rejected her latest proposal draft and informed her that Meredith's was coming together nicely.

Why was she such a colossal failure despite all her attempts to the contrary?

"It's an impressive sight, isn't it?" Liam stood next to her, hands stuck in the back pockets of his skinny jeans.

"It sure is."

"You seem a lot more reflective than most people I see here every day."

"I'm an architect."

"Ah. So you're looking at all of this and wondering, 'How can I create something this fantastic?'"

"Pretty much."

"It certainly is amazing. I've lived in Rome for the last three years while attending uni, and the sight never gets old." Liam peered at the missing part of the Colosseum's southern wall. "But only some things last forever. This Colosseum isn't one of them."

"It's lasted nearly two millennia. Not even a fire or multiple earthquakes over the years were able to take it down."

"And you admire that?" The tour guide's piercing gaze shifted to Crystal.

"Who wouldn't?" If only she could be as resilient. "The pure strength it takes to survive all of that is amazing."

Like Megan. How had her sister managed to remain so unscathed all these years? Sure, physically she'd been damaged, but emotionally she hadn't been hardened. The image of her frolicking in the waves, laughing, allowing joy to replace the sorrow she'd once known—it was something Crystal wanted for herself.

But how did she get it?

Liam rocked back and forth on his gray TOMS. "Did you know that only one-third of the original Colosseum still remains? Which means the original was not enough on its own. In order to ensure longevity, the structure had to be restored by forces outside itself."

What exactly was he getting at? "That's common for buildings this old."

"I find it fascinating, the parallels between

architecture and our lives, don't you?" He looked up, almost into the sun.

Then his gaze moved back to her. He must have noticed the confusion on her face. "Forgive me. I'm a philosophy student, and sometimes I get carried away." He flashed her a goofy grin.

Crystal laughed. "That's okay. I'm just not sure I know what you mean."

"Well, you see strength when you look at this great structure." Liam's voice took on a gentler tone. "But I see a facade. Something not built to last but with the appearance that it will."

"So are you saying there's no such thing as strength?" At one time Crystal would have scoffed at that notion, looking at herself as an example. Not so much anymore.

"No. There *is* strength. It just comes from a different source."

His rambling caught her off guard. "You've totally lost me."

"Just like the Colosseum needed restoration to remain intact, our souls need help from an outside source."

Oh. "You mean like God?"

"Call it God, call it Mother Nature, the Force, whatever you like. The point is, we all have our limits and we can't go it alone."

"Yeah, well, I've seen what kind of 'help' God offers—if he's even real—and I want no part of it, thank you very much." Crystal snapped her mouth shut. How was it she could admit something like that to a complete stranger but couldn't even talk to her loved ones about things beyond the surface?

"What do you mean?" Liam leaned forward, seemingly eager for more detail.

Crystal sighed. "I asked him to heal my sister over and over again. He either ignored me or never heard me in the first place because he's not there. By the time she got a heart transplant nearly twenty years later, it was too late. Our lives will never be the same."

"I'm sorry." Liam looked like he wanted to pat her shoulder, but he stayed as he was. "But fixing the circumstances of your life and restoring your soul are two very different things, aren't they?"

How? It didn't make sense. If God did exist and was really all powerful, the supposed "Great Restorer" like Nana always said he was, then why was her life falling apart now?

Liam glanced at his watch again. "My next tour is beginning in a few moments. I wish I had more time to talk with you. I always enjoy a good philosophical discussion."

"Good luck with school and work and everything." She tried to smile but it came slowly. Why had this conversation flustered her so much?

"You as well. Cheers." Liam shot her two

thumbs-up and strode toward the designated spot where tours began.

Crystal stopped staring after him and her eyes swept the lower walls of the Colosseum.

Upon further inspection, it was easier and easier to see the cracks in its foundation—cracks she hadn't seen before.

Chapter 19

July 7
Blog Post Title: Another Death-Defying
  Day: Running with the Bulls in
  Pamplona
Post Content:
  As two-ton beasts breathed down my
neck today, I finally found my heart . . .

Today she was totally, one hundred percent, going to die.

Megan sipped the coffee Crystal had snagged for her at a corner shop while she saved their place along Santo Domingo Street in Pamplona, Spain. It was only six thirty in the morning, but she'd been awake for hours—first lying in bed, thinking about what she had to do today, then heading outside at dawn to ensure they got a spot near the street. All around them, the crowd grew larger with each passing moment, pulsing with anticipation. A double fence constructed of wooden planks, posts, and boards lined the street, separating the crowd from the brick part of the road where bulls would chase thousands of runners in a mere hour and a half.

And sometime between now and then, Megan had to work up the courage to tell Crystal she was going to be one of them—and to actually do it.

Her sister thought they were here merely to observe the San Fermín festival, which lasted from July sixth through the fourteenth, though they only planned to stay a few days. Since Crystal had never actually seen Amanda's list, she didn't know that the girl had dreamed of running with the bulls. And apparently Mom hadn't mentioned it during one of her calls to "check in" along the way—aka, nose around to see how the girls were getting along.

"These people are nuts." Crystal took a swig of her coffee and stared at the runners gathering inside the barriers. Most of them wore white outfits with red bandanas, something Megan had noted when doing her research. She had a red bandana of her own stuffed into her back pocket.

"I know." And maybe she *was* nuts. Even though her doctor had cleared her to run a marathon if she wanted, he hadn't been thrilled when she'd mentioned this race—which actually only lasted something like two to six minutes from start to finish, and would only require her to run until either the bulls passed her or she made it to the Plaza de Toros where the bulls would be gathered and penned after the run.

She'd been exercising regularly for the last few years, but had never combined exertion with the pure adrenaline that would come from the fear of a bull breathing down her neck. What would that combination do to her heart?

Only one way to find out.

"I can see why Amanda wanted to come watch this." Crystal peered up at the old Spanish buildings surrounding them. People gathered in balconies along the corridor. The smell of chorizo emanated from the street cart behind them, making Megan's stomach growl. "It's exciting, even if I think these people are complete lunatics."

"It was always on my must-see list." Megan drained the rest of her coffee and tapped the cardboard cover with her thumbnail. "I remember Caleb telling me he was going to run it someday." Her eyes had bugged out at the thought, and he'd laughed at her reaction. It was probably the way her sister would react when she told her why they were really here.

Megan checked her watch. Almost seven, the time they'd close the gate for the runners. It was now or never. "I have something to tell you. And you're not going to like it."

Crystal swung her gaze toward Megan and her grip tightened on her own cup. "What?"

Megan shuffled her feet and rose up on her tiptoes. The gate was close. She could just make a break for it and Crystal wouldn't be able to stop her. But that would hardly be mature. "I'm running today."

"Running where? You mean, *there?*" Several people in the vicinity turned at Crystal's shriek and stared at them. Two younger girls whispered to each other and giggled.

"Yes."

"Ain't happening."

She'd known this was coming. "Amanda wanted to run with the bulls, not just watch. So . . ."

"So you amend the list."

"I can't." She'd already cheated at Machu Picchu. She couldn't do it again. "Please understand. I have to complete the list. If I don't run, I can't complete it."

With a shake of her head, Crystal gripped Megan's wrist with her free hand. "Meg, no. Your heart."

Those words would have struck fear in the old Megan. But the new Megan longed to be strong, someone who couldn't be held back by her health—or her own faults. Someone who could prove that more than a new physical heart had brought her here. "I'll be okay."

She started to move toward the gate. If she didn't hurry, she'd miss her chance. "Excuse me." She maneuvered around people and pulled the red bandana from her pocket.

"Megan!" Crystal followed her. "Out of my way!" Megan could hear people protesting and could imagine her twin pushing people aside.

Finally she felt a tug on her shoulder. "Stop. Wait."

Megan twirled. "You're not changing my mind, Crystal. I have to do this."

"You'll kill yourself! If a bull doesn't trample you, your heart just might stop working." Now her sister was visibly shaking, and her face contorted into a mask Megan didn't recognize. "Mom will never forgive me if I let you go out there."

Megan's hands flew in the air. "I'm not your responsibility!" Oh, why couldn't she keep the anger out of her voice? Her sister was just worried.

"Please, Meg." Crystal's nails dug into Megan's arm, desperate. "This . . . this is crazy."

Megan blew out a breath. She couldn't stand the sight of her sister suffering, but she couldn't let Crystal hold her back. Not this time. "I'm sorry." With a firm but gentle yank, she pried Crystal's fingers from her arm, turned, and raced through the crowd.

In front of her, a man began to close the gate. "Wait!"

He motioned her forward and she darted through. The gate clanged behind her, and her breath caught. The street was just as crowded on this side as the other. How in the world was she supposed to move out of the way of the bulls as they passed?

But she wouldn't think about that now. Instead,

Megan fastened the red bandana around her forehead.

She was officially a *mozo*. Megan tried to recall every moment of footage and piece of information she'd watched and gathered while preparing for this adventure. Six bulls would be released and run the length of four streets. Runners would either run faster than the bulls or dodge out of their way as they came barreling past. Six steers would also be released in an attempt to keep the bulls calmer than normal and running with the herd. Of course, she could be trampled by a steer just as easily as a bull, but at least the steer couldn't gore her like the bulls could.

She shuddered at the thought.

A man next to her with slicked-back brown hair stretched his legs, leaning into a lunge. He looked her up and down. "First time?" His accent sounded Eastern European. How had he known she spoke English? Maybe her American-ness was just that pronounced.

She laughed, a nervous trill floating on the air. "That obvious?"

He stopped stretching and came closer to her. "This is my seventh time. Don't worry. Everything will be A-OK."

Despite the anxiety fluttering in her stomach, Megan flashed him a thumbs-up. "Awesome."

"If you fall, tuck into a ball and stay down." She could smell onion on the man's breath. Sweat glistened off his brow. "Better to be trampled than gored. It's safer, though it won't mean no injury." The man flashed a thumbs-up back to her and stepped aside to continue his stretches.

She gulped. List or no list, she was certifiably insane to be here right now.

The huge clock overhead moved closer to 8:00 a.m., when the day's festivities would officially commence. Megan hopped on the balls of her feet. The anticipation that came with waiting was pure torture.

Would Crystal ever forgive her? Megan scanned the crowd for her sister's golden hair, but it was impossible to make out any faces. Everything was a blur of colors and smells mingling together.

Megan's phone buzzed in her back pocket. She pulled it out, and a shiver of excitement raced up her spine, one that had nothing to do with the pandemonium around her. A text from Caleb:

Today's your B-Day, isn't it?

She scrunched her nose. It wasn't her birthday. He knew that.

What are you talking about?

You know, Bull Day. Ha-ha, bad joke. Didn't you tell me that you'd be running with the bulls?

Yes! ☺   The run is about to start and I'm standing here wondering if I've made the biggest mistake of my life. LOL.

Nah, you got this. Wish I was there with you.

Because he'd always wanted to run it . . . or because he wanted to run it with her? A smile inched over her lips.

Guess I'll run it for you then!

No, Meg. Run it for you.

Crystal's words echoed back to her: *"This isn't just Amanda's journey. It's yours too."*
Megan's fingers hesitated, then flew over the face of her phone.

I will. Thanks, Caleb.

She locked her phone and stuck it back in her pocket. And then, just like that, it was thirty seconds till eight and someone in the crowd started counting down in Spanish. She joined in, her Rosetta Stone lessons from high school clicking in her memory. *"Diez, nueve, ocho . . ."*
Somewhere behind her, a rocket *whoosh*ed into the air and shouts rang up from the crowd.

The throng of runners pushed against her, and they became a collective muscle, leaning, leaning, getting ready to pounce. Should she look backward or stay focused on what was in front of her? How could she move out of the way if she didn't know what was coming?

Blood pumped through her veins, and instead of circulating the fear she expected, another feeling made the rounds inside of her. Amanda's heart in Megan's chest sang with the pounding of her blood, beating out a new rhythm Megan wasn't familiar with. The song invigorated her limbs, and as she readied her body to leap into action, a fuzzy calm tingled in her fingertips and toes.

So as she heard the scrambling of tennis shoes, the screams of pleasure and excitement from behind her, the pounding of hooves—and actually felt the vibrations beneath her feet—Megan let out a whoop herself. When she caught a glimpse of horns, she turned and let herself fly. Arms, legs, mind, body, soul, they all tangled together as she ran, her breath coming in hot bursts from within. The bulls were close on her heels, but in that moment, she wasn't worried about them.

And her heart, instead of giving out like she'd feared, wasn't just Amanda's anymore. Megan was laying claim to its strength, to everything it had been for Amanda, to everything it had the potential to be in herself.

A bull flashed by on her right—and then, like that, it was in the distance. Others raced past her and she kicked up her feet, letting her daily exercise speak for itself. The plaza loomed ahead, where thousands of screaming onlookers watched runners triumphantly race into the ring and then dash away from the loose bulls, who were immediately caught and penned.

And as Megan burst through the gate into the plaza, she couldn't help but raise her arms in the air. Because this victory didn't just belong to Amanda.

Like her heart, Megan had embraced it as her own.

Chapter 20

Guilt, despair, disappointment—all emotions Crystal had finally allowed herself to experience in the last few weeks.

But flat-out anger with Megan? That was a new one. And she had no idea what to do with it.

She pulled her carry-on suitcase from the conveyor belt, then slipped her flats back on her feet. Behind her, Megan walked through the security checkpoint, thanking the guard who let her pass. Her sister tugged on the edge of her bandana, which was wrapped around her head, her hair pulled into low pigtails. She smiled and laughed, and a new confidence brimmed in her eyes. How could she be in such a good mood when Crystal . . .

No. Crystal was fine. She wouldn't let Megan's stunt yesterday bother her. Who cared if it reminded her of all those times—

Not going there. "This way." With a turn on her heel, Crystal flounced past the checkpoint in the Spanish airport and into the adjacent hallway, not waiting to see if Megan followed. Every step she took made her feet feel brittle. Or maybe it was the ground that might break, like a fine layer of ice on top of a not-quite-frozen lake. She yanked her suitcase along behind her, searching for the gate where a plane would take them to Dublin.

"Hold up." Megan caught up beside her, her breath coming in puffs. "What's the rush?"

"Nothing." But still Crystal continued moving. She couldn't stop or the memory of the absolute terror she'd felt yesterday would overtake her and flood her veins with the red-hot emotion she was barely keeping at bay.

After the run, she'd been so relieved to see her sister whole. She'd even been kind of proud, because Megan had done something brave even when it was hard. Crystal let herself be swept up in the festivities, and together they'd joined a random celebration at a pub, where she'd had one too many *cervezas* and learned every lyric to the *Marcha Real*.

But today she'd awoken with a slight hangover, and she couldn't stop reliving that moment when Megan had told her she was not planning to watch but was going to run among rampaging beasts who'd love nothing more than to take a horn to her flesh. Seeing her sister with that stupid red bandana on her head this morning was a reminder of how close Crystal had come to losing her—not just yesterday but three and a half years ago.

What else was Megan going to do on this trip? What if her confidence turned into stupidity and she risked her health in a way that she couldn't come back from?

Crystal understood Mom's coddling a lot better now.

Not for the first time, Crystal considered calling their mother and getting her involved. But that might alienate Megan more and they could lose what little ground they'd actually made toward repairing their relationship.

So instead, she trudged onward inside this foreign airport, mulling how to move forward without losing her cool.

Next to her, Megan grew quiet. Together they walked past other tourists, some clearly on their way to enjoy the rest of the festival. One crowd of college-aged guys—American too, by the looks of them—whistled at Crystal and Megan as they went by. Crystal ignored them and hopped onto a moving sidewalk. For a moment she leaned against the railing as they traversed without any effort across the airport floor. High glass ceilings towered over them, revealing a cloudless, crystal-blue sky.

"Are you going to be mad at me forever?" Megan chewed her bottom lip.

Crystal had tried disguising her feelings, but apparently she wasn't as great at it as she once was. She placed her hand on her suitcase handle and started walking again, going twice as fast now. "I'll get over it."

They stepped off the moving sidewalk, and it took a moment to readjust to normal movement.

They'd landed across from a food court, complete with a café, a bistro, and—hallelujah!—a Starbucks. Crystal eyed the menu. "I'm getting coffee. Do you want something?"

"No, thanks. But I'll snag a seat at one of the tables."

"Sounds good." Crystal tugged her gaze away and led them toward the smell of wonderful bliss. She got into line and breathed in the scent of roasted coffee, letting it wash over her and cling to her pores and clothing. She ordered a mocha, waited for it to be made, and moved to the table Megan had chosen. They still had at least an hour before boarding, so she pulled out a chair and sat down across from her sister.

Megan fiddled with the napkin container. "Can we talk about it?"

Crystal took a sip of her coffee. It burned her tongue. "About what, exactly?"

"I just feel like there's a barrier between us. One that wasn't there before."

Was she joking? A tiny sliver of Crystal's control slipped away. "Come on, Megan. There's been a barrier between us for a long time."

"But we've been getting along on this trip so far." Megan frowned. It was such an unnatural expression on her face. "I just don't want to ruin that."

"I'll try to be less like Mom in the future. No worrying about you from here on out."

"That's not what I'm saying. You are obviously upset. For once, Crystal, will you just tell me how you feel?"

Conversations buzzed all around them, but Megan's words had no trouble smacking Crystal's ears. "You don't really want to know how I'm feeling."

"Yes. I do." Megan grit her teeth.

Crystal had been so afraid of upsetting the delicate balance she and Megan had been keeping. But Brian's words rushed back to her: *"You know, it's okay to have a knock-down drag-out. Sometimes that's what's needed to clear the air."* She didn't want to have this conversation, but they needed to.

It was time.

"Okay, I was furious with you yesterday."

"Why?"

"What do you mean, why? I told you. You could've had a heart attack. Or been gored. Or . . . died." The last word shuddered from Crystal's lips.

Megan's eyes filled with compassion. "But I didn't. I didn't die. I'm here. I'm whole. I'm fine."

"But you weren't." Crystal's heart stampeded her chest. "I still remember what it was like, you know. Always expecting a phone call telling me it was over. Thinking I'd come home from school to a tragedy. Wondering if I could have done

218

something different . . ." She trailed off when her voice turned raspy.

Her sister stayed silent for a moment. "I know I brought a lot of pain to the family—"

"It's not your fault you were sick all those years. You didn't choose that. But yesterday you did choose to run. This time you chose to put yourself in danger. It's like . . ." No, she couldn't say that. Could she?

"It's like what? Tell me."

"It's like you're purposefully being reckless because you have your life back, because you never got to be reckless before. But your decisions don't just impact you. Don't you ever think about how it affects the people who love you?"

Megan's lips flattened, and a spark of something lit in her eyes. Oh man. She hadn't meant for the words to come out so sharp, had only wanted to make Megan think. In reviewing them, she'd probably been too harsh. "I know this trip means a lot to you. But it was hard. Watching you run off. Having no control over whether . . ." Her voice trailed off.

Megan studied Crystal. "I'm glad you told me." She inhaled. "But now I have something to tell you."

"Meg—"

"Crystal, I need to say this." Megan's words were soft but decided.

Crystal's fingers tightened around her coffee cup. She nodded.

"You knew this trip was going to be outside of my comfort zone. You knew it would involve many things I've never done before. Maybe even a little bit of adventure and danger. If you knew that, and now you're balking at it, why are you here? Why did you come in the first place?"

Crystal wet her lips. "I wanted to help you."

"Are you sure about that?"

No, that wasn't the whole story. Of course Megan would realize that. "Fine, I wanted to fix what's broken between us. What . . . what I broke."

Tears leaked from the corners of her sister's eyes and she was quiet for a few moments. "So you just want to assuage your guilt? If that's why you're here, it might be better if you left."

"No, that's not—"

"Because I have to tell you, I've forgiven you, but I still can't believe you did it. You left me. My own twin, my sister, my former best friend. I woke up after my surgery, and you know the first person I asked to see? You. And you weren't there." Megan's hands shook and her cheeks were streaked with red. "You'd gone back to your perfect life, away from me, the only thing in your life that wasn't perfect. Like I was an inconvenience to your schedule, your life, a blip that you were tired of dealing with." She almost looked surprised at the words coming out of her mouth.

Crystal stared wide-eyed at her sister. Did she really think that's why Crystal had left? "You couldn't be more wrong. My life was—is—far from perfect."

"Don't say it like I should feel sorry for you." Megan buried her face in her hands, and her elbows smacked the iron table, knocking Crystal's coffee onto its side. The lid flew off and brown liquid burst from the cup, seeping through the holes in the table and onto Crystal's white shoes.

"Oh." Megan's eyes widened. "Sorry."

"It's okay. I'll be right back." Crystal quietly stood and headed toward the nearest restroom, her head fuzzy, her heart zipping. Her footsteps echoed on the large tiles as she approached the sinks, grabbing a few paper towels, wetting them, and running them across the tops of her shoes. The coffee slid right off.

Too bad the past wasn't as easy to wipe clean.

For a split second, she considered going home, leaving Megan in peace. But she'd already left once, and look where that had gotten them.

Would it be easy? No.

Could she make up for the past? No.

But maybe she could change the future. The only question was—how?

• • •

Never had Megan needed a friend more, someone who would listen and give her sound advice as she spilled her thoughts and emotions.

Correction: not just someone.

Caleb.

Surrounded by sleeping passengers, Megan leaned her head back and tried to get comfortable on the overnight flight from Spain to Ireland. A few overhead lights served as beacons for those who wished to read a book or magazine. The flash of a tablet screen flickered across the aisle as an American woman watched episode after episode of *Once Upon a Time*. To Megan's left sat a tiny Greek woman with bushy eyebrows and a huge mole above her lip. The woman's soft snoring joined the hushed chatter of the plane. The engine rumbled beneath Megan's feet.

On her other side, Crystal slept with her head against the window. After their emotional talk in the airport, Crystal had come back from the bathroom, muttered sorry, and stuck in her headphones. Megan had replied with an apology. She hadn't even known she really felt the things she'd said until they were flying out of her mouth. The shocked look on Crystal's face had kept Megan from continuing the discussion.

She really needed some perspective, and she

wasn't going to get it simply by sitting here and replaying their conversation over and over again. Caleb was probably asleep right now, but maybe she could write him an e-mail.

A flight attendant walked up the aisle with a trash bag, collecting empty pop cans and bags of mini pretzels. Megan gathered her garbage from the protein pack she'd eaten and tossed it in as the woman passed. Then she leaned over and pulled her laptop from its case, powered it up, connected to the plane's Wi-Fi, and navigated to her e-mail inbox. She opened a new message. Fingers hovering over the keyboard, Megan's mind raced. Where in the world could she start? Her thoughts were so jumbled.

She sighed and closed the draft. This was something she needed to have a real conversation about.

It was a long shot, but maybe Caleb was awake. She headed to Facebook and clicked on Chat, scrolling till she saw his name.

Amen—a green dot.

She double clicked and a chat window opened. Biting her lip, she started typing.

> Megan: I see I'm not the only one burning the midnight oil.

She watched the blinking cursor for a few moments. Would he answer? Maybe she'd

223

interrupted something important. But then an ellipsis showed up. He was writing her back.

> Caleb: Yep, I'm editing photos. They're not due to *National Geographic* till Monday, but I'm heading out to Scotland tomorrow.

Scotland? They were visiting there next week. Maybe they'd be there at the same time. Crystal's words rang in Megan's ears: *"Why don't you see if he can meet up with us along the way?"* And then her own thought that had followed—did she have a crush on her friend?

And if that was the case, did she have the courage to do something about it? She swallowed hard.

> Megan: How fun!

> Caleb: So . . . how was the run? Guess you made it outta there in one piece. ☺

> Megan: I'll admit I was scared senseless. But the pure rush, the freedom, the adrenaline—I can't really describe it. Trust me, you'll just have to experience it for yourself.

> Caleb: I intend to. What's up next?

Megan: We're headed to Ireland. On the plane right now, in fact. Have to kiss the Blarney Stone, stay in some castle, and do a few other touristy things.

Caleb: Make sure you visit the Cliffs of Moher if you get a chance. They're breathtaking.

Megan: That's on the list!

Caleb: Sweet. How's it going, having Crystal along?

Megan: We've had some good moments. But some rough ones too. In fact, we had a pretty big "discussion" just a few hours ago.

Caleb: What happened?

Megan: I finally got tired of her hiding her emotions from me, so I asked her to be honest. And boy, was she. And then I was in return.

Caleb: Sounds cathartic.

Megan: I'm not so sure. Maybe.

Caleb: What caused the "discussion"?

Megan: She got upset that I ran with the bulls. And believe me, I get it. I just had a heart transplant three years ago. I didn't even think I could do this. But I'm surprising myself every day. Amanda's heart is a lot stronger than my old one.

Caleb: What do you mean? Your old heart, your new heart—that doesn't matter. You're still you, Meg.

Was that true? She'd always imagined getting a new heart would change her, make her braver, give her wings to fly. But even now, after facing down the bulls in Pamplona, she couldn't seem to get past the fear that she'd never be enough on her own.

Megan: I guess I'm figuring out who that is.

Caleb: I know who that is. And I think she's pretty awesome.

Megan: Thanks. ☺

Caleb: I still feel really bad I wasn't there for your heart transplant or right afterward. If I'd known about it . . .

226

Megan: I didn't want to bother you. You were finally living your dream.

Except she'd tried to contact him. His mother said he was unavailable in some jungle somewhere. But Caleb would feel worse if she told him that.

Caleb: Meg, you know I would have been there in a heartbeat. No pun intended. ☺

Megan: I know, Caleb.

Megan stared at the screen. They'd gotten way off topic. She'd meant to get his perspective on her talk with Crystal. Instead, they'd delved much deeper into the past than she'd let herself think about for a while.

But that's what they did—go deep. He was someone she could totally be herself with.

What would it be like to explore something more than friendship with him? The thought seared her. She didn't have to think about that now, or decide anything. Maybe she could start by continuing to renew their friendship.

And that started by keeping a promise she'd made a long time ago.

Megan: Let's not let it be another five years before we see each other. I know

227

it's short notice, but how about we make that London trip happen like we always planned? Crystal and I plan to be there July 14–17. Could you by chance meet up?

He didn't answer for a moment. Across the aisle, the American woman shut off her tablet, folded her arms, and closed her eyes. Megan stared at her screen, eyes burning with exhaustion. What was Caleb thinking? What was *she* thinking, inviting him to hang out in London next week so last minute? People didn't do that.

She started to type something new, to assure him he didn't have to, that it was just a whim. It wasn't like she'd been thinking about seeing him again for days on end. But that was a lie.

Her fingers stilled. Then his reply popped up on the screen and relief *whoosh*ed from her lungs.

> Caleb: Absolutely! I can move some stuff around in my schedule. I'd love to see you again.

Megan bit her lip, feeling brave here in the privacy of Facebook land amidst an airplane full of sleeping strangers.

> Megan: The feeling is very mutual.

She paused.

Megan: I'll e-mail you our itinerary and you can let me know where you'd like to meet us.

Caleb: I'll check it regularly till then. Listen, I've gotta run soon—have to catch a little sleep. Big day tomorrow. But one thing?

Megan: Yeah?

Caleb: Don't be too hard on Crystal.

Megan rubbed her neck and sighed. She glanced at her sister. Even in her sleep she seemed fitful. Megan could sense she was unhappy—but about being here with Megan or life in general? Work was frustrating, she knew, but what else was going on?

Megan didn't understand her one bit. But she wanted to. Oh, how she wanted to.

Megan: It's hard not to get frustrated with her. For years, she didn't seem to care. And now, when I'm finally on the edge of a huge emotional breakthrough, she gets really desperate to stop me.

Caleb: Try to see it from her point of view. She's lived almost her whole life with a sister who was sick.

Megan: I know that. But on the flip side, she doesn't know what it was like being stuck in that hospital bed while she got to do everything I always wanted.

Caleb: That's true. But—hear me out here—you don't know what it was like for her either.

That's what Crystal had said: *"Your decisions don't just impact you. Don't you ever think about how it affects the people who love you?"* Her sister carried wounds from Megan's sickness too, wounds that ran too deep for Megan to see. Or maybe simply wounds that Crystal refused to let anyone see.

Caleb: Put yourself in her shoes. If you had a sister who had been sick her whole life, wouldn't you steel yourself against the fear that you might lose her?

Megan: Yes, of course. I've just always seen Crystal as so strong. Nothing seems to scare her.

Caleb: Everyone's scared of something. Except me, of course. ☺

She couldn't not smile at that.

Megan: Right. The Invincible Caleb Watkins.

Caleb: Ha-ha, I wish. I actually am afraid of something. That we really will stop talking again. I need a little Megan in my life.

Her cheeks warmed.

Megan: And I need some Caleb in mine.

Caleb: ☺ I'd better go. Glad we got to catch up.

Megan: Same here. Bye.

Caleb: Bye, Meg. See you soon.

Megan stared at the blinking cursor, her heart in her throat. She and Caleb were meeting up. Would it be awkward? Chatting just now had been as easy as ever. But what would it be like to wrap her arms around him again, see him flash a smile her direction, catch the sites of London with him? Possibilities welled in her mind and a grin overtook her.

But just as soon, the grin disappeared. What he'd said about Crystal, could it be true? Could the sister she'd always thought of as stronger really be afraid?

Megan snuck another glimpse at Crystal. Her hands were wrapped around her arms, where goosebumps popped along her skin. Megan closed her laptop, put it away, and snatched her jacket from beneath the seat in front of her.

She gently settled it over her sister, and the tension in Crystal's body disappeared.

Chapter 21

If staying the night in a Celtic castle in the heart of Ireland couldn't help Crystal relax, maybe nothing would.

From her spot next to the window, a lake glistened with the last bit of sunlight and spread across the ground like butter. To the right of that, green gardens and trees dotted the immense landscape. Since they were staying at one far end of the castle, she could see the other end of the stone structure wrapping around the grounds and turrets puncturing the sky, which was beginning to dot with pinpricks of light.

Crystal pulled herself away from the latticed white windows framed by gold curtains, away from a view that should have filled her with awe.

Instead, she slumped into the old-fashioned seat situated in front of a vanity and took her brush in hand. With each stroke of her hair, she willed the pain in her stomach to subside. The bags under her eyes were more pronounced than ever.

She missed Brian. She missed her job. And she and her sister couldn't be real for two seconds without losing it on each other.

Maybe that's why the last two days spent exploring Dublin had been so utterly exhausting. After their fight, they'd both apologized in the airport, determined to move forward. But standing still wasn't the same thing as moving forward. And as much as Crystal tried to figure out how to fix things, she couldn't.

That's probably why she missed work so much. The bombed Hoffman project aside, she'd always been able to get things done, to go after her goals and nail them. But this person staring back at her in the mirror? She didn't recognize her.

Crystal sighed and set the brush down on the vanity. Chunks of her long blonde hair rested in the bristles of the brush. Yikes. That wasn't good. Could an ulcer cause that or was something more going on?

She heaved herself out of the chair, gasping at the sudden lurch in her belly and moving to her bed. The ruffled blue bedspread was smooth beneath her legs as she climbed up and pulled her computer onto her lap. Crystal leaned against the puffed gold-and-robin's-egg-blue headboard, which was framed by curtains held back by golden knobs. For a moment she just sat, studying the paper that covered the walls, a pale yellow decorated with pictures of daisies.

As she powered up her laptop, Crystal could still taste the frozen chocolate mousse she'd inhaled after dinner. Of course, Megan wouldn't touch it because it wasn't "healthy" enough. Crystal's e-mail popped up on the screen and she deleted all the junk. Her fingers froze when she saw Tony's name on a message. She clicked and scanned the contents. It was short and to the point:

Crystal,
    We are going to go with Meredith's proposal if you don't send me something soon. I was hoping this time away would be restful and good for your creative juices. Was I wrong?

Tony

The tiny black words on the screen mocked her. She needed to brainstorm again. Maybe this time her brain wouldn't freeze.

Just then, the large oak door to their bedroom creaked open and Megan walked in. "You're still up." Somehow she'd had the energy to stay up late in the pub downstairs and chat with other tourists.

"I have to brainstorm more for that work proposal."

"Sounds thrilling." Megan made a face. "I'm going to go explore the castle." Her sister started changing from her dress into yoga pants and a fitted T-shirt.

"Why?"

"Because when's the next time I'm going to be in an Irish castle overnight?"

"True." Crystal closed her laptop lid and pulled

her legs up to her chest. The position soothed her stomach for the time being.

Her sister sat on the edge of Crystal's bed. "Would you like to come with me?" She asked the question with a timid, tentative voice. "You've been working every spare minute. You should take some time to relax."

Funny. That's exactly what she'd been trying to do all night—and couldn't. Maybe a change of scenery would be good for her. "I can maybe take a short break. Fifteen minutes."

Megan jumped off the bed and threw a sweatshirt over her head. "Dress warm. It looks like it might rain."

Crystal slipped into a sweater and tennis shoes. Together they left the room and crept down the red-carpeted hallway where other guests were staying. When they reached a dark corridor, Megan flipped on the flashlight from her phone. Her face lit like a kid telling a campfire ghost story. "Ready?"

Crystal couldn't help but offer a laugh at how ridiculous her sister looked. She pushed Megan along. "Go."

They walked down the hallway, taking in the tapestries and grand artwork hanging on the walls. Peeking into an entryway to the left, they discovered a huge ballroom with a wooden dance floor and high-backed chairs hugging the edges of the room. Floor-to-ceiling windows lined the far wall. They made their way over and found that one led to an outdoor balcony. With a push, they opened the doorway and stepped out.

Here they were met with an even more expansive view of the grounds. For miles, lush greenery surrounded them. Several stories below, a few guests milled about, some sitting around fire pits. The crisp air kissed Crystal's skin and a light rain fell, dotting her forehead and cheeks.

Crystal turned her palms to the sky. "Didn't you say you had to kiss a handsome guy in the rain? You should find one now, mark that item off."

Megan frowned, then opened her arms, tilted her head up, and stuck out her tongue. "But fresh rain tastes so yummy, and I'd rather be here drinking it up."

"You're such a little kid." Crystal couldn't help teasing her sister, and it felt good. Maybe they could find a happy medium, now that some of the junk was out in the open. Not really resolved but exposed. "But seriously. What if it doesn't rain again during the trip?"

"I'm sure it will. We can think about that later. Right now, let's just have fun." Megan twirled, then stopped, studying Crystal. "Have you had any fun at all on this trip?"

"Sure." But had she?

"When?"

"I . . ." But Crystal couldn't name a single moment of fun so far. It had all been fraught with grief and fear and anxiety. She used to have fun. When had she become this person? "I suppose I *am* a little more serious than you."

"A little more serious? You're always waiting for something to go wrong. When's the last time you let your emotions fly free and truly enjoyed yourself?"

All this time Crystal had thought it was better to stuff her emotions away—because that meant she was in control of them, that she had one less factor in life to worry about. But though unleashing her emotions at the airport during her fight with Megan had been painful, it'd also been liberating in a way.

"Come on. Spin."

The rain dropped heavier and a wind started to blow, whistling through the crack in the doorway behind them, but still Megan circled.

It couldn't hurt to follow her sister's lead for once.

After a moment more of hesitation, Crystal flung back her arms—and groaned as dizziness shot through her. She slouched forward and fell to her knees.

"Crystal?" Megan rushed to her side. "Are you okay?"

"I . . . don't . . ." Crystal stood, shaky, and pitched forward till the balcony railing hit her side. Though she stood still, everything else spun.

And her stomach, it was on fire, like a ball

of heat had come to life inside of her. She slid to the ground and heaved her dinner onto the concrete next to her. Rain ran rivers down her cheeks—or were those tears? Her head exploded with a blinding pain. "Something's wrong." Why couldn't she pick herself up?

But Megan had already whipped her phone out and was dialing. "Hello? Hi. We're guests here, and my sister is dizzy and breathing funny. She's grabbing her stomach. I don't know what's wrong. But we need an ambulance." She glanced around. "We're on the balcony outside a ballroom on the second floor. Okay." She lowered the phone and put her hand on Crystal's shoulder. "Help is on the way."

Crystal nodded, but even that small movement wrecked her system. She should have seen a doctor sooner about her stomach, but she'd been trying to take care of her job, her marriage, her sister . . .

All of her thoughts faded away as she slumped against Megan and blacked out.

Monitors beeped in the low-lit hospital room where Crystal lay in bed asleep, finally resting after a flurry of medical tests. Her hair was tucked underneath her head like a pillow, and her face had started to regain some of its color. Megan sat in the seat next to the bed, stroking her sister's hand.

Such a strange feeling—being the healthy one for a change. The strong one.

She pushed the thought from her mind. She'd never be stronger than Crystal.

Megan's phone buzzed on the table and she glimpsed Brian's name on the caller ID. She snatched it up so the vibrations didn't wake Crystal and slipped into the hallway of the little Irish hospital. "Hello?"

"Megan, hey. What's going on? Is she okay?"

When they'd been on their way in the tiny ambulance to the hospital, she'd left Brian a quick voice mail. Her sister had thrown up and fainted several times, and whenever she was awake she complained of an aching stomach and a pounding head. The doctors had rushed her back immediately, leaving Megan to pace the waiting room while they figured out what was wrong with Crystal.

The waiting had been awful. She'd texted Caleb, and he'd said he would be praying for Crystal. Instead of instantly shrugging off the statement, Megan found herself actually hoping that his prayers would make a difference. If nothing else, knowing someone else was praying comforted her.

Now Megan had to pass along the comfort to Brian. "She's going to be all right." She said the words as quietly as she could, since Crystal's room was just around the corner from the nurse's station. She didn't want to disturb any of the sweet nurses on duty. "Crystal has an ulcer. A pretty bad one but nothing that requires surgery."

"Really?" Brian breathed heavily into the phone. "Did the doctor say how long she's had it?"

Megan paced, her tennis shoes squeaking on the waxed linoleum floor. "He said it was fairly advanced. She's probably been dealing with it for months." Hadn't Crystal told Brian about her symptoms?

"She works too hard and is stressed out all the time. I should have seen this coming."

"It's not your fault. If anything, it's mine. She told me she'd been feeling poorly when we were in China, and I didn't make her go to the doctor."

"I doubt she would have listened."

"True." And Megan hadn't wanted to push.

"How long does she have to stay?"

"She can check out of the hospital tomorrow if everything goes okay tonight. They're going to put her on some meds that should clear her ulcer right up." Megan stopped pacing and leaned against the stark white wall.

"I'm glad it wasn't anything more serious."

"Me too. After this incident, I'm going to insist that she take it easy. No work for a while."

"Good luck with that."

His tone revealed more than Brian probably

realized. Crystal didn't talk much about her and Brian's relationship. Her words at the Spanish airport echoed in Megan's mind: *My life was—is—far from perfect.* Could she have been referring to her marriage?

Brian cleared his throat. "Are you going to cancel or rearrange your plans this week?"

"I'm afraid if we stay put all week, Crystal will just try to work more and not relax. But I think tomorrow we'll skip Galway and stay an extra day at the castle. And then as long as she feels up to it, we can head to London as planned on Saturday."

"That sounds like a good plan."

After they said good-bye, Megan headed back to Crystal's room. Her sister was still lying there, but her eyes were open, almost worried. They filled with relief when Megan drew closer. "I thought maybe you'd left me. And I wouldn't have blamed you."

That day in the hospital before Megan's surgery came to mind, when Crystal had fled and Megan had wondered if she'd ever see her sister again. But holding on to grudges didn't do any good. She'd told Crystal how it had made her feel. They hadn't really finished the conversation, but maybe now they could move past it. "I was chatting with Brian."

A frown flitted across Crystal's mouth. "What did he say?"

"He was worried about you. I told him you'd be your old cantankerous self in no time."

"Gee, thanks." Crystal stuck her tongue out at Megan. They both laughed, but then Crystal grabbed her side, grimacing at the movement.

Megan sat on the edge of Crystal's bed. A thread had come unraveled from the blanket. She picked at it. "You really scared me."

"I scared myself." Crystal stared at the blanket too. Above, a fan kicked on, blowing air through a vent where the wall met the ceiling.

Megan pinched the thread with her nail. "You need to take better care of yourself." She tried to keep the scolding tone out of her voice, but a tiny bit crept in.

Of course, maybe this was how Crystal felt about Megan and her health. And the fear Megan felt was probably only a fraction of what Crystal must have experienced over the years—and during the bull run. The thought sobered her.

"I'll try."

With a tug, Megan pulled the thread free of the blanket. She tucked it into her palm. "So what's stressing you out so bad you got an ulcer?"

Crystal bit her lip and her forehead scrunched, as if thinking deeply about how to respond. "My job can be stressful. Among other things."

It wasn't the revealing answer Megan had hoped for, but it was something. As long as Crystal didn't turn over and claim tiredness. As long as she kept talking. "Then I'm implementing a no-work rule for the next week."

Crystal flashed her a look of disbelief. "Nice try, Megan."

"I'm serious."

"So am I. I can't stop working for a week. I have too much to do." Her sister rubbed the bridge of her nose, sighed. "Tonight I got an e-mail from Tony. He's going to go with another architect's proposal if I don't send him mine soon. I'll lose my shot at senior architect and my dream project."

"Doesn't seem worth it if it's costing you your health." Megan's gaze roamed the tiny room. Hospital rooms everywhere had a different layout but the same basic feel to them: sterile, dead, often hopeless. "I've experienced what it's like not to have my health. Why would you risk it?"

Her sister stared at Megan, her mouth falling open. She closed it quickly. "I guess I never thought of it like that." Her hand rubbed her stomach, counterclockwise, then clockwise, like Mom used to rub their tummies as children when they'd eaten too much candy. "But I don't know how to not be an architect, you know? I love it. Being an architect lets me have a visible, tangible impact on the world. The things I design come to life. And sometimes they change lives."

The passion in her voice stirred something in Megan. "I wish I had something like that."

"Well, you're a writer. And writing also has the power to move people."

"All I've got right now is this measly little blog and one published article. It's not much."

"But it'll grow, and you'll have more opportunities come along."

"I hope you're right." Rain plinked against the window. "But back to you. I understand now a little more why you're passionate about your work. But why does being senior architect mean so much? You've talked a lot about that and achieving partner by forty."

Crystal's eyebrows knit together. "I suppose it's a sign, something that proves I've got what it takes to succeed."

"You've always been so good at everything. Weren't you offered a big scholarship after high school? Clearly you're extremely capable and intelligent. What further proof do you need?"

"Funny you should mention that." Her sister tugged the blanket closer. "Yes, senior year of high school I was awarded a scholarship that would have paid for most of college. I turned it down."

"What? Why?"

"Because when the board offered it to me, they said they knew all about your 'situation' and were awarding the scholarship to help our family any way they could. I wanted to get the scholarship for the 4.0 GPA I had, or the laundry list of extracurriculars I'd participated in, or because I'd written a killer essay—not because my sister was sick."

"Ugh." Megan's chest squeezed and her fingers rose to her neck, settling into the groove where she always checked her pulse. Habit. She stuck her hands back in her lap. "I'm sorry, Crystal."

"It's not your fault."

"It's not yours either." And Megan meant it. No one would choose to be sick. God was in control of that.

Maybe someday she'd understand his decision to make her well—or to allow her to be sick in the first place, only to heal her after losing twenty-plus years of her life to illness.

Not for the first time, she was tempted to ask him.

Would he say anything back to her?

Crystal's gaze met hers and her bottom lip quivered. But she broke their connection and lowered her bed with the remote that was resting on her lap. "I'm tired. Would you mind if I got some sleep?"

Megan rose and fluffed the pillow that lay under Crystal's head. "Not at all. But, Crystal?"

"Hmm?" Her sister's eyes were already closed.

Megan leaned forward and grabbed Crystal's free hand. "Repeat after me: I will not work for several days."

Crystal's eyes flew open. "Megan."

"I can't hear you." Megan squeezed Crystal's hand. "Come on. You've tried it your way. It landed you here. Why not try it my way?"

Crystal turned her gaze to the window, where her eyes seemed to follow the rain as it fell in drizzles down the pane. "I will not work for several days."

Now they were finally getting somewhere.

Chapter 22

It was too bad Crystal was missing this, because Galway was quite the treasure trove of awesomeness.

Megan crossed her legs as she sat in the grass at an overlook surrounded by a short stone wall, taking in the Corrib River below. To the left, rows of blue, yellow, and gray buildings stretched out toward the place where the river emptied into the Atlantic. A breeze worked its way through her hair, brushing strands across her cheeks. She let the smell of the sea roll over her as she jotted a few details from the day in her journal.

She hadn't wanted to leave Crystal behind today, but once they'd arrived back at the hotel in the wee hours of the morning and slept some, her sister had insisted on Megan taking the walking tour of the northern Irish city they'd already arranged.

So she'd spent the day with fifteen strangers and a tour guide named Bridget exploring sites like the Spanish Arch and sacred landmarks like the Collegiate Church of St. Nicholas. They'd promenaded down the gray-brick streets filled with colorful storefronts, watched artists paint masterpieces along the walkway, and listened to traditional Irish folk music in a centuries-old pub filled with open fireplaces and stone hearths.

It had been a delicious sort of day so far—and the fact she'd experienced it more or less by herself was all the more amazing. How far she'd come already from the girl who could barely handle an international flight alone.

Still, she should get back to Crystal soon.

Megan's phone interrupted the distant *ha-ha-ha* of seagulls. She dug in her backpack until she found the offending device. Kara. Why was her boss at the library calling? "Hello?"

"Megan! How are you?"

"Considering the fact I'm sitting by a river in Ireland journaling, I'd say pretty good. How are things there?"

"I'm barely surviving the summer rush. We've had a lot more patrons visiting lately, and the summer kids program is going full force. I really miss you."

She didn't exactly relish the idea of returning to work after this adventure, but it was nice to be missed. "Lucky for you I'll be back in less than three weeks." In the distance, a smallish white cruise boat with a red base approached from upriver.

"About that. I simply had to hire an aide to replace you for the summer, and she is doing a great job. I'm not sure I can justify offering you your position back. Maybe if Debra decides to quit once school starts, but I can't be sure she will."

Megan had known this was a possibility when she left. Still, she needed a job when she got home. Freelance writing wasn't going to pay the bills for quite some time, if ever.

"But I have something even better in mind."

That caught her attention. "I don't follow."

"Since Little Lakes is growing so rapidly and has started pulling in more patrons from surrounding cities, I just got approval from the city to add a new position—assistant librarian. And I can't think of anyone more qualified than you."

"But I don't have a degree in library science." And it was quite the step up from library aide.

The cruise ship got closer. Passengers topped the decks, some dancing, some lounging, almost all with drinks in their hands. Lively music lilted across the expanse of water.

"That doesn't matter. Your English degree is more than enough. The job is full-time and comes with a substantial raise over your current salary, plus better benefits, like a 401(k), paid time off, even some tuition reimbursement opportunities if you're ever interested in getting a master's in library science."

Before leaving on the trip, Megan had only worked part-time, about twenty-five hours a week. She'd kind of been counting on the other hours in the week to continue building her portfolio, even querying other online publications and magazines for freelance opportunities. But she could still do that with a full-time job, couldn't she?

Plus, a full-time job with more benefits would help her finish paying her medical bills more quickly, move out on her own, save for the future. Even if it wasn't her dream job, it'd be silly not to consider the possibility. "What would I be doing?"

"More administrative stuff than you currently do. I can send you the job description." A phone rang in the background. "So what do you think?"

"I'll have to think about it."

"Yes, of course. But the city wants me to hire someone quickly to get more help around here for the rest of the summer. So if you don't want the job, I need to post it and start taking applications."

"Okay. When do you need to know?"

"Next week, if possible."

The cruise ship glided out of sight, and the carefree vibe of the day tagged along.

If Megan wanted to land a writing-related job, Crystal was going to do all she could to help.

She tapped the arm of her Adirondack chair and soaked in the beautiful Irish sun, her computer resting on her lap. The castle loomed to the west, and its acres of greenery sprawled as far as her eyes could see. A large stone fountain bubbled, a group of businesswomen played croquet, and golf carts occasionally drove past, coming from or going toward the hotel's nine-hole course.

After an early discharge from the hospital, Crystal had parked herself in this chair all day. She'd convinced her sister to continue with their planned sightseeing of nearby Galway so she could build Megan a real website. It wasn't perfect, but it was definitely a step above the "measly little blog" she'd had before. Now, editors looking for potential writers wouldn't be distracted by the design and could focus on the content instead—which, frankly, was amazing. How had she never known how talented Megan was before this?

The website redesign plus the phone call Crystal had made earlier would surely give her sister an infusion of confidence, just what she needed to keep fighting for her dreams.

She added one final detail and saved the draft. Her fingers itched to check her e-mail, but she closed her laptop. She'd promised no work for several days. Once she'd informed Tony about her hospital visit, he'd said he could be patient for a while given her physical condition, though he'd clearly been unhappy.

Maybe she should head to the spa and really

take advantage of this chance to relax. Megan wouldn't be back until late tonight.

Crystal gathered her things and headed back to their room. She changed into her bathing suit and robe—the super-soft cotton wrapping around her body—and swung the door open. Megan stood in the hallway, her key card extended as if she was about to come inside.

"Shouldn't you still be out touring Galway?" Crystal opened the door wider, and her sister entered. Then she closed the door behind them and sat on the edge of her bed.

"I felt guilty leaving you alone all day."

"I'm good. Really." After eighteen hours on antibiotics, she was feeling so much better already. "Since you're done for the day, want to join me at the spa?"

"Sure." Megan slipped off her jacket and rummaged in her suitcase. "What did you do today?" She shimmied into her blue tankini.

Crystal snatched her laptop from the side table and opened the website design. "I mocked up a new website."

Megan's nose wrinkled. "For what?" She grabbed the second white robe from behind the bathroom door and began to swing her arms through it.

"For you. For your blog."

Her sister stilled. "What? Why?"

"Because yesterday you implied that you

weren't happy with it. I thought this might help." Crystal brought the laptop to Megan and handed it over.

Megan used her index finger to scroll through the mockup. She bit her lip and remained quiet for a moment longer than normal. Did she not like it?

"Of course, I can change anything you don't like. I was going for a travel motif, but—"

"It's perfect." Her sister closed the laptop and set it on the bed. "You didn't have to do that."

Megan's words said one thing, but her tone of voice said another. "I wanted to. Oh, and I totally forgot until today, but I have a friend from college who works at the *Minnesota Republic* in Minneapolis. She said she'd pass your résumé along to her editor. They don't have any job openings right now, but it doesn't hurt to have your résumé on file for future openings, right?"

"Wow. That's . . . great." Her sister smiled, but it seemed forced. She finished pulling on her robe and tied the sash tight across her body. "Are you ready to go?"

Hmm. "Sure."

They headed out the door and took the elevator to the ground level, walking to the spa. They entered a foyer that smelled of eucalyptus. Light jazz music swayed across the airwaves. A beaming redhead with porcelain skin greeted them and took their information. They deliberated over a handful of services and the receptionist scheduled them for facials, assuring them that they were lucky to have received last-minute appointments.

"Your treatment specialists will be ready in fifteen minutes. If you'd like to wait beside the relaxation pool, it's just down the hall."

They thanked the receptionist and made their way toward the relaxation pool. When they opened the door, Crystal could understand how the pool received its name. First, they were alone. Second, the pool itself was tranquil, as smooth as the satin sheets on the beds in their room. On the ceiling hung three seashell chandeliers. A tree of life mural stretched across the wall behind the pool. Six padded lounge chairs rested along the opposite wall.

Megan headed toward one and stretched out. She was much quieter than usual.

"What's wrong?" Crystal poured two glasses of cucumber-infused water from a large glass pitcher.

Megan played with the belt of her robe, flopping it back and forth on her lap. "Nothing."

"Now you sound like me." With a few quick steps, Crystal joined Megan and handed her one of the cups. "Spill it. And I don't mean the water."

Megan didn't even chuckle at Crystal's poor pun. "I really appreciate all the effort you put into designing the website and contacting your friend."

Crystal raised the glass to her lips and sipped. The faint taste of cucumber danced on her tongue. "I can tell."

"No, really." Megan's brow furrowed. "But the truth is, today I talked with my boss at the library. She said they can't offer me my old job back till fall, and maybe not even then. But she did offer me a new position." Megan explained what the job entailed.

"Are you going to take it?"

"Maybe." With the pad of her thumb, Megan traced a figure eight in the condensation on her cup. "I mean, I need a job. I can't just go home and loaf around."

"Why not take the job but continue to work on your writing and apply for other jobs on the side?"

"I could definitely keep trying to write on the side, but I'd feel bad agreeing to a job and then not staying on if something else came along that interested me more."

"I get that, though people do it all the time."

"True, but Kara has been so good to me over the years, even when I was such an unreliable worker during the height of my illness."

"But that means she cares about you and wants you to be happy. And it doesn't really sound like this is the job you ultimately want."

"It's not." Her sister stared at the mural on the wall. "But maybe I'm hoping for too much, trying to pluck too many stars out of the sky at once. I'm going to complete Amanda's list. And I started a travel blog. Those things are huge in and of themselves. If that's all I get to do, I'll be content."

"Content, sure. But happy?" Crystal raised an eyebrow at Megan. "You reach for those stars. You don't have to settle for just one, because you're strong enough to hold them all."

Megan's chin trembled. "I'm not strong, Crystal. Not like you."

Strong? Crystal couldn't keep it together at her job, had made a mess of her marriage, and had run the other way when emotions got too deep and the hurt too hard. "You're the one who lived with an illness for two decades. You're a survivor, Megan. There's nothing stronger than that."

Megan stared at her, eyes wide with something like wonder. "Then why am I so afraid?"

She chose her words with care. "I think maybe being strong doesn't necessarily mean you aren't ever afraid. It means you face your fears anyway."

But as Crystal said the words, she wondered who really needed to hear them more—Megan . . . or her.

Chapter 23

12. Try to make a guard at Buckingham Palace laugh.

My parents say I was such a happy kid . . . before. The goofy kind, who'd put underwear on top of my head and dance around when my favorite song came on the radio. Who'd make up bad jokes with terrible puns and laugh myself silly.

Uncle Joe stole that laughter.

After him, I think I went a whole year without laughing.

I don't remember it happening, not consciously. But I remember the darkness of life, how nothing felt good, how it all felt cold and confusing and scary.

And I remember my mom looking at me one day and saying, "I so miss your sweet laugh." I'll never forget her face, how it was sad and nostalgic and full of guilt.

So I started laughing again, for her. But I'm not sure it was ever real.

I want to laugh again. After all, they say laughter is the best medicine. There's something healing in laughing—and especially in laughing with someone else, together. Laughter breaks down walls, and maybe that's what we all need.

Maybe it's time to take the focus off myself.

Because when you try to make someone else laugh, you usually end up laughing too.

Chapter 24

July 16
Blog Post Title: Laughing in London:
Antics Across the Pond
Post Content:
London is everything I dreamed it would be and more. Today we discovered just how difficult it is to get a Buckingham guard to smile . . .

12. Try to make a guard at Buckingham Palace laugh.

Thank goodness the word *try* was part of this bucket list item, because members of the Queen's Guard were notorious for their poker faces.

Megan put Amanda's journal back into her pack. From where they stood in the crowd, she could see the wrought-iron gates and Buckingham Palace rising from behind. The gates were about to open for the day's tours, and they had to be inside to get close enough to talk to a guard.

The sun kissed her skin, and the few clouds in the sky were mere wisps. Everything she'd read said it often rained in London, but they'd experienced nothing of the sort since they'd arrived. She'd been hoping for—and dreading—the chance to mark *19. Kiss a handsome stranger in the rain* off her list. Crystal had suggested she could merely kiss a guy on the cheek, but that wouldn't really comply with the spirit of Amanda's list.

She was running out of time, but she couldn't deny the apprehension that overtook her every time she thought about kissing someone she didn't know.

Kissing anyone, for that matter.

Her thoughts sped rebelliously toward Caleb. Oh, for goodness' sake. He probably didn't think of her in that way. Maybe she'd know more once they finally met up again. But that wasn't till tomorrow. For now, she'd put aside her jitters and focus on the task at hand.

Today she was going to complete number twelve on the list, not number nineteen. And that would be that.

Beside her, Crystal studied a map of London they'd picked up from a visitor's center. "After this, let's be sure to head straight to St. James's Park."

"Sure, if you'd like." They had a busy day ahead of them, and the park seemed like the perfect place to catch a reprieve in the midst of it all.

Crystal peeked at her over the top of the map. "You sure are calm about all of this."

"I'll admit, comedy isn't my strong suit. I'm not really sure how we're going to get a guard to crack a smile, much less laugh."

"No, I mean about—"

"They're opening." A woman nearby shouted in excitement as the black-and-gold gates swung wide. The crowd behind them surged forward.

"Everyone just needs to take a chill pill." Crystal put her map away, and they let the crowd sweep them through the gates. Once inside, people dispersed toward the ticket counter, and finally they had some breathing room. "Over there."

Megan looked in the direction Crystal pointed and saw a pair of guards standing on either side of the doorway, each in front of a small house-like structure. They wore the regal red uniform, white leather buff belt, and dark-blue trousers with the iconic bearskin atop their heads. The one on the right had a baby face. "He looks like he just left high school."

"Let's talk to him then." Crystal grabbed Megan's jacket sleeve and started walking.

A few other tourists took pictures in front of the guards, so the sisters waited their turn. But now came the hard part. "How in the world are we going to make a guard laugh?"

"Don't look at me. I'm not funny."

"Understatement of the year." Megan winked at Crystal.

In response, Crystal's lips tipped into a smile. Before their time here, that smile had been a rarity. But over the last few days, Crystal's guard had slowly lowered. And it had all started because they'd finally let themselves get real about some things.

"I think maybe being strong doesn't necessarily mean you aren't ever afraid. It means you face your fears anyway." Her sister's words resonated in her head—and her heart. Megan still hadn't made a decision about the library job, but she'd need to soon.

"Didn't you come prepared with jokes?" Crystal brought Megan back to the present.

Megan shook her head. "I've been trying to come up with something, but . . ."

"I have an idea." Crystal strode toward the now unoccupied guard. He stood at attention, his gaze straight ahead. "I'm Crystal, and this is my sister, Megan. We're hoping you can help us with something."

That was her grandiose plan? To just ask the guy to laugh? The guard didn't even flinch. "Crystal, I don't think—"

"We're in a bit of a predicament." Crystal shook her head at Megan, as if to say "not now." "We have a task, and that's to get you to laugh. I know. I know. I'm sure many people have tried this. But we have a great reason." She proceeded to tell the guard about Megan's quest to fulfill Amanda's bucket list. And was it Megan's imagination, or were the guard's eyes softening? "Of course, we didn't want to be disrespectful of you, since you are a real soldier serving your country. We knew we couldn't pull any antics, or touch you, or whatever."

The guard's nose twitched. Maybe this was actually going to work . . .

Megan jumped in. "We'd be so grateful if you could give us a little chuckle. Or a small smile. We don't want to get you into trouble, though."

She and Crystal eyed each other and waited. The guard continued to stare straight ahead like a statue. They waited for five minutes. Finally, Megan sighed. "Come on, Crystal. The bucket list only said 'try.'"

Crystal frowned and nodded. She grasped the strap of her backpack and hoisted it higher on her back, then turned to the guard once more. "Thanks, anyway."

As Megan turned to head back through the gates, she heard it. A quick, low laugh. She and Crystal spun at the same time and looked at the guard, but his gaze remained on the horizon, his face a mask of stoicism. "Did I imagine that?"

"No. No, you did not." Crystal waved at the guard. "Thank you."

Megan and Crystal burst out giggling and made their way down the road from Buckingham Palace to St. James's Park.

Megan held a stitch in her side. "I can't believe we did it."

"I can. We're amazing." Crystal checked her

watch. "And we finished in plenty of time."

Why was her sister being such a stickler for the schedule? Megan couldn't even remember what they had planned for the day. She was just enjoying being together. "Let's take some time to relish the victory."

"I'm fine with that." As they reached the greenery of the park, Crystal ran her hand along the edge of a short wrought-iron fence with black loops at the top. A gray squirrel jumped onto the fence next to them, and as they continued down the path, a gorgeous pond came into view. People sat along the banks, feeding a variety of waterfowl.

Megan stopped and took off her shoes, tying the laces together and flinging them over her shoulder. Her toes stepped into the long grass, the blades tickling her feet as she continued walking. "I love that we're finally having fun together again. It's been so long. I've missed it."

"Me too." Crystal eyed Megan's bare feet, then took off her shoes as well. Her face displayed her pleasure at the change.

"How many nights did we spend giggling as kids and making mischief for Mom and Dad?" Even in the hospital—when she was able to be there—Crystal would try to entertain her with Mad Libs and all kinds of stories about the dumb guys she flirted with and silly mind games her friends would play. But eventually the laughter had been replaced with awkwardness and guilt, on both their ends.

"I remember having sleepovers in your room. I'd sneak over and we'd talk until midnight, or until Dad came in and gave us that look." Crystal watched two children flying an orange kite and an older woman giving instruction from behind. The kite's tail fluttered high above their heads, trailing green-and-purple swirls across the bright sky.

The memory was sweet—but tinged with grief too. "But then one day you just stopped coming. Why?" Megan asked.

Her sister's gaze moved back to her. Crystal chewed her lip. "Mom caught me coming to your room late one night. She was very gentle but told me you needed your rest."

Tears threatened to push their way through her tear ducts. "Oh." In an attempt to cater to her health, what other damage had been done unintentionally?

No more.

Megan looped her arm through Crystal's. "Let's not focus on all that. This day is perfect."

"You're right." Crystal straightened, seeming to shake off the sad memory. "Speaking of perfect, I'm still shocked at how calm you're being about seeing Caleb again."

"That's not till tomorrow." Butterflies threatened to take flight in her stomach and carry her away with anticipation.

Crystal got a strange look on her face.

The butterflies fluttered. "What?"

"We're meeting up with him today, not tomorrow."

"You're wrong."

"No, I'm not."

"Yes, you are." She'd written the date in her mind over and over again. "It's tomorrow."

They stopped at the edge of the pond. A black-and-green duck approached them. Crystal dropped her shoes to the ground and pulled off her backpack. The duck fled at the movement. Crystal dug around for a moment and her hand emerged with a notebook, which she opened and scanned with a finger. Then she turned the notebook toward Megan and pointed. "See? It's right there on the calendar. 'Caleb, July sixteenth, noon, St. James's Park.' "

Heat flushed Megan's skin and her fingertips got tingly. "Are you sure? I have the seventeenth in my head." She pulled out her phone and navigated to her e-mail exchange with Caleb.

July sixteenth, not seventeenth. Right there in plain English.

Megan groaned. "How did I make such a mistake?"

"I'm not sure." Crystal scrunched her nose.

"I mean, I know I'm not the most organized person, but you'd think I'd remember the date I was going to see . . ."

"The guy you have a mega crush on?"

"What?" Megan started pacing, the bright-red paint on her toenails standing out among the green grass. "Is it that obvious?" If Crystal could read her, then Caleb might as well.

"Uh, yeah."

"Fat chance of my feelings being returned. I mean, look at me." If she'd known the meeting was today, she wouldn't be wearing her hair in a ponytail, nothing but a tiny bit of lip gloss on her face, with jeans and a T-shirt on. Maybe it was silly, but she'd already laid out a cute new sundress for their meeting tomorrow.

Sure, she'd planned to renew their friendship, but it wouldn't hurt to give Caleb other ideas and see what his reaction would be. Now he'd see her lack of effort and probably not give her a second thought.

Her sister grasped her elbow. "You look fine. And besides, if Caleb doesn't see below the surface, he's not worth it. Still, confidence is the most attractive thing." Crystal dug in her backpack once again and produced some powder, mascara, and blush. "And lucky for you, I never leave home without my arsenal."

"You're a godsend." Megan closed her eyes as Crystal made quick work of applying the makeup.

"Now, turn around."

Megan obeyed and felt Crystal tug the ponytail

holder out of her hair. The bristles of a brush swept against her scalp, pulling at her hairs. When Crystal was finished, she handed Megan a small mirror. "Ta-da."

Her hair was now in a loose bun, which softened her features. Her makeup made her eyes pop and smoothed her cheeks. Megan handed the mirror back to Crystal and threw her arms around her neck. "Thank you, thank you, thank you."

"You're welcome." Crystal patted her back, then withdrew. "And looks like we finished just in time . . ."

Megan followed her gaze and her heart slammed into her chest. Caleb walked toward them. He wore a blue button-up plaid shirt with the sleeves rolled to the elbows, jeans, and a casual pair of boat shoes. A five-o'clock shadow on his cheeks and chin granted him a rugged appeal that was only slightly diminished by that pair of boyish dimples Megan knew so well. His grin told Megan a number of things—primarily, that when it came to Caleb, nothing had changed.

And yet, thanks to the blood coursing rapidly through her veins and the heat flushing her face, she also knew that everything had changed.

Next to her, Crystal whistled low. "Wow. He doesn't look the same at all."

Her "I know" got stuck in her throat. All Megan could do was watch her friend walk toward them. When he finally reached their location, he studied

Megan for a minute and then pulled her into his arms. "So good to see you again, Meg."

"Caleb." She placed her head on his chest. At six feet, he'd always been the perfect height for her to rest comfortably against him. His scent was different, some sort of spiced rum that sent shivers down her spine. The cotton of his shirt embraced her cheek with its softness. Megan listened and heard the *bum-bum* of Caleb's new heart beating steady inside him.

A throat cleared nearby, and it took Megan a moment to realize it was her sister. Oh yeah. Crystal was here with them. Megan pried herself loose from Caleb's arms—pried, because she wanted nothing more than to stay there in the safety that came, had always come, from being in his embrace.

She pushed her eyes upward until they met Caleb's green gaze. "Hi."

"Hi." It seemed like he wanted to say more.

She broke their connection and swiveled toward her twin. "You remember Crystal."

Caleb shook whatever he was feeling from his face and turned, his smile breaking out again. "Of course." He extended his hand and her sister shook it. Even though they'd met several times, her sister had never really known Caleb—not like Megan had. "Nice to see you again."

"Likewise."

"How are you?" Unsure what to do with

her arms, Megan crossed them over her chest. "Thanks again for making time to meet up."

"It's my pleasure." And his gaze told her it really was. Was he just being nice . . . or did he maybe feel the same way about her that she did about him? "What have you ladies been up to?"

She and Crystal told the story about making the guard laugh and filled him in on what sights they'd seen so far.

Crystal glanced at her watch. "Speaking of sightseeing, we were going to hit St. Paul's, the Tower of London, and Westminster Abbey today. Do you want to continue with those plans, or would you guys like to hang out alone?"

"I don't trust you not to work if you're by yourself," Megan teased. Besides, Crystal provided a nice buffer for Megan's fledgling feelings. It would be a lot less awkward with her there.

Then she glanced sidelong at Caleb. "What do you think?"

Caleb shrugged. "I came here to hang out with you, so whatever you've got planned, I'm in."

Megan tried not to read too much into his words.

Tried . . . and failed.

Chapter 25

What a difference half a week could make.

Crystal swallowed her pills with a glass of water, marveling at how much better her stomach felt since her episode in the Irish castle. She replaced her cup on the restaurant table, which was covered in a red cloth. She, Megan, and Caleb were having breakfast in an outdoor bakery. Her bland meal of toast and applesauce hadn't tasted particularly good, but her stomach didn't feel unsettled like it used to, so that was a plus.

All around them, diners' forks clinked against plates, waiters walked by to accommodate the morning rush, and sunlight warmed Crystal's hands.

Megan took the final bite of her egg white scramble and pushed her plate away. She inclined her head toward Caleb, who was sipping on his coffee. He'd just finished telling them a story of his time taking photos in the wilds of Africa. Her sister was clearly shocked that Caleb had come almost face-to-face with a lion and survived. "Weren't you terrified?"

A lazy grin spread over Caleb's face. "I mentioned that I was in a vehicle, right? On a safari?"

Relief spread across Megan's features. "I hate you so much right now. You scared me."

"Come on, Meg. You gotta live a little."

Crystal settled back in her chair and watched the interaction between Megan and Caleb. They seemed comfortable with each other, but there was something unspoken between them, something they needed time to explore for themselves. By themselves. Yesterday had been filled with sightseeing, and they hadn't stopped to talk much.

Maybe today she should give them an opportunity. After all, tomorrow they were moving on to the countryside, and Caleb would return to his photography elsewhere. "I'm feeling a little tired. I think I'll go back to the hotel for the morning."

Megan's head whipped around and she bit her lip. "Is your stomach hurting again?"

It felt so foreign for Megan to be worrying about Crystal. "I'm fine. Really."

"Maybe I should go with you." She glanced at Caleb, an apology written on her face. "I don't want you to be alone. What if you need an ambulance again?"

Clearly this wasn't going to work. Crystal would try another tactic, though it wouldn't be well received. "You got me. I need to work a little. I have some great ideas after seeing St. Paul's and Westminster Abbey yesterday."

Which, she actually did. Okay, maybe not great.

But an inkling of an idea, which was more than she'd had this entire trip. In fact, she felt like she was on the verge of a great discovery but had no idea how to break through the walls to get to it.

"Crystal." That one word was drenched with disapproval, and Megan's frown declared it openly. "You can't miss out on London to work."

"I have to work sometime. It might as well be today."

"We had an agreement."

"That I wouldn't work for 'several days.' It's been four. I've held up my end of the bargain." Crystal pulled some cash from her wallet and set it on the table, then stood. "Here's some money for the tip. I'm going to go now while these ideas are fresh in my mind."

Caleb pushed himself out of his chair. "I'm taking off tomorrow for a photo shoot, so I might not see you again." He walked around the table and gave Crystal a quick, friendly hug.

This was a good guy. "Have fun today. It's been nice catching up with you." Crystal maneuvered around the table and leaned down to give Megan a quick embrace. "I'm doing this for you."

The whispered words seemed to catch her sister off guard. "What do you mean?"

But Crystal just smiled and waved. Megan would have to figure it out for herself. She spun and headed back to the hotel, which was only a few blocks away.

Her light scarf fluttered in the breeze, filtering the morning air toward her exposed neck. Something about the way the sunlight flirted with the sidewalk, disappearing and then reappearing, about how the quaint shop windows hinted at the treasures that lay inside, about the Londoners and tourists milling past her, mixing and mingling together until she couldn't tell them apart—it all took a paintbrush to her insides and dipped her soul in a bright yellow she hadn't known in a long, long time.

Maybe Megan's no-work policy had been exactly what Crystal needed. Not that she could have done much work anyway, since her body had to recover a bit from her episode in Ireland and then traveling to London. However, it was time to start brainstorming again.

But for the first time in she didn't know how long, Crystal almost dreaded opening up her laptop and perusing her e-mails.

A slight panic built at that thought. She couldn't lose her drive. Not now, when she desperately needed it. This trip was turning into a good one, but when she got home, she'd regret missing out on the Lerner project. Just because things were going better with Megan didn't mean her desire to work on her dream project had diminished. In fact, as she'd allowed herself to open up emotionally little by little, her desire had only increased.

She quickened her steps and rounded the corner, glimpsing her hotel and making quick work of climbing the steps and entering the small lobby. Yes, she'd make a cup of tea and sit on her balcony. That was sure to—

"Crys."

Her footsteps halted. It couldn't be. But there, rising from one of the high-backed chairs near the lobby's fireplace, was Brian. A mixture of joy, fear, and something else burst through her chest, overwhelming her senses.

She had the urge to run to him, to bury her face in his chest and tell him how sorry she was. For everything.

But instead, she gripped the strap of her purse and stayed rooted to the spot. "What are you doing here?" It was all she could manage.

"I was worried about you. With the ulcer. And everything else." He'd reached her now, towering over her. She was suddenly transported to the first time they met. The firm where she'd been an intern in grad school had purchased tickets for the Fireman's Ball, and she'd been standing around a cocktail table with some coworkers, drinking a club soda, when he'd approached. He'd looked so out of place in his tuxedo, like he'd rather be wearing sweats and a T-shirt. But he'd come right up to her, all six five of him, and asked her to dance. Straightforward, no-nonsense, but with a twinkle of sweetness in his eyes.

He'd taken her breath away then, just like he was doing now.

"I'm f—" Oh yeah, he hated that word. "Okay. I'm okay."

His hands clenched and unclenched at his sides, as if he couldn't decide what to do with them. He finally reached out a hand and lightly touched her stomach. "You sure?" His voice was low and husky, and it was all she could do not to crumble inside.

"Yes." She whispered the word, afraid that if she spoke too loudly, the moment would end and he'd vanish. Because suddenly, though she hadn't expected him—and she hated the unexpected—the idea of him not being here was too much. "I've . . . missed you."

A smile spread, the same smile he'd given her countless times. He pulled her into his arms, tender enough that he wouldn't hurt her but fierce enough to communicate he wasn't ever letting go.

July 17
Blog Post Title: Hidden Treasures:
   Exploring London
Post Content:
   Who knew that a scavenger hunt around London could lead to the discovery of more than mere landmarks?

"What's the plan for today?" Caleb took the last bite of his breakfast and shoved the plate away, then washed it down with a swig of coffee.

"We were going to check the scavenger hunt off the list."

Her friend pulled the napkin from his lap and tossed it onto the table. He dug in his pocket, producing his wallet. "Scavenger hunt?"

She nodded. "Amanda wanted to complete a text message scavenger hunt."

"I guess I'm behind the times. What's that?"

Megan chuckled. "You get in teams of two to four people and follow clues that are texted to you. Once you solve one clue, the next is sent. It seems like a cool way to see parts of the city you might not otherwise."

"I'm all for exploring." Caleb placed his credit card in the billfold with the ticket. Megan started to protest and he waved her off. "My treat."

Always considerate. And the way he lounged in his chair, so casual, reminded Megan of countless hospital stays where they'd talked for hours. But she had a hard time reconciling the Caleb who had been there and the Caleb who sat here. He'd always been confident, but this Caleb—he was simply aglow with life.

And once again, his scar peeked from the top of his shirt. He never seemed to hide it.

Her fingers moved to the top of her own shirt, an adorable flowy button-up Crystal had loaned her for today. Her sister had looked at her askance when she'd insisted on doing up all the buttons, even though undoing a few wouldn't have been immodest.

But her scar was so ugly and she wanted to feel pretty, especially today. It was easier to keep it covered.

Megan ducked her head and cleared her throat. "We're registered already, so we can start whenever."

Rubbing his hands together, Caleb leaned forward. "Let's do this." Their waitress came to take his payment.

Megan pulled out her phone and texted START to the number she'd stored in her contacts. A few seconds later, the first clue popped up. "Across the street from luxury, a loving symbol of remembrance rests where the flowers walk. What is the sculpture at the bottom called?"

Caleb tapped his chin. "How much of this do we have to figure out, and how much can we use Google?"

"I think we can use our phones to find GPS information but not the actual answer to the question. We have to physically go to every location."

"All right then."

"Anything jumping out at you? You've been here before."

"True, but you're the real expert. How many times did you read that book I gave you?"

Megan smiled at the memory. "Too many to

count." She stared at the clue. "Luxury could be a castle. There are plenty here."

"Good thought. But maybe they'd use the word *royal* to tip us off." The waitress brought back his card and he signed, then tapped the pen against the table as he stared off in the distance. "What if it's talking about a specific borough? Isn't Kensington one of the most expensive places to live?"

"Here, let me record our ideas." Megan pulled out her notebook, flipped to a blank page, and wrote. Then she snapped her fingers. "Look at this part of the clue: where the flowers walk. Obviously, flowers don't walk. But I remember reading something about a flower walk in Kensington Gardens."

Caleb snatched her map off the table and dragged his finger until he located something. He swiveled the map toward her. "Harrods is right across the street. What's a bigger symbol of luxury than that?"

She took the map back and pointed. "And look. The Albert Memorial is in the gardens right next to the flower walk: a loving symbol of remembrance. Prince Albert died at age forty-two of typhoid, leaving behind Queen Victoria as a grieving widow. They were so in love." For a moment she wondered what that would be like— but then she refocused. "I say we head that way."

They walked to the nearest underground

Tube stop and took the subway to the gardens. When the monument came into view, Megan gaped at its opulence. A golden house-like structure covered the statue of Albert, angels ringing the top. She read the plaque explaining the monument. It said Albert was holding the catalogue of the Great Exhibition, which he helped to organize in 1851.

"Here." Caleb pointed to the plaque, where it explained the long stone frieze sculpture at the base of the podium. "It's called the *Frieze of Parnassus.*"

She'd gotten caught up in the grandeur of the work and had forgotten for a moment about the hunt. Megan typed the work's title into her phone and replied to the clue. An almost instant response came through. "Congratulations. You are correct. Here's your next clue." Megan couldn't keep herself from whooping. "We did it. Our first clue completed."

Caleb held out his hand for a high five. "Good teamwork."

Grinning, she slapped his palm. "Want to hear the next clue?"

"Oh yeah. I'm just gearing up." He bounced back and forth on the balls of his feet, Rocky-style. "Hit me."

No wonder everyone in the hospital called Caleb the class clown. She shook her head, biting her lip, and held up her phone. They continued their hunt, which took them to an obscure pub T. S. Eliot used to frequent, a bookstore with a map of the world on the floor, a fudge shop where Caleb bought four different kinds of chocolate— and where Megan refused even a bite—and several other locations.

Their final clue pointed them to find the last word on the plaque at the entrance to "a treasure of another country forever entombed in this monument." Megan had assumed that meant the mummies section of the British Museum.

But here they stood, after inputting the last word of every plaque they could find, and still they received the same reply: "I'm sorry. That's not correct."

"Guess we're not in the right place." Caleb ran his hands through his hair, holding them there while he put on his thinking face: lips screwed up to the left, eyes staring at the floor.

She plopped onto a bench, frowning. "Seems that way." But what *was* the right place?

He joined her, then took her hand in his and squeezed. It was a casual, friendly squeeze of encouragement—but her heart couldn't help but wish for more. "Don't worry. We'll figure it out."

"You think?" How silly she was getting so frustrated over a game. They could always request a hint.

"Hey, if we can survive heart surgery, we can do anything."

How did he do that—take such an obvious statement, one meant in lighthearted jest—and turn it into something her heart profoundly needed to hear? She studied him for a few moments, and the silence between them became palpable, a living, breathing thing.

Her eyes once again focused on his scar. And of their own accord, her fingers reached out tentatively to touch it.

He froze.

What was she doing? "I'm sorry." She pulled her hand back into her lap.

"I don't mind." He tilted his head. "It's just . . . I've never seen yours."

If any other guy had said that it would have sounded really creepy. But not Caleb. Because he got it. He got her. "Funny you should say that. I was just thinking this morning about how free you are showing off yours. Don't you ever get stares?"

"Sure, sometimes. I don't really notice anymore." He shrugged. "But it's my badge of honor, I guess. It's part of me, part of my story. Why pretend we're like everyone else when we're not?"

Oh, this man. She mulled his words over in her mind. "Good point." Megan hesitated. Trembling, her fingers found the top button of her shirt and pulled it through its loop. Then one more. She pulled the lapels of the shirt wider, exposing the thick, puckered skin below. Megan grimaced and resisted the urge to redo the buttons.

Her eyes moved to Caleb, who watched her with a look she couldn't quite interpret.

He reached for her hand again. "Meg." The word was nearly a whisper.

"Yeah?"

"I hope you know . . . You have never been more beautiful than you are right now."

Tears built in her eyes and she blinked them back. One fell, then another. His words found the raw places in her and soothed them like aloe.

"And there I go, making you cry. I'm always making you cry."

She laughed, wiping away the tears. "It's a good cry. Don't worry."

"Okay." He shifted in his seat. Her tears must still make him uncomfortable, all these years later. "Also, I think I've figured out the clue."

"What?" Oh yeah. The scavenger hunt.

Funny how she'd been here looking for one thing, and had found something else entirely: her courage.

Chapter 26

Amazing how a day with her husband could feel like a first date.

Crystal shoved her hands into her jacket pockets as she and Brian walked down the lane at Hyde Park. They'd spent all day taking in various architectural phenomena, like the Gherkin and the Houses of Parliament. In New York, there were some wonderful feats of architecture, of course, but inspecting such old treasures here for the first time brought something alive in her.

And seeing them wasn't just about work anymore. It was like that first trip to Washington, DC, all over again. She could feel the passion oozing back into her soul, refreshing what had been dry inside, refilling her tank of inspiration little by little.

In fact, even though ideas for the Lerner project swarmed, she didn't really want to think about work. Brian was only able to be with her for a week, so she was going to make the most of their time together.

"Thanks for not calling me a nerd when I drooled over Big Ben."

"If I didn't know that was a clock tower, I'd be jealous." Brian looked good in his brown leather jacket and red beanie. The temperature had dipped into the forties, and only a few people lingered in the park. "And you are a nerd, but at least you're a cute one."

"Why, thank you." Her nose tingled with the cold, but laughter burst through her lips and warmed her. Her stomach rumbled.

"Are you okay?" He'd been protective all day, making sure she took her medicine and didn't overdo it with the sightseeing.

"No."

"What?" Brian's eyebrows lifted. "Should we head back to the hotel?"

She giggled. "I'm not in pain, just hungry."

"Oh." His gaze swept the line of storefronts across the street. "Maybe that Mexican place is open."

"Mexican food in London?"

Brian shrugged. "Depends on how desperate you are."

"Not that desperate." Her eyes locked onto another storefront next to the restaurant. "But that—that, I can do."

"You're crazy."

"You love ice cream." She tugged on his arm. "Come on. I've got a sudden craving for chocolate chip cookie dough, and I won't rest until it's satisfied."

"Your hands are freezing." But Brian followed her across the street and into the shop. It was small, with a green-tiled counter and stainless steel display case showing off the variety of ice cream flavors they served. In the corner sat two tiny tables and some red plastic chairs.

The worker behind the counter looked up. "Closing in five minutes."

"That's okay, we'll be quick."

"I still say you're crazy." Brian leaned in to whisper against her hair, sending a shiver down her spine. All day they'd been flirting, but they hadn't so much as hugged since their initial greeting. Perhaps they were both feeling out the situation, seeing how or if their time apart had changed anything between them.

"You married me, so what does that make you?" She flashed a coy grin at him, then made her ice cream selection—a two-scoop cone with one scoop of cookie dough and one scoop of cookies 'n' cream. Megan would probably tsk at her for being so unhealthy, but considering Brian's selection of a waffle bowl with chocolate and sprinkles, he wouldn't judge.

They paid and thanked the cashier, then headed back to the park, sauntering down the dirt path, which was flanked by huge flower bushes. Every fifty feet or so, a wooden bench with slats sat waiting for company.

She watched Brian out of the corner of her eye and felt a splat on her shoe. Crystal glanced down and groaned. "Aw man." Her top scoop of ice cream had fallen from her cone and onto her leather boot. She kicked the ice cream off into the bushes. Her shoes would be ruined if she didn't get this cleaned up now.

Brian looked around, then gave her his ice cream to hold. "Be right back." He hustled off toward the nearest bench, where an older woman in a patched jacket sat. She grinned at him, then rummaged in her knapsack for something. He came back toward Crystal holding a huge stack of wipes.

He bent down and cleaned off her boot until all traces of sticky cookie dough ice cream were gone. He tossed the wipes into the garbage and took his ice cream back in hand.

Her boots were good as new. "Thank you."

"You're welcome."

Crystal licked her cone. The sweetness coated her tongue, and she begged it to hang on for a moment longer. They continued down the path, past the woman, and Crystal threw out her thanks. The woman smiled—her front two teeth missing—and waved.

Brian took another bite of his ice cream and then tossed the rest into a garbage bin. "I was right. It's too cold to eat ice cream."

"I love it." Yes, the cold bit into her lips, but it reminded her of something she'd forgotten all these years. Instead of numbing her, the cold woke her up. She was coming back to life, and she liked it that way.

"I hope Megan doesn't mind that I stole you away today, though it sounds like she was pretty well occupied." Brian stuck his hands into his pockets. "How have things been going between you guys?" Though she and Brian had managed a few brief calls over the last few weeks, there hadn't been much opportunity for deep discussion.

"Things have been . . . better." Crystal took the final bite of her cone, crunching it, cold from the remaining ice cream seeping into her gums. She filled him in on Pamplona, the fight in the airport, and the aftermath. Ever since that day in the Irish hospital, when Crystal had opened up about the scholarship opportunity, they'd been closer. Not perfect. But it was a start.

"Good." Brian's right hand snuck out of his pocket and pulled Crystal's into his, as if it was the most natural thing in the world.

A sudden ache hit Crystal—because it should have been. But sometime in the last few years, they'd stopped holding hands. Their relationship had become a series of one-off nights together and a few scattered dates here and there.

She'd been starving their relationship because she'd been starving herself emotionally. If she didn't let herself be vulnerable, let herself feel, then she had nothing left to give her marriage. The connection seemed clearer to her than ever before. How had she not seen it?

Brian continued. "It sounds like you're making good progress. I know it can't have been easy, but I think you did the right thing in coming. I can already see a change in you. Today I really was able to see your passion for architecture. You were like you used to be, back when we first met."

"I feel the change too."

Brian stopped and turned to face Crystal, his eyes searching hers. He took a lock of her hair and rubbed it between his thumb and forefinger. The tiny action nearly undid her. "I came here to check on you, but also because I couldn't stand the waiting and the wondering. It was torture, Crys."

"I know. I've hated being apart."

"Me too, but it was more than that. It's not easy to admit, but I've been so afraid that you'd come home and you wouldn't have changed."

She reached up and caressed his cheek. "I'm trying. I promise."

"I know. Today has been such a relief. You have no idea. For the first time, I have real hope again." He leaned in and kissed her, a kiss that spoke of passion simmering below the surface. Then he hugged her to his chest. "But I've realized something else. Maybe my expectations aren't fair. I can't put all the responsibility for change on you."

"You're not the one who needs to change."

Brian had always been the most caring and generous man she'd ever met. "I am. And I'm doing it. It may take me longer than I'd like, but slowly I'm letting myself be freed from the past."

And she was. But a fear niggled. How was it all going to translate when she returned to work, to life as usual? Would fixing things with Megan really be able to fix everything else? Or would she and Brian find that the same old problems persisted between them?

July 17
Blog Post Title: Hidden Treasures:
  Exploring London (continued)
Post Content:
  . . . The London Eye brings a whole new perspective. And it sure makes everything a lot clearer.

Megan was about to fly above London—although, really, hadn't she been flying all day?

Caleb gestured toward the doorway to the open pod on the London Eye, the city's iconic Ferris wheel overlooking the Thames. "After you."

"Thanks." She quick-stepped into the enclosed pod and he followed, along with about ten other people. She and Caleb snagged spots standing at the front of the pod where research had shown her the best views could be had. Once their pod rose into the sky, they'd see practically the entire city, including every site they'd already visited together. Like Trafalgar Square, where their scavenger hunt had come to a close a few hours ago.

Once everyone was loaded, the pod door closed and rose into the orange-and-pink sky. The pod provided a 360-degree view of the city, and the others inside crowded the windows, pointing and exclaiming in a variety of languages. Two little kids pushed their noses against the glass, their breath steaming it.

Megan couldn't keep the smile from her face. She turned to find Caleb watching her. "What?"

"Nothing." He faced the window once again, and their shoulders brushed. "I can't believe these last few days have gone by so quickly."

"I know." She watched the skyline rise before her eyes. The Thames flowed past, strong and bronze in the waning sunlight. Beyond that, Big Ben stood at attention and the House of Parliament seemed to watch them. "It's been so incredible seeing you again." More than incredible.

"I feel the same way."

She tugged her hair behind her ear. Was it her imagination, or had he gotten even closer to her? A child's giggle filled the air, and Megan pulled her gaze from his.

She cleared her throat, watching the last ray of the sun vanish. "So, remind me. What's on the horizon for you?"

"Tomorrow I head to Poland to take photos for a piece on the hidden treasures of Europe."

"That's right." Her mind jumped with the possibilities. "Will you be visiting Ksiaz Castle? Or maybe Roztocze? I've also read great things about Bialowieza Forest."

Caleb chuckled and shook his head. "Those are on my list, yeah." He turned and leaned against the railing, once again ignoring the scenery and watching only her. "I'm not sure when I'll be back in Minnesota to see my parents, so maybe we can meet up again before you head back to the States."

"I'd like that." She shifted on her feet. They were all the way to the top of the Eye. Now that the sky was dark, it was more difficult to make out individual landmarks. But with the buildings all lit up, the city stole her breath. Each landmark was a gem sparkling in a sea of the unknown.

"What about you, Meg? What's next for you?"

"Cambridge and Oxford, then—"

"No, I mean after all of this. After you've completed the bucket list, what do you plan to do next?"

"I'm not totally sure." She was leaning toward taking the library job, but he might be disappointed if she told him that. "Though Sheila said they've had a great response to my articles and she definitely wants more contributions from me in the future."

"That's amazing, Meg. You're really doing it."

"I have you to thank for that." She poked him in the ribs. "Not only did you hook me up with Sheila, but I wouldn't be here in the first place if you hadn't encouraged me to meet with my donor's family."

Caleb's grin rivaled the lights of London below.

Megan gripped the rail at her waist. It was cold but steady. "Before this journey, I was too afraid to have an adventure. But look. I'm here. I faced my fears. And I feel amazing for having done that. I'm stronger than I thought possible."

"I've never for one second thought you weren't strong."

"I did."

"What made you think that?" His gaze bore a hole through her defenses, and she turned to face him again. He tugged her hand from the railing and held it in his own. This time he entwined their fingers—a much more intimate grip.

She gulped, felt the pulse in his fingertips. "A lot of things."

When did she remember first feeling this way? "Once, when I was eleven, maybe twelve, my parents and I were watching Crystal play soccer. My sister moved with such grace and speed. She was fluid, like water pouring from a glass—strong, with purpose and precision."

"Sounds like Crystal." A squeeze from his palm encased her own.

She nodded. "That moment inspired me. I thought, *We're twins. If she can move like that, maybe I can too.* I hadn't fully come to terms with my illness at that point. I told my mom I wanted to try playing sometime." Her voice wobbled, and she felt the tears building. No matter how many times she thought about this moment, the emotions still enveloped her. "She said, 'Oh, honey, I wish you could too. But it's just not possible. It's not your fault Crystal was born with a strong heart and you were born with a weak one. It's just God's will for you.'"

Silence floated between them as the pod descended down the other side of the large white wheel. "No offense to your mom, but I hate when people say stuff like that about God's will."

"If it wasn't his will, then why did it happen?" Megan shrugged. "I guess there's really no point in dwelling on it."

"God can handle your questions, Meg. If you want to know, ask. A relationship is about trust, and trust is grown through communication."

By holding back her questions and not really praying, was she keeping God at arms' length? Maybe they didn't even have a real relationship. "I'll have to think on that some more."

Caleb's thumb stroked her hand, spreading his warmth. "Back to your mom and what she said." He raised his free hand to cup her cheek. "Megan Jacobs, you are one of the strongest people I know. It takes amazing strength to keep hoping when everything seems against you. You did that. Over and over."

His eyes riveted her where she stood. She couldn't move even if she wanted to.

"And it takes amazing strength to inspire a young guy to keep going, even when doctors tell him there's no way he's getting a second chance. You did that too."

"Caleb." Her hand rested against his chest.

"I mean it, Meg." His forehead touched hers now, and his breath breezed past her cheeks. "You saved me. Did you know that before I met you, I thought daily about ways to end my sorry life? I could swallow a bunch of pills, or sneak into my dad's office and get the gun from his safe, or break the mirror in the hospital bathroom and use it to—"

"Shh." Every word knifed her heart. She couldn't imagine this amazing man taking his own life. "You saved me too, Caleb. Gave me someone to talk to. You reminded me I wasn't alone."

"Meg." He was going to kiss her—and she didn't care about anything else, only wanted to explore these new emotions and drown in them.

But before the sweetness in his eyes could be translated to his lips, the pod jostled beneath their feet. She swung her attention toward the window.

They were back on the ground.

Once the pod door opened, fellow passengers began disembarking. One woman ushered her children away but flashed a small smile Megan's way.

A ride attendant gestured them off, ready to load the next set of passengers.

The moment had ended.

She dropped her hands, cleared her throat, and walked off the pod, touching her feet to solid earth once more.

Chapter 27

The last week had been magical.

But tomorrow Brian would head home. And even though he and Crystal had spent the week traveling and relishing their time together, they hadn't really talked about how things should change when they stepped from the pages of this fairy tale and returned to reality.

They needed to find time to have a big conversation before he left.

Crystal alighted from the Edinburgh tram, Megan and Brian following her onto the busy Scottish street in the heart of the city. All around them, tourists and residents bustled past, off to visit a variety of shops, restaurants, and attractions.

Her eyes were drawn immediately to the castle on the bluff overlooking Princes Street Gardens, a small park just across the way. The castle loomed over them, its majesty projecting its grandeur over the whole city. How strange and yet magnificent to have something so old, so awe-inspiring there for all to see.

"Wow." Brian nestled up beside her, his gaze directed toward the castle as well. "Now that's cool."

Megan approached on Crystal's other side,

nose in her guidebook. "This says the site has been occupied since the late Bronze Age, and that the buildings of the castle that are still standing date all the way back to the twelfth century. Incredible."

Incredible was right. In fact, they'd seen a lot of incredible sights during their fast-paced travel through Cambridge, Oxford, and the English and Scottish countrysides. Today they'd already visited the Museum of Edinburgh and taken an underground city tour of Mary King's Close.

The memory of Brian holding her near when she'd felt slightly freaked out about the tight quarters brought a smile to Crystal's lips. He'd even pulled her into a dark corner and snuck a few breathtaking kisses while the tour guide droned on about life expectancies in the eighteenth century.

This whole week had felt like a second honeymoon—except Megan was there, of course.

Her sister had been unusually chatty and upbeat, despite having to leave Caleb behind. Of course, she'd been on her phone texting with him every spare minute, and they were planning to meet up again in Paris later this week. Megan had confided in her how much she'd wanted to kiss him, how the moment had passed far too quickly and she was afraid they wouldn't find it again.

"Are you guys ready to head to the castle for a

tour?" Megan led the way toward the lush grass and short bush-like trees of the gardens. A paved pathway meandered throughout the park and up toward the castle. At the park entrance, a display of flowers burst from the ground, putting color into the day of anyone who passed by. Reds, yellows, purples, and blues waved in the breeze, inviting Crystal in. A large gold fountain glinted in the sunlight.

It was gorgeous—and the perfect place to have a good talk.

Crystal turned to Megan. "Would you be okay doing the castle alone?" And to Brian. "As long as you wouldn't mind skipping?"

Brian shrugged. "I'm good with whatever."

Megan nodded. "Me too. I'll text you when I'm done and we can figure out where to meet up." She waved and turned, heading off through the crowd.

"Everything okay?" Her husband's hand reached out to grasp Crystal's.

"Yes, but we need to talk. And I was afraid if we weren't alone, we wouldn't."

His hand tightened around hers. "Do you want to sit?"

"Let's walk for a bit." Hand in hand, they sauntered across the concrete path, past an assortment of large floral displays: one honoring Hans Christian Andersen, one celebrating the bicentenary, and one depicting a large clock—a reminder that even when it seemed like it should, time never stood still.

"I don't want you to leave tomorrow." She kept staring at the sidewalk. "Especially not without knowing where we stand."

A pause. "Where we stand is that I'm more in love with you than ever."

She couldn't help looking up at those beautiful, wonderful words. "Really?"

"Really. But our love for each other has never been the issue."

"You're right." She gnawed the inside of her cheek until she tasted blood. Because Crystal— she'd been the issue. "I'm learning a lot about myself these days. Mostly, that I don't have to be as strong as I thought I did. That I can be vulnerable, and that's okay." But so difficult. And so uncomfortable.

"Vulnerability isn't a sign of weakness. I think that's true strength shining through."

She paused. They'd reached the end of the sidewalk, the end of the park. They could keep walking, out into the crowd, away from their problems. Or she could sit down with her husband and face what she'd been hiding from all these years.

She tugged him toward an empty spot in the grass and they sat facing each other, still clasping hands. The shadow of the castle covered them.

"Brian, I'm scared. I think I've always been scared."

"Scared of what?"

"Scared of losing control—of myself, my situation, my life." She blew out a breath, trying to grasp for the words that would explain things she didn't even fully understand. "From the time my sister was diagnosed, our whole family fell into chaos. Things weren't the same anymore. We'd make plans, Megan would have an episode, and everything was canceled. I never knew if that episode would be fatal. Life was a big fat unknown."

"And you hated that."

She nodded. "I guess somehow I became obsessed with the idea that if I could control my own life, the pain of the unknown would be lessened, even nonexistent. That desire for control built inside me for years, but after Megan's surgery, it all came to a head. I became this robot, singularly focused on achievement, someone who avoided emotion because I was so afraid that it would rip me apart one tear at a time."

Brian's thumb stroked her hand and something inside of her broke.

"Crys, all the things you've done to try to control your life . . . They're only an illusion. You don't ultimately hold power over anything. Not really."

"I think I know that now." She pulled at a blade of grass with her free hand. "But I don't know what it means for our life. Because I still love my job, especially now that I'm finding my passion again."

"No one is asking you to give that up. I've always just wanted you to balance it with everything else."

"So what does that mean, realistically?"

Brian shrugged. "Making more of an effort to spend time together, I guess. Prioritizing relationships over work. Being open to discussion when things are getting too hectic."

She tilted her head, considered his words. "I can do that."

"And maybe also not just tabling discussions for 'later' when you don't want to address them at all." Her husband studied her. "Like about when to have kids."

"Or even . . . whether to have them." Had she really said that out loud? She pressed on. "Because you want children so badly. But I don't know if I do."

"You think I haven't figured that out by now?" Brian's words were soft, but they still bit into her soul. "What I don't quite understand is why. Is it because you can't control them?"

"Yes." A sob wracked her body, but she held in the tears. The memory of the little boy at the Wall of China surfaced. "But more than that, I can't

302

keep them safe. Like Mom and Dad could never keep Megan safe."

"Oh, Crys. I never thought about that."

Crystal turned around, and Brian propped her up from behind, wrapping his arms around her waist. She leaned her head back against his chest. "I don't know what to do."

"I don't either." Brian sighed against her hair. "I only know that I want a family. I don't have anyone to carry on my family name. No blood relations that I know about. I want that connection, that legacy."

Hearing the passion in her husband's voice—the deep desire of a little boy who only wanted to belong—made Crystal want to weep. How could she be so selfish? "Okay." She placed her hand on his forearm, choked the word out. "We can start trying when we get back home."

Fear clawed at her, scratching her insides and making her bleed. Oh, how she wanted to be free of this monster. But how? To think she could have lost Brian, that she still might someday, if she didn't figure out how to change . . .

"Crys, no. Not like this." Her husband's lips grazed her neck. "If we have kids when you don't want them, I'm afraid you'd resent me down the road."

She couldn't argue with that very real possibility, angry as it made Crystal at herself. "I don't know what you want from me." And she couldn't keep the frustration from her voice. She was tired, so very tired, of fighting. "I said okay. What else can I do?"

"Don't just dismiss the fear. Deal with it. Crys, you're so afraid of what could happen that you're not experiencing the joy that life has to offer."

She opened her mouth to reply, but no words came out.

"Look around you. If you had not decided to take a chance and come on this trip—if you'd stayed trapped in your 'perfect plan'—you wouldn't be here right now. I wouldn't be here right now. You'd be at work and I might be at home, packing my things because you'd pushed me away for the last time."

The fact that he'd even considered leaving made her blood run cold.

The fear continued to claw, making its way up her throat.

"But instead, we are here, and we're talking. And I see that you're finally struggling with the things that have been dormant in you for years. That makes me so proud of you. Know why?"

"No." Her voice trembled.

"Because it means you're finally facing the fear inside. It's been there all along. But do you feel it fighting back? You thought you were controlling it, but it was really controlling you. It's time to stop letting fear win. Wouldn't it be a better use of your time to leave the big stuff like control and worry to God and instead spend it reveling in all the opportunities for great joy he's given you?"

Joy.

What was it, really? She tried to remember a single moment of pure joy from the last three years, even the last twenty, and couldn't. Sure, she'd been happy at times, but joy?

It felt nonexistent, like a myth she could never quite grasp.

She hadn't noticed before, but music rose from a bandstand across the park. Some young dancers performed, their green-and-gold dresses spinning round and round. They whirled and twirled, and with every step created a dizzying spell that mesmerized her. While not every step was perfect—they were far from professionals—and there were moments when their spinning seemed out of control, that didn't detract from the beauty of their movements.

Could Crystal's life be like that? It *did* hold opportunities for joy. Her relationships with Brian, Megan, her parents. The possibility of children. Even work.

But it would mean throwing caution to the wind, tossing back her head, and spinning without always seeing where the dance would take her.

Chapter 28

19. Kiss a handsome stranger in the rain.

Kisses are a powerful thing, or so I'm told. I wouldn't know from experience.

Kissing is mysterious too. Because on the one hand, it's commonplace. People kiss all the time. But on the other hand, when I'm reading a book or watching a romantic movie, I don't care that it's commonplace. I still hold my breath in anticipation, waiting for that perfect moment when the characters will kiss and all will be right with the world.

Of course, that moment is made all the more perfect when it's raining. Rain has a way of making everything more magical. It's cleansing. It brings renewal of life.

Kissing also requires a measure of bravery. It means accepting a gift and giving freely of yourself at the same time. And what's braver than kissing a handsome stranger?

I feel like I've been dead for so long. And scared too.

So kissing a stranger in the rain sounds like just the thing to wake me up and make me brave.

Chapter 29

July 27
Blog Post Title: The Scariest Item on the
    List: Our Visit to the South of France
Post Content:
    If I had any illusions of coming across
as perfect (or fully sane) in this blog,
they will be shattered with the writing of
this post . . .

Rain was in the forecast.

She'd put it off long enough. They only had a little less than a week left before heading home. So today Megan had to tackle Amanda's nineteenth item on the list: *Kiss a handsome stranger in the rain.*

Megan stretched out on the padded lounge chair and watched the turquoise waves lap along the white sand of the French Riviera shoreline. Crystal had run off to grab a drink ten minutes ago and still wasn't back.

All around her, French residents and tourists alike read the latest magazines, chatted with friends in their bikinis, waded into the water, and drank champagne from crystal flutes. Sailboats and yachts dotted the horizon, going wherever the wind took them. The sun beat down from its mantel above, raining down bright hope for what the future would bring.

And yet, Megan couldn't help but feel despair rise in her chest. How was she going to do this? She was no flirt. Maybe if she channeled Crystal's confidence. Her sister was naturally good at getting people's attention.

The worst part was . . . well, Megan had never been kissed.

Almost kissed but not actually kissed. That moment in the London Eye with Caleb had been like fire crackling through her. Her whole world had tilted, and she'd seen it differently than ever before. She'd seen Caleb differently than ever before . . .

How was she supposed to kiss another guy when Caleb was at the forefront of her mind?

She picked up the big floppy hat Crystal had brought and placed it on her head, inhaling the coconut scent of her sunscreen. Megan couldn't do anything if it didn't start raining. She might as well relish this moment, so she closed her eyes. The heat plunged into her pores and deliciously devoured her, stopping all her thoughts and worries about what lay ahead.

"Meg, wake up."

Crystal's voice and a nudge to her shoulder shook Megan from her thoughts. Her body felt groggy, as if she'd slept. Maybe she had. She gazed around, her mouth cottony. People were abandoning their lounge chairs as drops of rain plinked from the darkened sky above.

Oh no.

"Let's go to the cantina across the street." Crystal pulled a pair of jean shorts over her bikini bottoms and pushed her sunglasses to the top of her head.

Megan shifted to a sitting position and gathered her belongings. Together they headed to the cantina, where a blast of cool air hit them as they entered. Inside there were rustic brown tables surrounded by people seated in wooden chairs, and a large circular bar at the center. In the corner sat a patchwork couch, and the walls were decorated with splashes of red and orange, festive colors to keep the party going all day and night. The lighting was low, matching the mood outside.

Crystal pointed to an open table in the back and they made their way that direction. As they squeezed through the crowd, Megan searched for a handsome man who might be willing to kiss her. What a joke.

Good thing she hadn't eaten much today, because her queasy stomach probably would not have been kind to her.

And it was more than just the typical nerves over doing something so daring. Caleb's eyes kept flashing in her mind, and they were wounded somehow. Kissing another man when all she wanted to do was kiss him seemed like a betrayal.

And yet, it was on Amanda's list, so it had to be done. Ever since Sheila Daily had suggested she publish the list in its entirety—for accountability and to build anticipation—readers had been excited to hear what would happen with this particular list item.

And a growing dread had built in Megan at the thought.

She bumped into Crystal, who had stopped abruptly at the table they'd seen. It was now being claimed by two handsome men in board shorts and no shirts. One had a wedding band on his left ring finger, but the other didn't. He looked up at that moment and flashed a grin at Megan.

If ever an opportunity could be called golden, this was it.

"Come on," she whispered to Crystal as she continued to move toward the table. Megan put on a smile of her own. "We were headed for this table, but it looks like you beat us here."

"Sorry. Crowded place." The man with the wedding band took out a menu and started perusing.

His friend swooped a hand through his blond hair. He was almost a dead ringer for a young Matthew McConaughey, with his tan skin and dimpled cheeks. "We've got room if you'd like to join us."

"We would, thanks." Megan pulled out a chair next to the man and glanced back at Crystal, whose wide eyes displayed her surprise. Her sister took the remaining seat with a mumbled thanks. "Do I detect American accents? Boston, perhaps?"

The non-married (or so she hoped) man passed them both menus. "Right on the money. Massachusetts, born and bred. I'm Greg, and this is Ryan. You've got an accent of your own. Midwest?"

"Minnesota." They shook hands. Greg's handshake was firm, but it sparked a memory of another man holding her hands on a Ferris wheel high above London. She cleared her throat. "I'm Megan, and this is my sister, Crystal."

"I can definitely see the family resemblance."

"We're twins. It's not hard to see." Crystal's lips flattened, and she studied Megan with open displeasure. What was her problem? Megan had to get this item checked off her list, and she would have expected Crystal to be way more helpful than this.

Megan turned her attention back to Greg. "Are you here for business or pleasure?" Megan took a lock of her hair and twirled it, something she'd seen other women do when flirting. Her own hair was a little short for the gesture, but maybe it didn't look as stupid as it felt.

Another grin fell across Greg's perfect face.

"We're both lawyers seeing to a client's interests here in the Riviera."

"Ah, so business then."

"Yes. But I wouldn't mind taking time for a little pleasure too." His wink sent Megan's eyes careening to her menu and a blush to her cheeks.

Beside her, Crystal harrumphed.

"What about you? What do you do?"

"My sister here is an architect, and I'm a library . . . Well, I'll be starting a new job as an assistant librarian when I get home." The day after they left London she'd called Kara up and told her the news. Megan just couldn't think of a good enough reason to say no. Besides, there were a lot of pros to taking the job. She just had to be purposeful about pursuing her travel writing in her spare time.

"I've always found librarians to be particularly sexy."

"Oh brother." Crystal said the words under her breath, and Megan gave her shin a slight kick. Not that she could really blame her sister for the reaction. Greg was a bit over the top. But she needed a handsome guy, and he was here.

A waitress came by, and they placed orders for the special of the day. Greg ordered a round of flights for the table, though Crystal refused hers. What in the world was up with her sister? Did Greg remind her of someone she didn't like? Yes, he was an unabashed flirt, but there didn't seem to be anything about him that screamed "creeper" or "serial killer."

Of course, that didn't stop Crystal from flinging little barbs at him throughout their meal and asking him pointed questions. He let them roll off of him and refocused his attention on Megan.

Megan, who, though it felt all kinds of weird and wrong, brushed her hand against Greg's arm and her foot against his leg, who tilted her head and laughed when he told a dumb lawyer joke, who was stepping so far outside her comfort zone—but wasn't that what this trip was all about, so Amanda's dreams could come true?

When they were finished eating, Megan leaned toward Greg. She had to be sure to get him alone so they could kiss in the rain, or all of this would have been for nothing. "Would you like to hang out for a bit? Alone?" Inwardly cringing, she forced the last word from her mouth.

His wide grin told her he wasn't opposed to the idea. "Sure. Let's get out of here." Greg reached for her hand and stood.

Before Megan could move, Crystal grabbed her arm. "I need to use the restroom. Can you come with me, Meg?"

Greg nudged Ryan, who had been texting or looking at his cell phone for much of the meal. "Women. They always need to hit the bathroom in pairs."

Ryan looked up and nodded, then swung his attention back to his phone.

Megan stood and brushed her fingers against Greg's hand. "Be right back. Can you meet me outside?" She felt utterly ridiculous.

He looked toward the door. "It's raining."

"I know. That's kind of the point."

His eyebrows shot up, but the corners of his mouth twitched and he let out a staccato laugh. "Sure, whatever you're into."

Crystal dragged Megan toward the restroom and shoved her through the door.

"Ow." Megan rubbed her arm. "What's wrong with you?" The waiting area inside the restroom was tight, and they hovered near the paper towel dispenser.

Her sister's eyes flashed, and she threw her hands on her hips. "What's wrong with *me?* What's wrong with *you?* I've never seen you act like that before."

"Act like what? It was just a little harmless flirting."

Crystal rolled her eyes. "Flirting is one thing. Megan, do you know what that guy thinks?"

"That I like him."

"That you want to sleep with him."

That queasy feeling roiled through Megan's stomach again. "What? No, of course that's not—"

"I know that, obviously. But he sure doesn't."

A toilet flushed in the small space, and a petite woman came out of the stall, her eyes darting between the sisters.

They were quiet until she'd washed her hands and left.

Crystal turned to face Megan again. "I'm assuming you're trying to check that kissing item off your list since it's raining. Am I right?"

"Of course." She would never act like that otherwise. Especially not with how she felt about Caleb.

"You could have just found someone and said, 'My sister dared me to kiss a cute guy in the rain. Want to help me out?' "

Megan slumped against the wall. "I didn't think about that."

"Now you've got to go tell that man you don't really want to take him out into the rain to do who-knows-what. You just want a kiss."

The thought of kissing Greg now made her feel like running into one of these bathroom stalls and retching. Crystal must have seen the look on her face. She gentled her voice. "I can go tell him if you'd like."

For a moment Megan was tempted to let her. But this was her mess. She'd clean it up. "No, I'll go."

"I'll be inside if you need me."

"Thanks." Megan left the restroom and weaved through the crowd until she reached the door.

She opened it and saw Greg standing under the awning. When he caught her eye, his face lit up, but now she knew why. Could she still kiss him regardless?

He grabbed her hand and led her around the corner to an alley, then wrapped his hands around her waist, backing her up against the wall of the cantina, where they were exposed to the sky but not much else. Whoa, he moved fast.

The rain came down in sheets around them.

Greg lowered his lips to her ear. "What did you have in mind for our little adventure?"

She shivered and tried to wiggle out of his arms. "I'm afraid I may have led you on unknowingly."

He frowned. "What do you mean?"

"I only wanted to kiss you in the rain. Not . . ."

Instead of loosening his hold, Greg pulled her even closer. This felt nothing like when Caleb had held her. Her lungs constricted, making it hard to breathe.

Visions of Frank trying to accost her in the Peruvian hotel flashed in her brain. She'd only gotten away because someone had happened upon them. But right now there was no one else in sight.

Megan pushed against Greg's solid chest, but he didn't move an inch. "Let go." Her teeth began to chatter. "I want to go back inside."

"Why, baby?" He moved his hand, and it

started to creep up her shirt. His fingers were ice on her stomach. "It's fine. We can kiss."

Megan would get her kiss from a handsome man in the rain, but not like this.

She wrapped her arms around Greg's neck and yanked, bringing her knee up into his groin. He groaned and crumpled. She ran around the corner, slipping on the slick concrete but getting right back up. Then Megan fumbled with the front door to the cantina and stumbled into Crystal's arms.

Her breathing was heavy, but her heart felt strong. Because, this time, she hadn't relied on anyone else to save her.

She'd only needed herself.

Chapter 30

The proposal was perfect.

Crystal sat back in her chair and stared at her computer. Here she was thinking she'd have absolutely nothing to present at the pitch a week from Monday, and instead, she had the ideal proposal. It hadn't taken hours and hours of brainstorming or looking at architecture to unlock her inspiration.

Instead, the joy of letting herself *feel* had pushed against the bridge she'd erected around her soul, washing it out with its gentle streams.

Into it she'd poured the changing lights of the Taj Mahal, the longevity of the Roman Colosseum, the grandeur of Edinburgh Castle— and the whimsy of a girl in love. The community planned within the pages of this proposal would knock Jeff Lerner's socks off. She still couldn't believe the perfect combination of modern and old world had blended together in her mind to spark such creativity.

But it hadn't just happened in her mind. She'd let it penetrate her heart, and therein lay the difference.

On the hotel desk, her phone vibrated. Though it was late here, it'd still be daytime in New York, so she wasn't surprised to see Tony's name on the caller ID—despite the fact it was Saturday. Somehow she'd convinced him to still consider her newest proposal, even though he'd been determined to go with Meredith's. He was probably calling for an update.

"Crystal speaking."

"Tell me something good."

"I just finished it."

"I'm glad to hear it. I've been waiting to see that proposal all week."

"Well, it's done. Don't get your knickers in a knot."

"My knickers?" Tony chuckled. "Where are you, London?"

"Paris, actually. We just arrived this afternoon. Going to explore for a few days before heading home." Then she'd have nearly a full week at home before the pitch on August 6.

"I need to talk to you about that, actually." Tony paused. "Mr. Lerner asked us to move the pitch up a week. To this Monday."

"As in the day after tomorrow?" No, no, no. Now that she had the perfect idea, she should be the one to present it.

"Exactly. I need you to get on a plane as soon as possible. And don't forget to send me your proposal so I can look it over and get everything prepared on our end. You just worry about getting here."

"I can't. My sister is counting on me, Tony."

She'd made a commitment to see Megan through to the end. She couldn't leave now.

"I'm counting on you too, and I've been more than patient, Crystal."

She sighed. "I know you have but—"

"And do I really have to remind you what's riding on this? You versus Meredith. Senior architect. My reputation is on the line for backing you all these weeks while you've been gone. Don't make me look like a fool."

"You're killing me, Tony." But he was right. She couldn't abandon all her responsibilities at home just because she and Megan had made plans here. Crystal checked her watch. Perhaps they could squeeze in the last few bucket list items in the next twelve to eighteen hours and then she could hop a plane home. It wouldn't be ideal, but at least she'd fulfill all her obligations.

"I'll be on a plane tomorrow." She maneuvered her computer mouse and clicked to open an e-mail, attaching her proposal and hitting Send. "And I just sent you my proposal. I'm really proud of it, Tony. It's . . . me."

"I hope so. Because Meredith has come up with quite a doozy herself."

The possibility of losing to Meredith still rankled, but her confidence in this proposal overwhelmed any fear she had that it would be rejected. "May the best proposal win."

"Atta girl. Let me take a look at this and I'll

dash off any questions I have to you before I leave today. Just make sure you're back in the office early Monday. The meeting is at one. On second thought, tomorrow afternoon would be even better if you can swing it. Come straight here from the airport. Meredith and I will be here going over the final details."

"I'll have to check with Brian." It would be a Sunday, after all. And he wouldn't appreciate her running off the moment she got home.

Papers shuffled in the background. "Gotta run. Let me know when you land."

"Will do."

The call ended, and Crystal pushed back from the desk. This hotel room was more cramped than the others, but it had everything she and Megan needed. Outside their window, the most romantic city in the world called to her, life pulsing on the streets below. She took up residence next to the window and looked at the Eiffel Tower in the distance, stroking the pane and tracing the lights with her fingertip. How she wished Brian were here with her, experiencing the sight.

"It's pretty, isn't it?"

Crystal whirled to find Megan coming through the doorway.

Her sister tugged off her jacket and threw her purse onto the bed.

"Beautiful. Did you enjoy your evening?"

"Yes. I can't believe you missed the Louvre. I

stayed until they made me leave." Megan's eyes were bright and her cheeks flushed. She seemed a lot better today than yesterday, when she'd had to fight off that stranger in the South of France. Crystal had marched outside, determined to kick the guy's butt, but he still lay crumpled against the wall, groaning.

And that's when she'd finally, fully realized—Megan could take care of herself.

"I'm glad you enjoyed it." The conversation with Tony fresh in her mind, Crystal tugged at the curtain to the right of the window. "How would you feel about venturing out again tonight?"

"I don't think I'm up for it. We've got a full day tomorrow." Megan sat on the edge of her bed and massaged her neck.

Crystal sighed and walked to her own bed. She grabbed a pillow and sat down, hugging it against her chest. "I just got a call from Tony. He said I'm needed in New York this Monday."

"What?" Megan's hand stilled and she pulled it into her lap. "Why?"

"The pitch I've been working on has been moved."

"Can they do that?"

"Unfortunately." Crystal curled and flexed her bare feet. "The client requested the earlier date. He has no obligation to select our firm for his project, so we have to accommodate his schedule."

Megan worried her bottom lip. "Can't they tell him their architect is out of the country?"

"It doesn't work like that."

"But, Crystal . . ."

"I know it stinks. I was thinking we could go see the Eiffel Tower lights right now, and maybe catch a really early mass tomorrow, and then be done."

"I didn't kiss a handsome stranger in the rain." Disappointment still shone in Megan's eyes over her failed attempt.

"You can do that at home. It doesn't have to be in a specific place. Minnesota will work just as well as Paris."

Megan's lips twisted and she sighed. "I guess you're right. I just wanted to have it all done while you're here with me. And readers are expecting it."

"But you can't control when it rains." Crystal peered at Megan, whose eyes clouded. "I don't see a way around it, Meg. I need to get home."

"You're really leaving?" Her sister didn't have to say the rest of what she was thinking: *You're leaving . . . again?*

The memory of that moment in the hospital—when Crystal hadn't had the courage to stay with Megan in her room—taunted her. And though they'd touched on the incident during their fight in the Spanish airport, they'd never talked about it again.

Crystal had never apologized, not really.

Her lungs deflated, and she sucked in a breath. "It's different this time." A muffled siren outside raced past their window. Crystal stood and paced. "Back then, I was a coward. I was selfish. You have no idea how hard it was to live with the guilt, that it was you and not me. I was strong and you were weak, physically speaking. It was like I stole that strength from you when we were inside Mom's womb. And then there was the fear that you—the person I loved more than anything in the world—might disappear from my life at any moment."

Crystal's hands shook as the truth finally slipped from her, and she stopped moving, slumping against the wall. "I couldn't deal with it, Megan. And I'm sorry. I know you said you forgive me, but I don't know how. I am having a hard time forgiving myself."

Megan's mouth formed an O and she blinked rapidly.

But instead of tears flowing from her sister's eyes, a light shone. Understanding. Hope.

Megan got up, silent, and faced Crystal. "Of course I forgive you. It's forgotten." They stared at each other for a long moment, and Megan slipped her arms around Crystal's shoulders.

Could the past really be wiped away like that, her deeds not held against her any longer?

But Megan's next words were even more

shocking. "Now will you forgive me? I . . . didn't know. That you felt that way. And I didn't try very hard to see things from your point of view."

"There's really nothing to forgive. None of this is your fault."

"Please, Crystal?"

"Okay. I forgive you." Crystal squeezed her sister back and then pulled away. She cocked her head. "Are you really all right with me leaving in the morning?"

"I wish you didn't have to, but I understand."

"Thank you." Crystal stopped pacing and locked her gaze with Megan's. "At least this time I'm leaving hopeful, not scared. And I'm leaving behind a beautiful, confident woman who is fully capable of doing this on her own."

"For the first time, I kind of believe that." And then came her sister's tears. "But even if I'm capable, I'll always need my sister. So please promise it won't be three years before I see you again." Megan lowered herself to the edge of her bed again, tapping the spot beside her.

Crystal sat and leaned her head on Megan's shoulder. "Promise."

There was that feeling again, nestling inside her.

Joy.

If things between her and Megan could get better, *and* she landed the Lerner project, *and* she and Brian continued their forward motion when she got home—maybe she *could* have it all.

Maybe she could even give God another try. He was important to Brian, after all, and Nana had always said he was in the business of miracles. If this moment between her and Megan wasn't a miracle, what was?

Above all, maybe Crystal had been wrong. Maybe the past didn't have to be a bitter mark always marring the surface of her heart. Maybe life really could be an amazing adventure, one not of her own making, but the kind that comes from toil and heartache and love.

Especially love.

Chapter 31

July 29
Blog Post Title: The Jewel of France:
  Notre Dame
Post Content:
  Have you ever felt like you were meant to be somewhere at a certain time? I hadn't . . . till today.

Megan took another sip from her paper cup. The hotel room java didn't have the pizzazz she'd hoped for, but it was better than nothing. And she needed it. She and Crystal had stayed up late talking, then managed four hours of sleep before her sister caught a 7:00 a.m. flight.

She got up from her seat at the tiny hotel desk and flung open the curtains. The sun shone bright. At eight, the streets of Paris were already bustling below. And was it her imagination, or did she smell the delicious scent of chocolate and fresh bread baking?

Today was going to be good. She'd complete as much of the bucket list as she could, and she'd get to do it with Caleb.

Maybe they'd even get to finish what they started on the London Eye. If their flirting via text all week was any indication, her growing feelings for Caleb were mutual.

A knock reverberated in the room. She shook off her nerves and walked to the door, flinging it open. "Hey." Her attempt at a casual greeting resulted in a squawk. She cleared her throat.

Caleb stood with his hands in his jeans pockets, an easy smile on his face. "Hey, yourself." He gathered her in his arms and nuzzled his nose into her hair. "You smell good."

The electricity between them charged her whole body.

He pulled away and tilted his head. "Are you ready to venture out?"

Megan resisted the urge to throw herself back into his arms. "I am. Hang on." She dumped the rest of her coffee down the sink, tossed the cup in the garbage, and snatched her purse. "Crystal had to leave unexpectedly this morning, so it's just you and me."

"Is everything okay?"

"Oh yeah, just work stuff. She had to get back home." Megan gestured to the door, but Caleb stepped aside, indicating she should go first. The light pressure of his hand on her back guided her out.

"Sorry to hear that." They started walking toward the elevator bank.

"Are you?" Megan turned her face toward his and cocked an eyebrow.

He laughed. "I'm not sad to have you all to myself, but I'm guessing it must have been tough on you. I'm sorry for that."

She smiled and nudged him with her elbow. "It was at first. But we talked—all night, in fact—so I'm okay. Surprisingly, the idea of finishing my trip alone doesn't freak me out like I thought it would."

"I wouldn't exactly say you're alone."

"True." She reached out and squeezed his arm. "I'm glad you're here."

"So am I." He snatched her hand and held it all the way down the hallway, to the lobby, and onto the metro, where they caught a train to the stop nearest Notre Dame.

As they approached the white-washed building with two turrets reaching for the sky, Megan couldn't breathe.

And it had nothing to do with her physical condition—more like her spiritual one.

"It's gorgeous." She stared at the cathedral in front of her. Why was this different from all the other holy buildings she'd visited during this journey? Her neck hurt from craning, but something about it just made Megan long for . . . more.

"And you're only seeing one side." Caleb rested his hand against her back and led her around a bend. "You have to see the famous flying buttresses. And then the view from across the River Seine—it's magnificent."

Caleb was right. Each side had something different and new to offer. At first, she exclaimed with each discovery as she gazed up at the centuries-old church, but then she grew silent, just grateful to see it all for herself. "Let's go inside."

As they scooted through the doors, an ethereal sort of quiet struck. Sconces were lit along the various columns of the Gothic cathedral. The arched ceiling rose high above them, and her eyes were drawn to the front, where the pipes of a grand organ nestled just under a beautiful arched display of stained glass. People moved about the church, some filing into wooden seats, some gazing about in awe.

Yes, this was a tourist attraction, but it was more than that. It pulsed of something holy.

She got the feeling Caleb was watching her, so she swiveled her gaze toward him. "What?"

He leaned closer and whispered, "I'm just taking a mental picture of this moment."

"Why not take an actual photo? It'd last longer." She pointed to the professional camera slung around his neck.

"I seriously doubt that."

She gulped. There it was again, that serious tenor to his voice that told her they had a lot left to discuss.

"Come on. The mass is starting." Caleb tugged her gently toward a pair of seats near the back.

Megan had been to mass a few times with her grandmother as a child, so she was slightly familiar with some of the traditions, which were a lot different from her Baptist church back home. Still, when the entire service was in another language, it made it difficult to know what to do.

She and Caleb followed the crowd when people stood or sat, and she hummed along when she recognized a tune.

But mostly she allowed herself to finally try praying for the first time in forever.

Hey, God.

This feels so strange, to be talking to you so informally. To me, you've been this sovereign deity in the sky, someone with an iron will who decides what happens here on earth. And you are. And you do.

But I think maybe you're more than that.

My experiences have shaped how I view you—and how I view myself. Maybe I've been mad at you a little for making me weak. But how can I be mad at you when you turned around and saved me?

Although if you hadn't saved me, would I even be justified in being mad at you?

Would I still say you are trustworthy even if you hadn't saved me? Do I believe your trustworthiness—even your goodness—has to do with me? Or is it something steadfast, that can't be changed no matter what happens to me?

I don't have the answers. Maybe I never will. But I'm seeking.

As the mass continued, Megan quieted her soul. After all, as Nana used to say, *"You can't hear the Lord speak if you don't listen."* What she hoped to hear, she wasn't sure.

And then something in her shifted.

It was as if God was nudging her toward . . . something.

Like the nudging she'd felt when she'd wanted to wear a dress that exposed her scar. Or when she'd knocked on the Abbotts' front door, about to meet them for the first time. Or when she'd stood with Caleb on the London Eye, nearly kissing him.

Bravery. That was it, wasn't it? He was nudging her toward bravery. And she'd been resisting.

Resisting because she'd been afraid that she wasn't enough. That she could never be brave like Crystal. That she didn't have what it took to live life as an adventure.

But wasn't life an adventure in and of itself? Three and a half years ago, she hadn't thought she'd live long enough to find out. But God had given her back her life. He'd given her abilities, which should be used, not buried. And then opportunities had come along, like the chance to take this journey and write for Sheila Daily.

And once again, the ball was in her court. What would she do with these opportunities? Clutch her old weakness, or reach out for the new strength she was discovering in herself?

The mass ended and people rose to leave, but Megan stayed. Her hands remained in her lap, and she didn't realize she was biting her lip until she tasted the tiniest bit of blood.

Something was holding her back from the freedom to be found in bravery.

Her hands moved to her purse, unzipped it, reached in, and pulled out her notebook—the one with weeks and weeks of recorded heart rates. Beside her, Caleb remained silent, as if sensing she needed time. Megan ran her fingertips over the smooth surface of the notebook, filled with pages of useless knowledge.

This notebook wasn't keeping her safe. It was only a ritual to make herself feel better about the big, scary world of unknowns regarding her health.

Megan stood and laid the notebook on the seat where she'd been sitting. She held her hand out to Caleb. "Ready?"

He took her hand, and they walked together out the doors, into the sunshine of a day brimming with possibilities.

Chapter 32

25. Give my heart away.

I've always wanted to fall in love.

Of course, I wonder if someone like me could ever trust another person so completely that my secrets fall away and don't matter anymore. And even if trust wasn't an issue, how can I ever be brave enough to tell a guy all about my past?

The other day I asked Mom how she knew she loved my dad. Her answer still rings in my head: "He helps me be the bravest version of myself."

And so, I think in order for me to ever truly live, I will someday have to do the hardest thing of all: give my heart away.

Chapter 33

July 30

Blog Post Title: Crepes, the Eiffel Tower, and Fulfilling a Dream I Didn't Know I Had

Post Content:

The best things in life are the ones that surprise you . . .

She was almost done with the list. And then how would she go back to normal life?

Megan walked beside Caleb down the streets of Paris, pausing occasionally to browse the windows of bakeries and little gift shops. Yesterday, after visiting Notre Dame, they'd hopped a train to Versailles and explored King Louis XIV's garden and gilded palace. Even though it hadn't been on the list, Caleb had convinced her she simply had to see the smaller city. Since they had another day here in Paris, she'd consented. Today had been a flurry of sightseeing, and finally they were approaching the Eiffel Tower.

To complete Amanda's list, Megan only had to stand beneath the tower, observe its lights at night . . . and kiss a handsome stranger in the rain. Crystal was right. She might have to wait until she was home to finish the last item.

Although if the clouds on the horizon were any indication, she may have a chance to finish it tonight—if she could find a handsome guy willing to kiss a stranger.

And if she was willing to do it in front of Caleb. Ugh.

"I can't believe this is our last day here." A breeze kicked up, and Megan pulled her jacket tighter around her shoulders.

"I know. It's flown by." Caleb would leave tomorrow for his next photography assignment—an extended trek across Tibet that could last up to two months—and she'd return to Minnesota. Her new job would begin a few days later, and she'd dive back into reality.

Hopefully, all the things she'd experienced here wouldn't simply become distant memories. She wanted more than anything for the lessons she'd learned to become part of her life, and she fully intended to keep pursuing her dream of writing. It may go a little slower than she'd like, but she had a clear vision and wasn't going to let anything stop her this time.

"What are you looking forward to the most about Tibet?" She walked by a creperie, where a baker stood in the window creating crepes. He mixed batter in a bowl, then poured the thin delicacies onto a skillet. As a customer exited, Megan caught a whiff of sweetness and couldn't help but sigh. She yanked her gaze away and kept walking.

Caleb halted his pace and turned. "Did you want to get a crepe?"

"What? Oh, no." Despite all the temptations along this trip, she'd managed to avoid rich foods and stick to her strict diet. Giving up her notebook was one thing, but a diet change actually could wreck her physically. No sense in tempting fate on her last day here. "Let's keep going. The Eiffel Tower isn't too far ahead."

"The Eiffel Tower can wait. You can't leave Paris without eating a proper crepe." Caleb grabbed her hand and pulled her toward the creperie's door.

She tugged back. "No, really. It's fine."

"Megan, you're a stick. You can afford a little flour and sugar." Caleb pushed out his lip and widened his eyes in a pathetic attempt at a sad puppy face. "Pretty please?"

She couldn't help the laugh that bubbled from her. "Don't even try to pull that old trick."

"Oh, I'm trying." Caleb squeezed her hand. She tried to ignore the way it made her tingle. "But I won't force you. I guess some people just aren't real tourists, because a real tourist experiences all that a culture has to offer."

She rolled her eyes. "Fine. I'll have a tiny bite from your crepe. Happy?"

"I'll take it." They headed inside. Chocolate éclairs, croissants, muffins, and more were artfully arranged in a glass display case at the counter. "What kind do you want?"

"It's your crepe, remember?"

Caleb's mouth quirked to one side. "Right."

He indicated she should find a table and then headed to the counter to order. Megan located a booth in the corner, next to the window. As she waited for him to join her, the fading sunlight disappeared and the lights of the shops around them began to glow. Was this really the last night of her journey? She didn't want it to end.

She didn't want to return to real life. And she didn't want to leave Caleb.

"Here you go." Caleb slid into the booth across from Megan and placed a platter with a rolled crepe at the center. It was filled with sliced bananas and drizzled with chocolate and powdered sugar.

She picked up a fork and carefully slid it through the crepe, sure to snag a banana. One small bite wouldn't hurt, right?

"What are you so afraid of?"

"Getting sick again." The answer popped out so fast she didn't have time to think about it. Her eyes met Caleb's, and understanding gazed back at her.

"I get it. But one crepe won't do that to you."

"My doctor said I should maintain a healthy diet and exercise. I want to do everything in my power to never return to that hospital room, Caleb."

"Hey." He reached across the table and grabbed her hand, something he'd been doing a lot lately. He ran his thumb over her knuckles one by one. "If anyone understands, it's me. But I decided several years ago not to let my condition rule my life. I eat healthy, because, yeah, it's important. But if a bad heart didn't kill us, the occasional indulgence certainly won't."

She paused. "I know it's stupid to feel this way, but if there's any way to prevent going through that again, I will."

His calloused thumb continued over the ridges of her hand. "It's not stupid at all. We've been through something others can't understand. But what are you gaining by keeping such a tight hold? God chose to spare your life. Don't waste it by not really living."

What he said nearly matched her thoughts at Notre Dame word for word.

The tears built behind her eyes. But no. She wasn't going to cry. This once, she'd stay strong. "It's just a dumb crepe."

But it wasn't. It was a symbol. Just like exposing her scar. Just like leaving her notebook behind. Each one was a loosening, a flinging away of the old Megan.

With her free hand, she picked up the fork again and shoved a bite of the pastry into her mouth. And oh, the sweetness that popped on her tongue. The chocolate and banana blended together perfectly, and she might have moaned a little as she savored every moment until swallowing.

Caleb nodded and grinned. "Told you."

"Hush." She offered him a bite, and he pulled it off the fork with his teeth. Then she speared herself another piece and they ate, talked, and laughed until it was gone.

Megan stood. "Let's go check off another item on this list."

Caleb followed her out the door. He shoved his hands back into his pockets, and they continued toward the Eiffel Tower. The monument got closer and closer, until it loomed over them in all its grandeur. The white lights were striking against the black sky, and something about standing underneath this tower—well, she felt invincible.

As she lifted her face skyward, a drop of water hit her on the forehead. "Uh-oh."

"What?"

"I think I felt—" The sky interrupted her with a release of rain. Megan shrieked and looked for cover.

Caleb pointed to a nearby restaurant and threw his arm around her, as if he could keep her dry. They took a few steps, but Megan halted. "Wait." This was the perfect opportunity. Except for the fact that Caleb was here.

There was no perfect answer. She just had to finish the list.

Her eyes darted around, but she couldn't find anyone nearby who wasn't racing for shelter, much less a handsome stranger.

"What are you doing?"

Megan's wet hair stuck to her face. "I have to find someone to kiss."

Caleb stopped trying to drag her to dryness and warmth. He tilted his head. "Uh, what?"

He must not have seen the full list she'd posted online. "For Amanda's bucket list. The last item—I have to kiss a stranger in the rain." The rain pounded on the sidewalk, and she felt like she was shouting. "I thought I'd have to wait until I got home, but it's raining, and it's the last night, almost like it's a sign. Maybe I'm supposed to get the whole thing done now."

"You have to kiss a stranger?" A shadow passed over his eyes, that same look he got whenever Megan's nurse had made him return to his room during one of their late-night visits in the hospital.

She shrugged. "Forget it. There's no one around anyway. Come on." Megan started walking toward the restaurant, the water squishing between her toes inside her shoes.

"Megan, wait."

She turned. The rain ran down his cheeks and drenched his white shirt and jacket, defining the muscles in his broad chest. His hair was plastered to his forehead. He was a mess.

An achingly handsome mess.

She rejoined him. "What?" Her teeth chattered.

He pulled her into his arms. "You're freezing."

She laid her head on his chest, soaking in his warmth. "I know."

"And you're supposed to kiss a stranger in the rain." Despite the din of honking cars and the onslaught of rain, she could hear his heartbeat beneath his chest—rapid, like hers.

"Yes."

"What about me?"

She pulled her head up and gazed up at him. "Did you miss the part where I said a stranger? You're not a stranger."

"I sort of am. We both have new hearts, so that makes us different people than we were when we first met. And this journey has changed you— you aren't the same girl I knew in the hospital. And I'm not the same guy."

Megan couldn't peel her eyes away from him. "You want to kiss me?"

"Do I have a pulse?" Caleb stared down at her. "Any man would be crazy not to."

Oh.

At the moment she didn't really care if it counted for the list or not. But maybe it could. The heart she'd heard beating only moments ago, it was new to her. This Caleb—he meant more to her than he ever had before. Together, they were strangers, on the edge of embarking on a new journey.

She held his steady gaze, the rain clinging to his eyelashes. Every nerve in her body was on fire despite the cold. And then she felt that inner nudging again, toward bravery, toward life. Toward Caleb.

"Meg? Say something."

"Shut up and kiss me."

Caleb grinned and bent his face toward her. His lips covered hers, and suddenly she wasn't standing still but flying. Caleb's arms traveled from her waist up her arms, up her neck, to her cheeks. He held her face delicately in his hands and pulled away to look down into her eyes. "Hi. I'm Caleb. It's nice to meet you."

"I'm Megan." She placed her hands on top of his. "And *that* was the best greeting of my life."

Crystal straightened the stack of proposal copies on the conference table for the fifth time. The room was empty, but in just a few minutes, the twelve seats in front of her would be filled by Jeff Lerner and his associates, not to mention Tony and at least one other partner.

She paced the room and picked a stray piece of lint off her black blazer. Her heels clicked on the tile floor as she walked to the window. The room could use some more light. With a flick of her wrist, Crystal pushed a button and the blinds opened, revealing a hazy New York summer day. The skyline always took her breath away, but today it lacked a little something. Perhaps that was a natural result of traveling. She'd now be comparing Manhattan to Rome, Paris, and London—the other great cities of the world.

In the window's reflection she could see herself. The humidity in the room and outside was enough to make even her straight hair frizz a bit, but she'd done her best to ensure a professional appearance. There would be no repeat of her last presentation in this room. Today she was refreshed, ulcer-free, and ready to tackle the next stage of her career.

On the table, her phone buzzed. Crystal darted to see who had texted her. It was from Brian:

Good luck on your presentation today. I love you and am proud of you, no matter what the result. Dinner at Le Chalet at six? Then maybe afterward we can relive Edinburgh.

Her heart fluttered at the memory of their last night together. She hadn't seen him since arriving home, as he'd been starting a twenty-four-hour shift when she landed. Though she'd swung by the station on her way into the office, he'd been out on a call. She'd eaten a late dinner at the office with Tony and Meredith instead. Her arms ached to be wrapped around Brian again. They still had plenty to discuss, but her heart was feeling more ready than ever to move forward.

A smile flit across her lips as she wrote her reply:

I'll be there. Be prepared for the night of your life.

His response came swift:

Can't wait.

"What are you so happy about?" Tony walked into the room, glasses lowered to the tip of his nose.

"I'm just prepared for a great presentation, that's all."

"Good." Tony checked his watch. "Where is Meredith? She should be getting—"

"Right here, boss." Meredith careened into the room, her arms stacked high with presentations bound in the same folders as Crystal's. Crystal hadn't had a chance to look at Meredith's design in detail, but she couldn't help overhearing the whispers of adoration some of the first-year associates had spouted in the break room earlier this morning.

At six feet tall, Meredith didn't need the three-inch heels she wore, but coupled with her fresh new suit, they gave her a commanding presence.

She flashed Crystal a smile, as if to say, "May the best woman win."

"Excuse me, sir?" Jamie, the intern, stuck her head into the conference room. "Your one o'clock is here."

"Perfect." Tony rose. "I'll be back, ladies."

In the moments while he was gone, Crystal and Meredith double- and triple-checked that the projector and computer were functioning properly. Then Tony led in a group of men and one woman. "Mr. Lerner, I'm pleased to introduce two of my architects, Crystal Ballinger and Meredith Wilson."

Jeff Lerner was younger and much more casual than Crystal had imagined, given his amount of success and his net worth. He looked to be in his late thirties, early forties, wearing jeans, a Beatles T-shirt, and a blazer. He came forward and shook both of their hands, his wide grin evidence of his good will. "It's so nice to meet you all. Let me introduce my associates." He rattled off the names of his six male associates and then turned to the woman. "And this lovely lady is my wife, Jenny."

The shy woman bowed her head toward them and held out her dainty hand. She seemed younger than Mr. Lerner, closer to Crystal's age. It was highly unusual for a business meeting to include a wife, but perhaps she worked on Lerner's team.

"Now that introductions are complete, why don't you all take a seat and get comfortable?" Tony motioned toward the chairs, and everyone did as he asked. At the last moment Steven Perretti, another partner, slipped in and stood in the back of the room. "We know how valuable your time is, Mr. Lerner, so we prepared two separate pitches to give you a taste of the different designs our firm can support."

"That sounds wonderful. Pitch away."

Tony nodded and turned to Meredith. "Meredith, why don't you start us off?"

Meredith grinned a thousand-watt smile and picked up her stack of proposals. She passed them around and launched into her pitch to convert the James Lawrence building and surrounding area into a highly modern community, one with the feel of IKEA on steroids. It was very well designed, and Meredith had thought of everything, even a state-of-the-art indoor park where children could simultaneously play and learn. Throughout the presentation, Crystal peeked at the client to gauge his reaction. He seemed to be tracking with Meredith and her design.

After Meredith finished her spiel, Lerner and his associates asked numerous questions. Crystal's pants began to cling to the back of her sweaty legs. She had to remain calm, something that was a whole lot easier before she'd gotten in touch with her emotions.

At long last, her turn arrived. She popped out of her chair and threw everyone a practiced smile. "Thank you for that amazing presentation, Meredith." She passed Lerner's team her own proposal. "When I thought about this community, I considered where I would want to live. I thought about what made something a home—because if you don't feel at home in your community, where can you?"

The smiles and nods gave her courage to continue. "Then I thought about where I currently live, and how unaccommodating it is to that idea of community. Not because people are unfriendly but because there aren't many places to gather and foster the community people crave. I live in a typical flat in New York City, after all."

She flipped to the next slide of her presentation, which included a map of the proposed property. "One thing you'll notice about my design is that I took great care to incorporate several opportunities for true community, especially spaces that people can make their own. For example, mural walls where they can claim their place in the community permanently. Within the houses themselves, big gathering spaces instead of tiny nooks no one ever uses. Et cetera."

She continued explaining her ideas, referring less to her presentation and speaking more from her heart. Megan would be proud of her. "The James Lawrence building has held a special place in my heart for a long time, and I would consider it an honor to help realize its full potential."

"This is all extremely interesting." Mr. Lerner leaned forward, elbows on the table and chin in his hands. "Tell me, what inspired this design?"

"I just returned from a fabulous trip to Europe with my sister." Crystal couldn't help using her hands to emphasize her emotions. She could literally feel the passion bursting from her fingertips. "There I was struck by the idea of the old and new mingled together, how there was a perfect harmony to it. How the new kept things interesting but the old provided the lasting effect that we want for our lives. And that's the essence of this community." She tapped the proposal. "I would want to live here."

"And so would I." Mrs. Lerner—Jenny, was it?—straightened in her chair, and her eyes shone with something indescribable. She turned to her husband. "Jeff, this is it."

Mr. Lerner patted his wife's hands where they were folded on the table. He turned back to Meredith, Tony, and Crystal. "I didn't tell you this, but we are planning to be the first residents of this new community. I know it's often not smart to mix business and pleasure, but we haven't found a community that holds all the values we want. We longed for something fresh, but as Jenny likes to remind me, not everything new and modern is always a good thing."

Meredith shifted in her chair.

"With that said, we would like to partner with you to get the design finalized and get the building of this community under way." Lerner smiled wide as he looked at Crystal. "The second design, that is."

"I'm so pleased to hear that." Crystal could barely say the words without her voice cracking.

She'd done it.

They all shook hands. Tony would send the contract that afternoon, and Mr. Lerner would sign it once his lawyers looked it over. Then Crystal would work closely with his team to get a final design approved before construction began.

Jenny Lerner approached Crystal. A tear skimmed down her cheek. "Thank you. I couldn't have envisioned a more perfect place to raise my children."

"You are so welcome." Crystal tilted her head. "How many do you have?"

"Oh, none yet." Jenny's cheeks tinged pink. "But hopefully soon. How about you?"

"Kids?" Her conversation with Brian in the Edinburgh park rose to her mind. They hadn't broached the subject again, hadn't come to any conclusions yet—just exposed her fears for what they were and left them writhing on the floor of her heart. "No. We haven't . . . I'm not sure . . ."

"I'm sorry. It wasn't my place to ask." Jenny

squeezed Crystal's arm. "Thank you again." She turned and joined her husband and his entourage.

Jenny's presence had brought a certain lightness to the room, but as soon as she left, it was stuffy again. But why should it be? Crystal should be on cloud nine. Everything she'd wanted to achieve, she had. The reality settled in. She turned to Tony. "Well?"

He glanced at Perretti, who nodded. He grinned and stuck out a hand. "I'm pleased to offer you the position of senior architect, complete with a new office, salary raise, and some new responsibilities."

"Really?"

"Really."

A thrill raced through her, strong and sure. She took Tony's hand and pumped it up and down, then threw her arms around him in a fierce bear hug.

Tony pulled back and threw another grin downward. "Since when are you a hugger?"

"I've changed, Tony. Haven't you noticed?"

"I have." Her boss stroked his beard. "Hopefully enough to get out of here early to celebrate?"

"Sure. That'd be fun. I have dinner plans at six, but we can hang out until then."

"Perfect. I've got to get that contract sent off, and then I'll round up the troops. Let's aim for four." At her agreement, he headed back out the door and down the hallway toward his office.

The rest of the room had already cleared. She snatched her phone and called Brian—voice mail. He must be at the gym or something. Crystal walked back to her cubicle and sat down. Though her head was racing with all the possibilities, she should probably tackle any e-mails that awaited her attention.

Crystal fired up her computer and started working. Before she knew it, she looked up and the clock said 5:02. "Oh no." She stood and headed down the hallway to Tony's office. "Did you see what time it is?"

Her boss glanced at his computer clock. "Yikes. Sorry. There was a bit of a hold up from legal on the contract so it took longer than expected. Let's go now."

She couldn't miss her dinner with Brian. "I have plans at six."

Tony waved his hand in the air. "Cancel. This is a big day. People have probably already left for the bar. Plus, you've worked for this for years. It's time to celebrate."

"I haven't seen Brian since I got home."

"Invite him to join us." Her boss put his laptop into a bag and gathered his keys, wallet, and other belongings from his desk drawer. "I'll round up any stragglers and we'll head to Smith's on Fifth."

What could she say? The entire office had made plans to celebrate her promotion. She'd have to get creative. "Give me a second to let Brian know."

She walked down the hallway, pulled out her cell phone, and dialed.

"Hey, Crys. How did it go?"

"Did you see my voice mail?"

"No, sorry. I was out running errands and must have missed it. So?"

"I did it. I landed the account—and got the promotion."

"I knew you could do it. I'm so proud of you." He paused. "I'm dressed and about to head out the door for dinner. I want to be sure they've got our special table reserved like I requested. Sounds like we have even more to celebrate than you returning home."

She chewed her lip. He wasn't going to like this. "I really hate to do this, but is there any way we can move it back a bit? Or reschedule for tomorrow night? My team is going out for drinks to celebrate."

His silence said volumes. Then, "I haven't seen you yet and I'm on the schedule tomorrow."

"That's right. I forgot." She pulled her hair from behind her shoulder and wrapped it around her finger. "I don't know what to do, Brian. I want to go to dinner with you but—"

"So come to dinner with me, Crys."

"It's not that simple. Everyone has already headed over to the bar."

"Let them celebrate without you for once."

"They're celebrating me! I have to be there." Why couldn't he understand? But it probably looked like the old Crystal flaring up. "This isn't like before. I'm not doing it to get ahead. I just think it's impolite to stand everyone up."

"Except you're standing me up."

She cringed. He was right. But before she could respond, Tony came around the corner, coat flung over his forearm and laptop bag over his shoulder. He gestured toward the elevators and mouthed, "Let's go."

Crystal held up a finger. If everyone could just give her a moment to think . . .

"You know what, Crys. It's fine. Just go to the bar. We'll talk when you get home."

Something in his tone flashed a warning to her brain, but the impatient look on Tony's face held a warning of a different kind.

"I'll make it up to you tonight. I promise. And I'll try to get out of there as quickly as possible."

Brian hung up without saying good-bye. For a moment Crystal just stared at her phone.

Tony cleared his throat. "Ready?"

One hour, max. That's all she'd stay. Enough time to throw back a glass of wine and bond with her team. Then she'd scurry home to Brian, and she could show him this was just an anomaly.

She wasn't the same person who'd left over a month ago. She'd changed, and this scenario didn't prove otherwise.

"Ready."

Crystal followed Tony out of the office and toward Smith's on Fifth, her heart pleading with her to go the opposite direction.

Chapter 34

The rain had stopped about twenty minutes ago, but Caleb had yet to release Megan's hand. After that magical moment beneath the lights of the Eiffel Tower, he'd pointed to the top. "Let's go up."

"It's not on the list. We don't have to."

"Isn't the list done?"

"Yes." Megan had expected a rush of relief, but it wasn't there—it was probably just covered by other more prominent emotions right now.

"Then it's time to start making your own list."

They'd stepped inside a store to wait out the rain. The owner passed them a few towels and they'd dried off as best they could. Then they'd hit the street again and got in line to ride the elevator to the top level of the Eiffel Tower. Once they'd ascended, Megan was struck by the brilliance of the city. She and Caleb were much higher than they'd been in London, and the city stretched as far as her eyes could see. The rain had left a crispness in the air that spoke of new beginnings.

Megan approached the railing. Caleb came up behind her and settled his arms around her waist, resting his chin on the top of her head so she was thoroughly nestled against him. Years ago, she would have thought it the strangest thing in the world to be standing with her best friend like this. But now . . . it would feel strange not to.

"How long, Caleb?"

"Till what?"

"No. I mean, how long have you wanted to do that?"

"Since the first day we met."

She pulled away so he was beside her and she could see him, his arms still around her waist. "Be serious."

"You don't think I am? Megan, I've had a crush on you since day one. But I was pretty sure you never looked at me twice in that way." He leaned toward her and planted another kiss on her lips, soft and sweet. "I still can't believe it's real."

"Me either." Her head felt fuzzy and her heart leaped.

Caleb turned his attention to the horizon. "Look at that, Meg."

"What?" There was so much to see.

"All of it. The flickering lights. The stark darkness higher in the sky. The way it hums and moves and breathes. The city is alive."

Clouds moved to reveal the full moon. It seemed bigger and more radiant from up here. "Hmm, you're right."

"This is the view of the rest of your life if you want it." Caleb's warm breath brushed over her skin at his whispered words.

"I do. I do want it."

"Then come with me to Tibet."

"What?" She veered back from him, the magic of their stolen moments broken. "And do what, exactly?"

"Write the stories I'm photographing. Just like we always planned."

Oh, Caleb.

She couldn't put off telling him about her new job any longer. "I wish I could, but I committed to taking an assistant librarian position and I start later this week." She told him the basics about the job.

"Is that really what you want to be doing with your life?"

He leaned in and touched her forehead with his own. Oh, she could get lost in those eyes.

"I don't plan to stay there forever. This job is merely a stepping stone. Plus, I made a commitment. I can't back out now."

"Sure you can. Tell your boss that you've changed your mind."

He didn't make it easy on a girl. "Even if I felt okay about doing that, I have the rest of my hospital bills to repay. That's reality."

"I'm not suggesting you live like a pauper." Caleb pulled back and frowned. "I actually get paid pretty well. All my travel expenses are paid for, and I make money on top of that. You would too."

"But you work freelance jobs, right? That doesn't sound very stable. I need a job I can count on." Sure, Mom and Dad didn't require rent, but she'd like to be able to move out sooner than later. And she couldn't do that till the bills were paid.

One thing at a time. Her dreams would fall into place eventually.

"It's stable enough. God's provided everything I need, Meg."

"That may be, but there are other factors we didn't consider when we were kids. Don't you ever worry about traveling places where there aren't any heart specialists? Are there even adequate hospitals in Tibet? What if you relapse while trekking across the Tibetan Plateau?"

"I could relapse anytime, anywhere. But I don't want to let fear dictate my actions."

"I don't either." Nothing was as terrifying as the thought of relapsing—but there was a difference between trusting God to provide and being needlessly reckless. "But it's something to think about."

Caleb's hands moved to grip the railing in front of them, the veins bulging. "Megan, I love my life, and I don't mind the risks. But it's always been missing something. You. We dreamed this dream together. Don't you want it anymore? Are you really okay with just returning home and giving up?"

Now, hold on. "I thought long and hard about whether to take this job. It's not about giving up. It's about being practical and taking the next step. I still plan to work on my writing on the side. Meanwhile, I'll be paying off my bills."

"But you could be doing both at the same time if you came with me."

Something about Caleb's proposal made her want to leap forward without thinking. Something else held her back. "I have responsibilities. I can't back out on the job, which means I can't go with you to Tibet."

This was all moving too quickly. She couldn't think straight. "But maybe I could look at my schedule once I'm settled at the library, and we could plan a trip together, doing exactly what we always said we'd do. Little by little, we could work toward our dream."

"Lying in that hospital, we had nothing but time to make plans. And now that we can live them out, why wait?" She felt the pressure of his hand on her shoulder and moved to face him again. "Besides, how do I know that you won't stand me up like you did in London the first time?"

That comment knocked the wind from her. He'd forgiven her—but clearly, the fear of rejection hadn't been forgotten. "I wouldn't do that. Not now. Especially not now." Not when things between them had changed so much.

Behind them, a guard called out a five-minute warning. The tower would be closing soon.

"You don't know what you'll do once you've returned to your old life."

She wanted to argue, but words failed to come. What if he was right?

Her arms twitched, wanting to reach out and touch him again. She dug her hands into her jacket pockets. "I don't know what to say. Can't we just figure this out once I'm home?"

He stared at her for a moment, his jaw taut. "I don't think that's a good idea. For years I've dreamed of this, of us. And now it feels like we're at an impasse. If we leave things open-ended . . . Well, I just can't keep the hope alive anymore, Meg."

Oh, how her heart hurt as it tugged her two ways: toward Caleb and adventure, and back home to responsibility . . . and safety.

And suddenly she couldn't stay here anymore. Her newfound courage had fled.

"I'm sorry. I'm so sorry. Be well, Caleb. Take care of yourself. I . . ." She turned and slipped into the elevator just as it was closing. It descended quickly, pulling her back down to earth. As soon as the doors opened, she shoved through the crowd and flew down the street toward her hotel.

What was wrong with her? After all she'd conquered, why was she running?

It was Caleb's words: *"You don't know what you'll do once you've returned to your old life."* That was the crux of it, wasn't it? It was nothing to go on a trip and complete someone else's bucket list, to live out someone else's dreams—not when compared to quitting everything that was comfortable and familiar and trying to live out her own. She thought she'd come so far, but it had all been a farce, not a real test of courage at all.

Megan started to run down the streets of Paris, zigzagging between parked cars, people, animals, whatever lay in her path. She splashed through puddles, mud bursting up to hit her pants.

But she couldn't outrun the fear.

Which meant one thing. All those years ago, her mom had been right. Megan had a weak heart.

And it had nothing to do with the one beating inside her chest. Even though it had seemed like God was urging her toward courage and strength, she didn't have what it took to be truly brave.

Crystal couldn't believe it was ten o'clock and she still wasn't home.

She clutched her purse in her lap as she swayed with the movement of the subway train. She glanced at her watch again and groaned. They hadn't arrived at the bar until closer to five thirty. And of course, everyone wanted to buy her a drink. Several glasses of wine later, Crystal had a throbbing headache.

At least five times Crystal had risen to head home, worried about what Brian was thinking, but another partner would appear or her coworkers would force her to do karaoke with them or something else would prevent her from leaving.

Once she'd finally peeled away from them all, she discovered the subway was under construction on her normal route. She'd had to detour and then was stuck on the train for nearly an hour waiting for some accident to clear. A text letting Brian know her predicament received silence in return.

She prayed with everything in her that he'd understand.

Finally, the subway arrived at her stop, and she jumped from her seat and flew out the doors and up the stairs as quickly as her heeled pumps would let her. From there she ran home, despite the blisters forming on her toes. When she swung the front door of her flat open, darkness met her. A meow was the only greeting she received, and then Sybil was rubbing against her legs. Maybe Brian was already asleep or not here at all. Crystal headed through the apartment's living room and kitchen, toward the bedroom.

And there he was. He sat nearly motionless on the edge of the bed, staring at the ground.

"Brian?" Did he hear the fear in her voice?

His head turned toward her, robotic, mechanical.

"How was the celebration?" His tone cut her with its mixture of exhaustion, loneliness, and disappointment.

With a wince, she flipped on the light and sank down next to him on the bed.

He moved to the chair in the corner. The separation made her ache.

"Brian, look at me. Please."

She could see the struggle play across his features, but he refused.

"I was only going to stay an hour, but things got . . . complicated. Will you forgive me?"

"I don't know how."

"I'm sorry. Believe me, I wanted nothing more than to be here with you. But people kept arriving as I was trying to leave and . . ." The excuses sounded so lame even as they left her lips.

He ran his hand along the back of his neck. "It doesn't sound like you'd do anything differently." His voice wasn't angry. It was breaking. "You wouldn't choose me over them."

"I was in a tough spot, people pulling at me from all sides." Her own words pinched at her nerves. "That came out wrong. Of course our marriage is more important. But this was a one-time thing, Brian. I'll do better about making our time together a priority. I promise."

"The thing about promises—you have to keep them occasionally, or people stop believing you."

Ouch. "I'm trying. I really am."

Brian stood and headed toward their closet. He wheeled out a suitcase. His suitcase. There were tears in his eyes.

Whoa, what? Crystal shot to her feet. "What's that for?"

"I'm leaving."

"You can't leave. I just got home."

"And what's changed?" He stopped, dragging his hand across his jaw. "I can't stay here, just hoping things will be different. I thought the trip would change things. After Edinburgh, I thought we'd finally gotten back a piece of us we'd lost. Sure, it wasn't perfect, but it was progress. But you're back and the first chance you got, you threw it all away."

"You're right. I screwed up. I'm sorry." She approached and tentatively touched his arm. "Give me another chance."

"Crys, I love you more than anything on this planet." His voice broke, and his chest shuddered.

His words gave her hope, made her bold. She threw her arms around him. "Then please. Stay." Her vision clouded, and she buried her face in his strong form.

With gentle hands, Brian unwrapped her arms. "I thought maybe, after all this, we wanted the same things. But *this* is not the life I want. I want to know . . ." He backhanded a tear. Oh, sweet man. How she'd wounded him. She'd take it all back if she could.

He blew out a breath. "I want to know that my wife cares just as much as I do about what happens to this marriage."

Every word he said was a barb, and she no longer had a wall around her heart to stop them from piercing deep. "I do care. I swear, Brian. I will make it up to you."

"Actions speak louder than words. You can't make up for it, Crys."

But that's what she'd thought with Megan— and Megan had forgiven her. Brian would too. Wouldn't he?

"That opportunity for joy? It's gone. Maybe forever." He whispered those last words.

"Forever? What do you mean?" He couldn't be saying . . . Surely, he didn't want a divorce.

His jaw ticked. "I don't know."

"How will things get better if you go?" She reached for his hand, but his stayed by his side. Eventually she dropped her own, then tucked it underneath her other arm.

"I don't know if they will." His voice was sad. So very sad. He grabbed the handle of his suitcase and started down the hallway toward the front door.

Crystal hurried after him. She wasn't giving up without a fight. "Wait."

Brian turned, shoulder slumped.

"You can't leave. I won't let you."

"Oh, Crys." He shook his head. "When are you

going to learn? You don't control everything."
He turned and went through the front door, into
the hallway—and maybe out of her life for good.

And there wasn't one thing she could do to stop
him.

Chapter 35

The nine-hour flight from Paris to JFK International had been torture. Pure torture.

The guy next to her had snored really loud. The couple across the aisle wouldn't stop making out. And Megan had stared at her computer screen the whole time, willing the words for her final blog post and article to come. She had a deadline with Sheila, after all. But it was too painful to relive.

The deadline came and went.

Yes. Torture.

The original plan had been to fly straight home after her last day in Paris, but she wasn't ready for that. The irony. She wasn't ready to move forward with Caleb, but she also couldn't fathom moving back in with Mom and Dad.

She'd stopped in New York to see Crystal instead.

Her sister didn't know she was coming. Megan had tried calling her, but couldn't get her on the phone. It'd just have to be a surprise, one she hoped Crystal and Brian didn't mind.

Megan approached their apartment—Mom had been more than happy to supply Crystal's address, adding, "I'm so glad you're finally visiting her" for good measure—and lifted her hand to knock on the red door. The sound reverberated in the empty hallway. Megan checked her watch: 6:00 p.m. Hopefully Crystal was home from work. If not, Megan would just go find a quiet coffee shop and try not to fall asleep.

Nothing happened on the other side of the door. Maybe her knock hadn't been heard. She pounded again, a little louder.

"Megan?" She twirled around to find Crystal in the hallway behind her, briefcase clutched in one hand, keys in the other. "What are you doing here?"

"Surprise."

Her sister bit her lip, then pulled Megan into a hug.

"I'm sorry to intrude. I tried calling. Just thought I'd stop and see you on my way home. And . . ." Megan's voice warbled, but Crystal didn't seem to notice her distress.

Crystal let go of Megan, put the keys in the lock, and opened the door. "It's good to see you. Come on in." Her sister snatched one of Megan's suitcases and rolled it inside.

Megan followed with her other luggage. As they made their way into the living room, she checked out Crystal's chic apartment with yellow curtains, black leather furniture, and granite countertops.

"Did you get my message? I was hoping to stay the night." Megan plopped onto the love seat. "But I can find a hotel if it's not convenient for you."

"No, I didn't see it. But don't be ridiculous." Crystal took Megan's things down the hall and after a few moments emerged from a room to the right. She lowered herself onto the arm of the couch. "I'm glad you're here. You just took me by surprise."

"If you're sure. Do you want to go out for dinner? I haven't eaten yet."

"We could order in." Crystal picked up her phone. "Chinese okay?"

"Even better." Megan removed her flats and stuck them under the coffee table. "Will Brian be home soon?"

Her sister paused, and Megan thought she saw a tick in her jaw. But Crystal just shook her head. "No."

"Gotcha." Maybe he was working. Or maybe there was more to the story.

The room grew silent as Crystal perused her phone. "There's a new place right up the road. I'm going to call. What would you like?"

"How about beef and broccoli?"

Crystal nodded and dialed to order the food. Megan found the guest room and changed into her pajama pants and a T-shirt. She texted their parents to let them know she'd landed safely and would head their way tomorrow. After a quick glance at her e-mail, she saw several from Sheila Daily. Cringing, she opened the most recent message.

Megan,

I'm surprised you missed your deadline and didn't let me know why. You've ignored my calls and e-mails, and I can only assume you've had some sort of emergency. Write or call me to let me know you're okay, will you? And please let me know when you can turn in your last article. I know readers will be anxious to see your list completed.

Sheila

Sheila thought Megan had had an emergency. How could she tell her the truth—that she'd missed the deadline simply because it hurt too much to put her heart on the page at this moment?

Megan clicked Reply, but after a few minutes, she deleted the empty draft and closed the laptop lid.

Crystal stuck her head into the room. "Want to help me bake cookies?"

"Sure." Maybe Megan would even eat one. But as soon as the thought came, an image of eating crepes with Caleb surfaced. Would everything remind her of him now?

Megan followed Crystal into her kitchen. Crystal opened the fridge and dug around, emerging with butter and eggs. Then she rummaged in her cabinets for flour, baking soda, salt, and sugar. She got out a few plastic mixing bowls and began measuring and dumping.

"Why are you here, Megan?" She didn't look up, just kept measuring and dumping, measuring and dumping.

"Seeing my sister wasn't enough of a reason?"

At that, Crystal looked up and quirked an eyebrow. "I'm glad to see you, but it seems like there's something else on your mind."

"Fine." Megan picked up a hand mixer, and Crystal handed her the bowl. The whir of the mixer filled the small kitchen as Megan beat the butter and sugar together. They blended together into a creamy base. "I wasn't ready to face my life post-adventure."

"Post-adventure?" Crystal cracked an egg into the bowl. "Or post-Caleb?"

Megan positioned the mixer over the egg and watched as it flew apart, melding with the creamed butter. "Both."

"What happened?"

Megan told her everything. As she let go of the story, cookie dough slowly formed in the bowl with the addition of flour and the other ingredients. "I so badly wanted to be strong and brave, but I just couldn't say yes to him."

"He was asking a lot of you, so it's not like you were wrong to say no." Crystal reached for the bowl. She gripped a spatula and folded chocolate chips into the dough. Her folding quickly became stirring—rather vigorous stirring. "Though sometimes the men in our life ask for something very reasonable, and if you say no, even without meaning to, you can end up ruining your life."

Her voice broke, and the bowl slipped from her fingers onto the tile floor. Crystal just stared at the splattered cookie dough but didn't move to clean it up.

Megan blinked in rapid succession and studied her sister. "Why do I feel like we're not talking about me anymore?"

Crystal finally reached for paper towels. She bunched them in her hand and sank to her knees, but didn't move to actually wipe up the mess in front of her.

"Sis? What's going on?" Megan had been so wrapped up in her own misery, she'd missed something. Something big. She knelt, grabbed some of the towels from Crystal's hands, and swiped the floor, capturing stray pieces of dough.

Crystal rocked back on her knees and sat, leaning her head against the cabinets. Her hands still clutched a few clean towels. "My marriage is falling apart. Brian . . . He left me yesterday."

"What do you mean, left you?"

"I think he might want a divorce." Crystal continued to stare at the overturned bowl.

Megan righted the plastic bowl and put her dirty paper towels inside. She eased the rest out of Crystal's grasp, then placed the bowl onto the counter above them. "I'm sure that's not true. I saw how in love you two are."

"That's not enough."

Crystal told her about the promotion, and their fights, and all the trouble that had led up to that moment. She'd been holding on to so much pain and till now, Megan hadn't even known she needed comfort.

"I've ruined everything."

Megan squeezed Crystal's arm. "You made a mistake." She pulled her knees to her chest. The tile was cold under her bare feet. "He'll realize it and come around."

"Maybe."

They were both quiet for a while.

Then Crystal turned to Megan. "I didn't mean to make this conversation about me." Her voice was soft. "Back to you. You said you wanted to be strong and brave. That made me think. When we were in Rome, at the Colosseum, our tour guide said something profound about strength. Maybe it would help you to hear it."

"What did he say?"

"Essentially that we can't be truly strong on our own. That there's another source of strength out there. I still don't know where I stand with God, but you seem to have a stronger faith than I do." Another squeeze. "Anyway, I think he was saying that God wants nothing more than to restore us, whatever that means."

Megan had originally thought God made her weak. And then she'd been sure that he was calling her to be strong.

Was it possible he was calling her to something else entirely?

She couldn't lay here in their bed and smell his cologne for one minute longer.

Crystal sat and tugged her hair free from the ponytail holder. It fell around her shoulders, and she brushed the tangles with her fingertips. She flipped on her bedside light, flooding the room. Then she pulled a notebook and pen from the side table. Megan slept in the room next door, so Crystal was quiet as she crept to the rocking chair.

Pen poised over the paper, she finally thought of the perfect title for her list: *Operation Get Him Back*.

And then she thought. And considered. And debated with herself.

Two hours passed and she still didn't have a single clue how to get Brian to come home. It was like the Lerner proposal all over again.

She was stuck.

She tore the paper from the notebook, crumpled it, and tossed it to the ground. Crystal grit her teeth against the tears threatening to spill. No. She wouldn't. Not this time. The last time she'd given free rein to her emotions, they'd strangled her. She wouldn't, couldn't go back there.

Except, how did she close the floodgates when an entire ocean of love and raw regret pounded against them?

Crystal stood and wandered to the closet. She felt for the light and flicked it on. Brian's side was mostly empty, but he'd left his cooler-weather items behind. She lifted a gray sweater from the hanger, pulling it over her head. This was the sweater he'd had on when he proposed. It made the blue rings around his eyes pop. Crystal clutched a mound of the fabric and brought it to her nose, inhaling the scent of her husband.

Though he may not be her husband for much longer.

She sank to the closet floor and leaned against the wall, but something jutted into her back. "Ow." Crystal turned and saw an old box with *Crystal's Stuff* written in bold permanent marker across the top. Curious, she worked back the flap, and her eyes met the item on top—an antique jewelry box Nana had given her before she'd died. Crystal hadn't thought about this old thing in years.

Carefully, she extricated the box and examined it. It was pink and delicate, with inlaid gold panels. She remembered seeing it in Nana's room when she was a child, opening it and watching the tiny ballerina inside start dancing. Over and over again, she'd crank the box and listen to the classical strains of music, watching the ballerina dance, knowing that one motion led to the other. Knowing that even if she wasn't in control of what happened to Megan, she could control the fate of the ballerina.

Until one day, when she couldn't.

Crystal had been eleven, staying with Nana again while Megan and their parents traveled to another state to get second opinions at a different hospital.

The box sat just where it always did, on the vanity in Nana's room. Crystal made her way over, lovingly stroking the box's cover. It may be small and it would sound dumb to anyone else, but here was something that never changed. She could count on coming to Nana's and finding this box in the same spot.

She cranked the box's small lever on the right side, then popped the lid. But something was wrong. The music trotted along like normal, but the ballerina was slow, sluggish. Maybe she just needed a little tug—

Crystal gasped as her tug snapped the ballerina right off her base. Her fingers trembled as she tried to reattach her, but it was ruined. She'd broken it.

"Everything okay in here?" Nana's voice behind her made Crystal whirl around.

"I . . ." Crystal held out the ballerina, shame forcing her gaze to the floor. "I was trying to fix it. I'm sorry."

"Oh, my dear." Nana came closer, knelt, and embraced her. "There's nothing broken that can't be fixed."

If only that was true.

Crystal pulled away and stared at the ballerina in her hand. Her hair was deep brown like Crystal's and Megan's, and she wore a blue tutu. Crystal had always imagined the ballerina was her. But blue was Megan's favorite color. And the ballerina wore a huge smile—just like Megan, who'd never stopped smiling despite all the fainting spells and hospital tests and the fact she couldn't play sports anymore.

She dropped the tiny figure to the ground.

Nana picked it up. "I'll be right back." A few minutes later, she returned with superglue. Carefully, she dotted some on the bottom of the ballerina and placed her atop her perch. When she let go, the ballerina stayed.

Then Nana turned. "Not everything is as easy to fix as that, I'll admit. Life isn't perfect. It's messy. It doesn't follow a pattern or a plan. Thankfully, we know the

Big Guy in charge." She reached down and squeezed Crystal's hand. "And he is the supergluer of souls."

Crystal's fingers shook as she cranked the lever and opened the box now, nearly twenty years later.

The ballerina still danced.

And in that moment, Crystal wanted to as well. No matter what the risks, no matter if she ever got Brian back, no matter if something awful happened to Megan or anyone else she loved— she had to believe that joy still existed.

And it began with trusting not in herself but in someone who actually had the power to put broken things back together.

Nana and her parents believed. Megan did too, though she'd clearly had her struggles. And her beloved Brian . . . His faith had never wavered.

Maybe it was time for Crystal to embrace something beyond herself. Because clearly, trying to be the one in control had only broken the ballerinas in her life—and inhibited Crystal's ability to dance.

Crystal placed the jewelry box on the floor and rose. She walked to Megan's room and opened the door. A black comforter covered her sister's sleeping form. With a light step, Crystal headed toward the empty side of the bed. She lifted the sheets and crawled beneath them, nestling herself next to Megan.

Her sister awakened and rolled to face Crystal. "Hi." Then she sleepily slung her arm around her—just like when they were little.

That was all it took. Crystal closed her eyes and finally, at last, let someone else witness her tears. The sobs came fast and loud.

"Oh, sis." Megan pulled her tighter and stroked Crystal's hair. "It's okay. It's okay. It's going to be okay."

She snuggled into Megan and heard her sister's heart beating, strong against her ear. Her tears leaked onto Megan's shirt and stained the pillow beneath them. Finally, Crystal's body relaxed, and she fell asleep at peace for the first time in years.

Chapter 36

Maybe for the journey to finally be over, she had to be back here, where it began.

Megan gazed up at the Abbotts' huge home from the front yard. The late-summer rays reflected off the windows. A wind chime rustled in the warm breeze, a promise that autumn wasn't too far off.

She'd been home for three weeks and had expected to feel different somehow. Accomplished. Freed. But life had continued along at a clip. She'd settled into her new job at the library with ease.

Patrons still came in and out, many of them exclaiming over how much they'd loved following Megan's blog. They'd ask what was next for her, as if expecting her to set off on another grand adventure any day now.

But that wouldn't be happening. Given the fact she'd never returned Sheila's e-mail, Megan had blown the chance for more articles with *Travel Discovery Nerds*, and she hadn't queried any other publications. Sure, she'd eventually written a quick final blog post very generally describing her completion of the bucket list, but it was weeks after returning home and it was a sad letdown to her epic adventure.

She'd hoped she could at least go back to life as usual. But that wasn't happening either. Ever since that night at Crystal's, Megan had been thinking about what her sister had said: that God wanted to restore her.

But if that was true, why did she still feel so . . . incomplete?

Then last night she'd come across Amanda's journal, buried in her still-unpacked suitcase. Perhaps she needed to return it in order to feel a sense of completion.

She took a breath and rang the Abbotts' doorbell, clutching her purse strap. After a few moments, Charlene Abbott answered. She wore her hair down today, and it curled around her shoulders. "Megan." She reached out her hand and pulled Megan into a hug. "You dear girl."

"Hi." It was a flimsy reply, but what else could she say?

Charlene released her. "Come in, come in." She led Megan to the sitting room and sank down on the couch, patting the seat next to her.

"Thank you for letting me stop by on such short notice."

"You are always welcome here, Megan. Gary is out of town at a medical conference, but he would have loved to see you."

"You'll have to tell him I said hello."

"I will certainly do that. Would you like some sweet tea? Coffee? Water?"

"No, I'm fine, thank you. I won't take up a lot of your time."

"Don't be silly." Charlene tilted her head. "I know that journey must have been difficult, but I hope you also know it meant the world to us. Reading your blog posts, following along, it was almost as if . . ." She trailed off, her voice catching. "It was almost as if we were watching Amanda do those things. And we will be forever grateful to you."

"You're welcome. It was fun." She laughed softly. "Not all of it, but I learned a lot about myself. I'm still learning, but it kickstarted the process."

"I'm glad to hear that."

A few moments of silence filled the void between them. In the corner, a large grandfather clock chimed four o'clock.

"I actually came by to return Amanda's journal." Megan pulled it from her purse. She stared at the picture of the Eiffel Tower on the front of the journal and quickly flipped it over, then held it out.

"Thank you." Charlene reached for it and breathed a sigh when it was back in her hands. "It's such a poignant piece of Amanda's soul."

"It was beautiful. And I couldn't believe how many things we had in common." Megan folded her hands in her lap. "I only wish things had ended happier for Amanda. She had all these hopes and dreams. And her awful past. I just . . ."

"You need to read the last entry."

"I did. I read all the way to the end multiple times."

Charlene shook her head. "She filled this journal to the brim, but started another. She only got to write one entry in it, but it was the most precious thing she could have written. In fact, we had it framed. I'll be right back." She stood and left the room. A few minutes later she returned holding a floating frame that encased a piece of paper. "Read it, if you like. I'll give you some privacy."

"Thank you. For sharing her with me."

Charlene placed her hand over her heart. "It has been our immense pleasure." Then she left through the swinging kitchen door.

Megan turned back to the frame she held in her hands. There were two pages in Amanda's recognizable writing. It was dated just three weeks before Amanda passed away.

Uncle Joe died last week.

I was in math class when I got the note that Mom was picking me up early. I gathered my things and headed to the front office, and when I saw her, I knew something was wrong. Her hair was a tangled mess, her mascara smudged under eyes, and—the kicker—she was wearing yoga pants. Mom never wears yoga pants outside the house.

She opened her arms, I went into them, and

she held me while she sobbed. "It's over," she whispered into my hair.

Mom is broken to pieces, but I also sense that she's relieved. Relieved she doesn't have to worry about how he might react when he gets out of prison. Relieved she doesn't have to face him again. Relieved I can move on.

But it's not over for me.

I always thought I'd have this big confrontation with him. Yes, I had to testify at his trial, but I don't count that. I wanted a face-to-face, just-the-two-of-us, adult-me-and-remorseful-him confrontation where I told him how he'd made me feel. How he'd set me back. How his actions had changed the course of my life forever.

I guess I thought that would bring me peace. That I'd finally be rid of the demons that visit me in my dreams—if I could only stand up to him and declare my freedom from him, to his face. I figured it doesn't count if it's done in a counselor's office in the light of day, with others helping me.

Except, I've been thinking. Maybe it does count.

What if life isn't about that big moment, but a lot of little moments that add up along the way? Could the total of those moments equal peace?

Or maybe peace is found somewhere else.

Amy once shared with me that her own peace comes from Jesus. Such a weird thought. How can peace come from some dude who lived two thousand years ago?

When I said that to Amy, she showed me something in the Bible. It was a verse in Isaiah that she said applied to Jesus. It meant a lot to her so I wrote it down: "God's Spirit is on me; he's chosen me to preach the Message of good news to the poor, sent me to announce pardon to prisoners and recovery of sight to the blind, to set the burdened and battered free, to announce, 'This is God's year to act!' "

Amy pointed at that part toward the end: "to set the burdened and battered free." She said, "Amanda, don't you get it? That's you. That's me. That's all of us. Jesus came to set us free."

I find myself unable to step through the door to freedom. But why? Do I like my prison cell or something? Maybe I'm just comfortable there. I know what to expect there. There, I've found my identity.

There, I've let fear chain me, but I can see the key. It's hanging on the far wall. I lunge and strain and groan, but no matter what I do, I can't seem to reach it.

I told Amy that. And she said, "That's the beautiful thing. You don't have to reach it yourself. Your chains have already been unlocked. You just have to choose whether to remove them."

Finally, I have a choice. I guess I've had one all along.

So I'm ready to take that first small step, to taste my freedom, to leave this dank prison of the past behind. To run and not grow weary, to walk and not faint . . .

And oh, how the sunshine kisses my skin, in a way I never thought it could. It's better, deeper, and more brilliant than all my dreams combined.

Megan stared at Amanda's cursive scrawled across the final page. Like Amanda, she'd been reaching so hard for the key—and failed to notice how loose the chains shackling her really were.

And she could either embrace the freedom in front of her or shrink away into nothingness inside the prison she'd created for herself.

"I choose life, Amanda. Like you, I choose life."

Chapter 37

"I can't remember the last time I was out here in the summertime." Crystal looked deep in thought as she gazed out across the Minnesota lakeshore, surrounded by an assortment of tall pines and other plant life.

She'd lost about ten pounds since their trip, and her color appeared paler than Megan remembered. It wasn't surprising, since it'd been nearly five weeks since Brian had left. Megan asked occasionally about how things were going, but didn't want to keep bringing up a sore subject.

Megan watched as the sun lowered on the horizon. She opened the doors to the Jeffreys' boathouse, the hinges protesting with a groan. Their friends had been letting Megan and Dad borrow their rowboat for years. "And you barely made it for this one." Labor Day, the unofficial end of summer in Minnesota, was just two days away, and Crystal had come out for the long weekend.

"I had to put the final touches on the Lerner project." Her sister helped Megan drag the rowboat to the lake's edge. "The community is going to be even more than I had originally dreamed. I wish I could move there myself."

Megan grunted as the wood dug into her palms. "Why don't you?"

"It's intended to be a family community." Crystal straightened and dusted her hands on her jeans. "The homes are too big for just me." Pain glinted in her eyes, and she busied herself with grabbing the oars from their rack on the wall.

"Oh." Poor Crystal. "Have you spoken to Brian lately?"

"No." Her sister stepped into the boat, rocking and then getting her footing before she sat. "I'm trying to respect his wishes and give him space."

Megan handed her the oars and then pushed off, jumping into the boat in one fluid motion. "That's got to be rough."

"You have no idea." Crystal pumped the oars, bringing them out into the middle of the town's small lake. "I feel in limbo all the time. Work is the only thing keeping me sane right now. This project has been a godsend. But the managerial stuff that comes with being senior architect isn't all it's cracked up to be."

"You don't like it?"

Crystal sighed. "It's just a lot to keep up with, and I don't get to spend as much time on regular projects. I'm hoping it'll slow down soon. On the other hand, it keeps me from thinking too much about Brian."

"Have you called him at all? Told him you want a second chance?"

"I've considered texting or calling a few times, but I always talk myself out of it. I keep thinking he will talk to me when he is ready."

"I don't know. Don't you think you should do something to fight for him?" Megan bit her lip. "Not that I'm the love expert or anything like that." Not even close. She'd let the perfect man slip through her fingers. But she was done with regrets. Life was about moving on now, doing all she could to embrace the freedom she'd been given.

Crystal stopped rowing, her breathing a bit labored. The water lapped against the edge of the boat and a bird cawed. The smell of grilled hamburgers wafted from one of the lake houses nearby. "When he left, he reminded me that I don't control everything. I'm afraid he will take any move on my part as an attempt to control the situation."

"But how will he know you've changed if you don't show him?"

"I don't know." Her sister's brow scrunched, and she began rowing again. "Tell me about you. Have you decided to apply for that editorial assistant job in Minneapolis?"

"Actually, yes." Since reading Amanda's journal last week, she'd been waiting for God to show her what her "first small step" should be. When Crystal's friend had sent her the job description and Crystal had forwarded it to Megan a few days

390

ago, she'd taken it as a sign. No, the job wasn't a travel writing position, but it would put her on a path to do what she really wanted—much more so than the library job, which so far hadn't challenged her or interested her.

Still . . . "But after applying yesterday, I feel restless."

"What do you mean?"

"I don't know. I keep thinking back to our trip. At the end of it, I expected to feel some great triumph. I completed the list, and yet I feel . . ."

"Like you didn't?" Crystal tilted her head in contemplation.

"Yes." Megan grabbed the oars to take her turn. She yelped at the sudden pain in her hand.

Releasing the oars, she peered closely at her palm in the fading sunlight. A splinter had embedded itself just under her skin. She tried to dig it out with her nail but had no luck removing it.

"Megan."

Her head popped up to look at her sister, whose voice had taken on a curious tone. "What?"

"You feel like you didn't complete the list because you didn't."

"What are you talking about? Yes, I did." Megan studied the splinter again. How could she get this sucker out?

"Wasn't there an item on there that you said had already been completed by Amanda?"

" 'Give my heart away.' She did that when her heart was donated to me." Megan curled her injured hand and pulled it to her chest, felt the *thump, thump* beneath.

"But you said you wanted to complete the bucket list in its entirety." Crystal's hands waved in the air as if she were conducting an orchestra. "You have to do it all yourself. Megan, you have to give your heart away. In fact, I think you already have—you just haven't admitted it."

Megan's heart picked up speed, a cadence of truth pounding beneath her fingers. "Caleb . . ." Just his name on her lips made her flinch. She hadn't heard from him since Paris—but she hadn't reached out either. "He's probably moved on."

Isn't that what he'd basically said? That he couldn't keep hoping, which probably meant he'd stopped entertaining any ideas about the two of them being together.

The idea hurt her insides. She opened her palm again and desperately pushed against the splinter. It remained stuck, and the skin around it grew puffy and red.

"Here." Crystal took Megan's hand in hers and used her long nails to slide the tiny piece of wood from her skin. The relief was instant. "Something I'm learning lately is that you don't give love just because you know you'll get it back. You have to give your heart away. That's what the list calls for. It doesn't call for you to be in a relationship or get married or have babies together. You have to take the first small step. That's the only part you can control."

A chill ran down Megan's spine. "What did you say?"

"You have to give your heart—"

"No, not that part. You said I have to take the first small step."

"Yeah?"

Megan laughed, smoothing a finger over her now splinter-free flesh. "Okay, God." The whispered words flew across the lake. "I'm listening."

Crickets and cicadas played them a symphony as the sisters walked back to the house under the glow of a full moon. The house came into view— such a familiar sight, but one that hadn't been part of Crystal's world for a long time. Its simple white paint with blue trim was peeling, in need of a fresh coat, but the flower garden surrounding the porch blossomed with Asiatic lilies, Shasta daisies, and asters.

No matter what had happened in their lives, Mom had never let that garden go.

Megan hadn't said much since they'd left the boat behind. Crystal hoped it meant she was finally going to get back in touch with Caleb. Her sister deserved happiness more than anyone she knew.

As they got closer to the house, Crystal spied a figure on the swinging bench. Mom sat wrapped in a blanket, a mug nestled in her hands. The bench rocked with a gentle sway as she stared off into the distance.

Crystal had eaten dinner with Mom and Dad after arriving this afternoon, but hadn't spent time alone with either one of them. Mom in particular had seemed surprised at the changes in Crystal—both physically and emotionally. Thankfully, she hadn't even questioned the fact Brian hadn't come with her. Perhaps Megan had filled her in on the current state of things.

The women climbed the steps of the porch, and Mom's gaze moved to them. She smiled, and for the first time in a while, the worry lines around her eyes seemed dimmer. "How was the boat?"

"Good, Mom. Really good." Megan bent and gave her a kiss on the forehead. "What are you doing out here alone?"

"Just thinking." She brought the mug to her lips and sipped. "I have hot chocolate. Would either of you care to join me for some?"

"Actually, I'm going in. I have something important to do that can't wait." Megan sneaked a glance at Crystal, a tentative smile possessing her lips. Then she headed inside.

"How about you?" Mom looked at Crystal too, her features open and inviting. Other than giving her updates several times a week via e-mail and sometimes by phone while out of the country, Crystal hadn't talked with Mom much lately. In fact, today was the first time they'd even seen each other since Megan's surgery.

One conversation couldn't change everything between them. But it was a start.

"I don't need any hot chocolate. But I'd love to join you."

The look of pure delight on Mom's face nearly made Crystal weep. Because . . . she'd missed her. Maybe a girl never stopped wanting her mom, however much they fought or disagreed. Crystal settled herself on the swing next to Mom, who threw part of the blanket over her lap and squeezed her knee. For a few moments, they simply rocked, watching the stars twinkle over them and listening to the near silence.

"It does my heart good to see you two finally reconnecting. That's been one of my constant prayers."

"You certainly did what you could to encourage a reconciliation over the years." Crystal chuckled, thinking back to all their mom's attempts to get her and Megan to talk. One had finally worked, though Mom couldn't have known how asking Crystal to talk Megan out of going on her trip would change things.

"I guess God had his own timing on that one." Mom set her mug on the ground. "I never said thank you."

Crystal maneuvered her eyes to face her. "Thank you for what?"

"For going with Megan. I worried less, knowing you were there." Mom blew out a breath. "After all this time, you'd think I'd have stopped my fretting. But worrying about Megan is like breathing. It comes natural."

What could Crystal say? She'd always known Mom's life revolved around Megan. To expect it to stop just because Megan was well would be ridiculous.

"I've always worried for you too, but not in the same way." Mom lifted her hand and brushed Crystal's hair behind her ear. The touch was so soft, so tender.

Crystal bit the inside of her cheek.

"You were the one who made things happen. So capable. So practical. But that comes with a cost sometimes."

Maybe Mom knew her more than she'd thought. "You don't have to worry about me, Mom. I'm better than I've been in a long time." Which was ironic, considering her situation at home. But even though she missed Brian with a fierceness that scared her and it nearly drove her batty wondering what was going to happen, there was peace too, knowing she wasn't in charge of fixing it.

Mom kept stroking her hair, and Crystal couldn't stop herself from lowering her head and leaning it on Mom's shoulder. When was the last time they'd sat like this? The scent of Mom's Chloe perfume lingered in the folds of her sweater.

"A mother can't help worrying for her kids." Mom's voice faded back into Crystal's reality. "Although God's been teaching me a lot over the last few months about the difference between worry and concern."

"What do you mean?"

"When I worry, I am telling God I don't trust him. I fret about things I can't control. I used to think worry was just part of my emotional DNA, something I couldn't change. But the Bible tells us not to worry. It's an actual command. Your father reminded me of that. Gently, of course." A soft laugh. "If we're told not to worry, then there's got to be a way to make it happen."

Crystal frowned. "But how can you simply turn it off?"

"I used to wonder that too. That's where concern comes in." Mom's lips tipped into a smile. "We can tell God our concerns. It's like worry, but we are telling him we trust whatever outcome he has planned. And trust that he will provide peace and comfort whatever happens."

"But . . ." The question got stuck in Crystal's throat, fighting for release. "How do you trust him with certain things? Like your children's lives? How did you not go crazy all those years

Megan was sick?" *And how would I not go crazy with worry if I ever had kids?*

"Who said I didn't go crazy? I didn't always trust him. There were so many moments I crawled to God in prayer, imagined myself beating my hands against his chest and wailing, telling him exactly what I thought about what he was doing in Megan's life. In all of our lives."

Oh, Mom. "Do you ever regret having children? All that heartache and worry . . . It seems like too much to bear." The question was out before Crystal could stop and consider whether she really wanted to hear the answer.

"Never." The word came swift. Mom turned Crystal's chin till they were staring into each other's eyes. "God continually reminded me that he cares even for the sparrows—and that he cared for Megan even more than I did. And though I spent years counting Megan's heartbeats, wondering if the next would be her last, I knew deep down that nothing I did would keep her heart beating. That wasn't in my hands. So with every beat of her heart, I've had to learn to trust him more and more."

"But how?"

"By focusing on what *was* in my hands—the ability to choose to live every moment full of joy. Even the hard moments."

That word again: *joy.* And the fact that it was a choice.

"You and your sister, along with your father, have brought me more joy in my life than I'd ever imagined. You were God's special gift to me. A gift I didn't even know to ask for."

Longing rose up in Crystal's soul. She'd backed away from the idea of such a gift, thinking only of the pain it might cause. But imagine . . . What if she could accept it instead?

"Do you hear me, Crystal?"

"Yes." A tear slid down Crystal's cheek. "I hear you."

Chapter 38

September 1
Blog Post Title: The Actual Final Item on
  the List
Post Content:

I know my last post was titled "The Final Item on the List." But today, with my sister's help, I realized something.

I wasn't done after all.

See, when Amanda's dear parents handed me her list, they said she'd completed *25. Give my heart away.* I worked on completing the first twenty-four items during my trip. And I did. But when I got home, something felt undone. I didn't feel like I'd accomplished everything I was supposed to do. I tried filling the void with regular life, thinking if only I could get things back to normal, I'd start feeling normal again.

But this journey has changed me, more than I even knew. Normal doesn't exist for me anymore.

That's when Crystal reminded me that I'd set out to complete the whole list— and I hadn't. And while I can't give my heart away in the same way Amanda did, I can in the metaphorical sense.

In fact, I already have.

Deep breath

I've been burying my feelings, because they're new and I didn't know what in the world to do with them. The feelings elated me, but scared me at the same time. People think I am brave because of what I've been through in my life, but I'll let you in on a little secret: falling in love drains my courage much more quickly than facing death ever did.

Yes, falling in love. There. I said it. (Well, wrote it.)

During my trip this summer, I fell in love with my best friend. I've always loved him, though not in this way. Back then, I loved him for being there during my hospital stays. I loved him for making me laugh when no one else could. I loved him for giving me travel books and dreaming with me. I loved him for bringing me hope that life someday would be different.

And then, when life *was* different, I turned away from it. He lives life in such a bold, carefree way, and I didn't know how to be either of those things. I admire him so much. But more than that, I love him.

401

Yes, Caleb Watkins—I love you.

I love you for the way you challenge me. For the way you show me the holy side of things. For the way you bring art to life in a kiss. For the way you fight for me. For the way you hold nothing back. For all that you are and all that you will be, you have my heart and you always will, whether you're in Minnesota or Paris . . . or Tibet.

And even if you never return this love, I can be comforted in knowing that I did all I could to give my heart away.

Amanda, your list is complete. Thank you for the opportunity to learn about myself through your journey. Thank you for being all the things you were.

Most of all, thank you for giving me your heart. It is strength and it is breath and it is life to me. I couldn't have asked for a better one.

Megan read and reread the words on her computer screen. Her fingers itched to erase the entire post—but no, this was what needed to happen. She knew that as sure as she knew her own name.

She hit Publish and watched the post go live.

Chapter 39

Autumn was here, and things were back in full swing at the office. Crystal clicked on yet another e-mail that told her about a fire she needed to put out. Now that she was senior architect, she did more managing and less creating than before.

The ache behind her eyes was becoming as commonplace as her never-ending e-mail inbox.

Jamie came waltzing into Crystal's new office, a stack of papers piled high in her arms. "Where did you want me to set these?"

"What are they?"

"The proposals Meredith and Jason are submitting for the Sloma project."

"Right." Crystal rubbed her forehead. Her normally neat desk had become inundated with paper. Paper, paper, everywhere. She maneuvered a few piles around to create a clear space. "Here is fine."

"Great." Jamie set the papers down and straightened the chic blouse Crystal had bought her in London. "Do you need anything else? I can grab you a sandwich from the cart downstairs. Your two o'clock appointment will be here in thirty minutes and I noticed you haven't eaten lunch yet."

"Oh." When had she had time? She'd worked

so late last night, she'd slept here. It was actually better than trekking home to her empty apartment. Then she'd been up at four this morning and going ever since. In fact, other than the coffee she'd forced down her throat, she'd had nothing to eat or drink since sometime yesterday.

But it wasn't just busyness. This was what grief must be like, when she actually let herself feel.

Jamie still stood there, waiting for an answer.

Crystal cleared her throat. "No, thanks. I'm good."

The intern nodded and left. Crystal had started to dig into one of the stacks of papers when Tony entered. He looked her up and down. "Did you sleep here again?"

"Yes."

His gaze turned sympathetic, and he tapped his finger on one of the piles on her desk. "I know it's more responsibility and a lot to get used to. But soon you'll get the hang of it."

Would she, though? She'd always imagined becoming senior architect would be more satisfying than it had turned out to be. And with Brian still gone, she only felt dead inside.

Well, that wasn't completely true. There was a flicker of hope that lit inside of her whenever she thought about the jewelry box and what it meant. Someone else was in control. She just needed to keep moving forward and letting herself feel, mend.

Of course, another part of her bucked against her newfound hope. It told her if only she tried, she could make a plan and bring Brian back. Ever since her sister had asked what she'd done to fight for him, she'd wondered if she *should* be doing something. Not just sitting around, waiting.

But then she'd read something, or see something, or hear something. And it would remind her to be still—and trust.

"Hello, earth to Crystal." Tony knocked against the desk and Crystal jumped. "Did you hear me?"

"Sorry, no." She must be more tired than she thought.

"I said I want to see your edits on the Greyson proposal by the end of the day."

That particular proposal had been in her inbox for two days and she hadn't so much as peeked at it. "That might be a little difficult."

"I know you can make it happen." With a quick check of his wristwatch, Tony waved good-bye and turned to leave.

In the past she'd loved to make it happen, had relished watching things bend to her will. But did she really want this anymore?

A sudden dawning. The flame of hope flickered once more.

"Tony, wait."

He stuck his head back into her office. "What is it? I'm late."

"I know, but I have to tell you something."

Crystal stood, in a daze. Was she really about to do this? "Can you close the door?"

Her boss adjusted his glasses and frowned, but did as she asked. "I don't like the sound of that."

She moved around the desk and approached him. "You've been an incredible mentor to me, Tony. You've pushed me, challenged me, and made me a better architect. You've always believed I would make a great partner, and you helped me get here, where that goal is within reach someday."

Tony tilted his head. "What's going on, Crystal?"

"A lot. A lot is going on. In my mind, in my life, in my heart."

"And where is all this leading?"

"To . . . quitting." Her hand lifted and covered her mouth momentarily. "Well, not quitting totally. But I'm not sure I want to be a senior architect anymore. At least, I don't want all the extra work that comes with it. This job, it isn't what I thought it'd be. I miss creating. I feel like all I do now is manage the junior associates and I don't have the time to spend on my own projects. I miss having a vision and bringing it to fruition. I miss . . . well, I miss joy. And right now, this job doesn't bring that to me."

Tony took in a deep breath. "That is definitely not what I expected to hear."

"I know. It's not what I expected to say."

Crystal rushed on. "I understand if you don't think it will work for me to revert back to my previous position. Even if you'll let me do that, I'll need a lighter workload. An understanding that this job isn't my whole life. It's important—that's not what I'm saying. I just don't want to be married to it anymore."

Tony took her in, as if considering what she'd said. "I'll need to approach the partners about this, discuss how to proceed." Her boss took off his glasses and rubbed the bridge of his nose. "But I have to warn you. They may decide they don't want to keep someone around who isn't fully committed to this company. We like to have ambitious people working for us. It keeps our firm on the forefront of the restoration niche."

In the past a statement like that would have knocked the breath from her. But now . . . "That's a risk I'm willing to take."

He narrowed his eyes and gave a gruff nod.

After Tony left, Crystal sat there, drained. She checked the clock, called Jamie, and asked her to cancel the rest of her afternoon appointments. Then she grabbed her purse, leaving her laptop behind, and hurried out of her office, out of the building, into the early-autumn air.

Today was the first indication that fall was on its way, with a crisp breeze brushing across her cheeks and blowing strands of hair into her mouth. It had been too long since she'd really noticed the changing of the seasons.

When she arrived home, Crystal flung off her work clothes and pulled on her pajama pants—and, just because, one of Brian's T-shirts. Even though he hadn't been home in six weeks, she could still catch a whiff of his scent.

She settled on the couch and flicked on the television, flipping mindlessly through the channels. Nothing caught her interest, so she turned it off. Blaring silence met her.

Maybe she should call Brian. Her actions today would show him she'd changed.

She reached for her phone.

Be still . . .

The quiet whisper across her soul nearly strangled her, but she set the phone down and burrowed into the couch, pulling a throw blanket over her. She could feel herself drifting, drifting . . .

"Crystal?" The voice seemed out of a dream.

She popped her eyes open and saw Brian squatting next to where she laid on the couch. He reached out his hand to touch her forehead. His hand against her skin assured her that he was real. "Are you sick?"

She shook the grogginess from her head and sat up. "No. Why?"

"Why are you home then? It's four in the afternoon."

"I . . . Wait, why are you here?" She was having trouble forming thoughts, but that one came to the forefront. He was dressed in his blue EMS shirt and a pair of jeans. His hair was recently cut, but the scruff on his chin indicated he hadn't shaved for a few days. He looked even more attractive than usual.

Brian hopped up and ran a hand through his cropped hair. "I came to get the rest of my stuff."

A weight dropped in her stomach. "Right." She pushed her hair behind her shoulders. Words formed on her tongue—words of pleading, words of apology, but nothing sounded right. So she just sat there, staring at him.

He shifted his weight. "How have you been?" Eyes averted from her, he began fumbling to straighten the magazines on the coffee table.

How to answer that question? She thought of a thousand answers, but only one came out. "Sad."

"Even though you have the job of your dreams?" He stood and looked at her. "Sorry. That was uncalled for."

"I deserved it." Crystal bit her lip. Should she say something? Was she manipulating the situation by telling him? She waited for another nudge to be still. Feeling none, she decided. "I actually told Tony today that I didn't want to be senior architect anymore."

His arms folded over his chest. "Why?"

"There were a lot of reasons why. Mostly, it

wasn't what I thought it'd be." She paused. "A lot of things aren't what I thought they'd be."

"Like what?"

She folded her legs beneath her. "I never thought I'd reconcile with Megan and my parents. Never thought we'd be here either, on the verge of losing everything . . ." Her throat clogged. "But I'm realizing that things won't always go according to my plan. Sometimes that's good, sometimes that's bad, but I'm done trying to control my circumstances. Believe me, there were so many times I thought up ways to try to get you to come home. But I've been trying with all my might to restrain that controlling instinct in me."

"Just like that?"

"No, actually. It's been a process. But you being gone has given me plenty of time to think. And feel. And realize you were right all along." She stood. Her hands ached to touch him, but she held them together in front of her instead. "I love you, Brian, and I want to make our marriage work. But I've realized I can't make anything happen. Not on my own."

A faint light blew across Brian's features, but it was gone in an instant. "I want to believe you've changed. But how can I?"

It was a fair question. "I can't control what you believe. I can only ask you to trust me. But whether you decide to come back to me or not, I'm determined to live my life with better priorities. I want a life that will bring me joy. True joy, not the temporary kind that comes from achievement, but the kind that is rooted in something other than myself."

For a moment her husband just stared at her. "Who are you and what have you done with my wife?"

Her lips formed a soft smile. "I haven't done a thing. It was all God. I was broken and didn't even know it. He superglued me back together."

Brian unfolded his hands and cupped her face, searching her eyes with his own. "Really?"

"Really."

"I've missed you. The real you."

"Me too. You have no idea."

His thumb stroked her cheek. "I shouldn't have stayed away like I did. That didn't help the situation. Will you forgive me?"

"If you'll forgive me." Was this really happening? Had everything really worked out as she'd imagined—even better, in fact?

He bent his head to hers and kissed her, reverently, as if all of this might disappear.

She'd asked him to trust her, and he had. Maybe she could make a show of good faith too. Not because she needed to, but because she wanted to give her husband a gift.

"I'll be right back." She ran to her bathroom—their bathroom—and found what she was looking for. Then she came back to where he stood in the living room and held out the small package.

He strode toward her and looked at the circular pack of pills in her hands. His eyes widened as he realized what they were. What they meant.

"I have to tell you the truth. I'm still afraid. But I know what to do with those fears now." She dropped the birth control pills into the trashcan and slipped her arms around her husband. "So. Want to make a baby with me?"

His lips took on a devilish grin and he scooped her into his arms. "I thought you'd never ask."

Chapter 40

"I still can't believe you're leaving us." Kara wheeled her chair toward Megan behind the librarian's desk.

"Me either." Megan placed her last framed photo into her box. It joined all the little knickknacks she'd accumulated at her desk over the years—posters of her favorite books, *Pride & Prejudice* notecards, pictures with frequent patrons, and more. "But I want to thank you again for being so understanding."

"I just want you to be happy." Kara got up and threw a hug around her neck. "We're going to miss you. Not only here in the library, but in Little Lakes."

"I know. It's crazy." A few days after Megan had submitted her application for the *Minnesota Republic* editorial assistant position, she'd traveled to Minneapolis for an interview, then been offered the job soon after. Having an in with Crystal's friend had been helpful, as was the fact the daily paper was looking to fill the position quickly.

"I still can't believe I landed it." Megan folded the box tops together.

"I'm so happy for you." Kara chewed her bottom lip. "So . . . anything else?"

"No." It had been nearly two weeks since Megan had spilled her soul in a blog post for the whole world to see—and she hadn't heard a word from Caleb.

Her boss cringed. "I'm sorry, sweetie."

Megan shrugged, tried to let it roll off her shoulders. "I guess it wasn't meant to be."

"He's an idiot then." Kara straightened. "Let's change the subject. Are you all done for the day?" She checked her watch. "We close in thirty minutes, so you can take off early if you need to."

"No, it's kind of nice no one else is here. I told Debra she could leave early if she'd let me reshelve the travel books one last time."

"I totally understand." Kara sat back at her computer and started clicking her mouse. "I'll be as quiet as I can."

Megan laughed. "Thanks." She moved from behind the librarian's desk and headed for the cart of books the new library aide had left for her. In the distance, she heard the jangle of the bell over the library doors.

As she maneuvered the metal cart down the Travel aisle, her eyes skimmed the books on the shelves. So many of the places discussed in these books—she'd seen them in real life. Experienced how they looked in the fading sunlight. Lived their history through tours and imagined what it would have been like to see them built.

Her eyes stopped on one title: *Visiting Tibet.*

An invisible force drew her hands toward the medium-size travel guide. She pulled it from its place on the shelf and opened to the middle, where several pages of glossy photos showed mountain peaks capped with snow, huge palatial dwellings with red roofs, azure skies over totally desolate landscape . . .

"As beautiful as it is, there's one downfall to visiting Tibet."

The book fell from Megan's hands, and she swiveled on her heel—and there stood Caleb, looking sheepish and just as handsome as he'd been atop the Eiffel Tower.

Somehow she found her voice. "Really? And what's that?"

"There's really shoddy internet service there." He pushed the metal cart aside and came closer to Megan. Her back hit the shelf behind her.

He was here. And he was leaning one arm against the sturdy shelf and bending over her. She could smell the minty toothpaste on his breath.

She tried to act casual. It wasn't working. "Did you have a nice adventure, other than the internet situation?" Her voice shook.

"You know, it wasn't as great as I thought it'd be."

"Oh?" Her heart fluttered inside her chest.

"Yeah. See, I started dreaming of another

adventure while I was there. So it really wasn't all that satisfying." His mouth quirked.

He was baiting her. Fine. She'd bite. "And what adventure would that be?"

"The one that starts and ends with you, Meg." With his free hand, he brushed her bangs from her eyes. "I'm sorry I didn't get here sooner. I'm sorry I let you leave in the first place, as if a life with you wasn't a big enough dream for me. I was so stupid. But I came as soon as I read your post."

"It's okay." She bit her bottom lip, and it drew his attention.

"No, it's not. Because I should have told you a long time ago how precious you were to me. I should have—"

"Shh." Megan placed her fingertips over his lips. "I'm learning that 'should haves' belong in the past. Tell me now." She smiled. How was that for brave?

He leaned even closer, until their noses touched. "You so poignantly named all the reasons you love me, but I only have one for you. Megan Jacobs, I love you because you're you. And that's enough for me. It's always been enough for me."

And then his lips met hers, and a glimpse of the brilliant dream Amanda had written about swooped in, leaving freedom in its wake.

Acknowledgments

Before I became an author, I had no idea how much work went into the creation and production of a novel. I am so grateful to each of the following people who helped this book become what it is today:

Rachelle Gardner: You never gave up on me, and you never let me give up. Thank you for believing in me when I didn't. Having you in my corner is a huge blessing. #BestAgentEver

Karli Jackson: You saw my vision for this book and helped to sharpen it. Your suggestions and edits took this story to another level. It has been such a pleasure working with you. Thank you!

The rest of the Thomas Nelson team, specifically Becky Monds, Amanda Bostic, Jodi Hughes, Kimberly Carlton, Kristen Golden, Paul Fisher, Allison Carter, Kristen Ingebretsen, and anyone else who touched this book: THANK YOU for your professionalism and for believing that Megan and Crystal's story should be heard.

Mom: I will never forget all the love and confidence you poured into me every moment we had together here on earth. Thank you for being my biggest fan, even all the way from Heaven. Your legacy lives on in the character of Megan, who exuded joy and hope even when faced with death.

Dad: Like the father in this book, you have always spoken truth and love into my life. Thank you for building me up and telling me I could do this. And thanks for that rocketeer story you wrote when I was a kid. You'll never know how much it meant that you got involved in my hobbies. ☺

Nancy Harrel and Kristin Walker: Once again, you are both supermoms to me! Thank you for watching the kids when I was on deadline and for treating me as one of your own daughters. I am blessed to be learning to do life from such wonderful women.

Gabrielle Meyer, Melissa Tagg, Alena Tauriainen, and Susan May Warren: Thank you for helping me to brainstorm this book! I am so grateful for such beautiful souls to walk this writing path alongside me.

Elliott and Theodore: I thank God for you two every day. You are my greatest gifts and I am so thankful that in spite of my fears, God chose me to be your mommy.

Mike: Thank you for your continued sacrifice so I can pursue my dreams. I love you.

My readers: I know that there are many books you could choose to read, so the fact you picked this one up means the world to me. I pray your heart is blessed.

And finally, thank you for the freedom you give, Jesus. Help us all to be brave enough to claim it for ourselves.

Discussion Questions

1. Which of Megan and Crystal's destinations would be your top pick to visit someday?
2. What items are on your own personal bucket list and why?
3. Megan lets fear hold her back from pursuing her dreams. Have you ever experienced something similar?
4. How did growing up with an ill sister affect Crystal? What are some healthier ways she could have coped with it?
5. What role did Megan's parents—particularly her mother—play in her perception of herself and her illness?
6. Amanda writes a bucket list in order to overcome challenges from her past. Does this idea of replacing painful moments from her past with joy and hope for the future resonate with you? Why or why not?
7. Megan feels pulled between safety and adventure. When was a time you experienced a similar struggle?
8. When Crystal finds the music box, she is reminded of something Nana said to her once: "Life isn't perfect. It's messy. It doesn't follow a pattern or a plan. Thankfully, we know the Big Guy in charge. And he is the

supergluer of souls." In what ways had Crystal attempted to superglue her own life back together? In what ways have you seen others (or yourself) attempt to do so after a tragedy or hardship? What does it look like practically to trust God to superglue us back together?

9. Megan struggles with wondering why God allowed her to live when Amanda died. She also wonders why she had to wait twenty-plus years to be healed. Have you ever wrestled with a similar question? What conclusion did you come to?

About the Author

Lindsay Harrel is a lifelong book nerd who lives in Arizona with her young family and two golden retrievers in serious need of training. She's held a variety of writing and editing jobs over the years, and now juggles stay-at-home mommyhood with writing novels. When she's not writing or chasing after her children, Lindsay enjoys making a fool of herself at Zumba, curling up with anything by Jane Austen, and savoring sour candy one piece at a time.

Connect with her at www.LindsayHarrel.com.

Center Point Large Print
600 Brooks Road / PO Box 1
Thorndike, ME 04986-0001 USA

(207) 568-3717

US & Canada:
1 800 929-9108
www.centerpointlargeprint.com